CHRISTMAS AT THE LITTLE PARIS HOTEL

REBECCA RAISIN

Boldwood

First published in Great Britain in 2024 by Boldwood Books Ltd.

Copyright © Rebecca Raisin, 2024

Cover Design by Alexandra Alden

Cover Photography: Shutterstock

The moral right of Rebecca Raisin to be identified as the author of this work has been asserted in accordance with the Copyright, Designs and Patents Act 1988.

Every effort has been made to obtain the necessary permissions with reference to copyright material, both illustrative and quoted. We apologise for any omissions in this respect and will be pleased to make the appropriate acknowledgements in any future edition.

A CIP catalogue record for this book is available from the British Library.

Paperback ISBN 978-1-83533-510-9

Large Print ISBN 978-1-83533-511-6

Hardback ISBN 978-1-83533-509-3

Ebook ISBN 978-1-83533-512-3

Kindle ISBN 978-1-83533-513-0

Audio CD ISBN 978-1-83533-504-8

MP3 CD ISBN 978-1-83533-505-5

Digital audio download ISBN 978-1-83533-507-9

Boldwood Books Ltd
23 Bowerdean Street
London SW6 3TN
www.boldwoodbooks.com

For Jax
My loveliest creation

1

1 NOVEMBER

Opposite the Jardin du Luxembourg, on Rue de Vaugirard, you'll find the world's ugliest hotel. My hotel. Even the stunning Gothic architecture can't distract from the level of disrepair evident through the window. If I squint hard, I can envision what it *will* be like with a little TLC and a whole lot of euros.

Or is that just wishful thinking?

'Spoils of *le divorce*,' my younger cousin Manon says. Only two years separate us, but at times it feels more like decades, as if I'm ancient at thirty-eight compared to my freewheeling family member. Manon doesn't take life as seriously as I do, and I envy her ability to not give a damn whenever she comes to a fork in the road.

I let out a theatrical sigh. 'It's a disaster. An unmitigated disaster.' Not only did I lose my husband Francois-Xavier, but I also lost in the divorce proceedings and wound up with this eyesore as part of the settlement. I don't want to say the French favour their own when it comes to dissolving a marriage and dividing the assets, but they clearly do. I might be half-French but, in this case, it wasn't enough, not when I was up against his colossal family. Note to self: don't marry into a clan of litigators.

Manon clucks her tongue as she peers into the window. 'We're stuck in a time-warp. The seventies called and they want their avocado-green drapes back.'

The colour scheme is a retro chic horror story and not one you see in Paris often. For very good reason...

It's hard not to let bitterness take over. Francois-Xavier took off with another woman and is enjoying an extended tropical island holiday (financed by yours truly) while I'm going to have to reside in a hotel that may just collapse around me like a house of cards. But stay here we must. Even during messy, noisy renovations.

L'Hotel du Parc has a distinct air of dilapidation about it, at least from this angle. 'I'm all for budget stays, but this...' I let the words fall away.

With the sale of the hotel came four backpackers who agreed to stay on for a reduced rate to keep an eye on the place until the divorce finalised. They've asked to stay while we revamp, which I'm happy to do since any money coming in, no matter how nominal, all helps at this point. 'I didn't realise the backpackers were having to avoid piles of junk like that.' I point to the detritus through the window.

'It's not *that* bad,' Manon says. This is coming from a woman who uses the floor as a wardrobe and probably wouldn't have even noticed the refuse if I hadn't pointed it out. 'I'm sure their rooms are fine and, being free-spirited nomads, they're probably ecstatic to have accommodation in the centre of Paris for a fraction of the usual cost.'

'*Oui.*' Manon's right. They're probably loving it, and each couple has their own room and private ensuite, which is more than what they'd get at a hostel for the same price. 'Still, it's unsightly.'

'Easily remedied. And, sure, the décor is hideous but that's cosmetic. By the looks of it the place simply needs a massive tidy up and a design makeover.' Manon takes a step forward and runs a fingertip along the outside of the window, which comes away grey. 'See! Everything just needs a good scrub.'

I hope she's right because funds are limited. Just selling the hotel isn't an option, as it turns out Francois-Xavier overpaid for the property by a fairly large margin, so the current forecasted sale price wouldn't even cover the excessive mortgage. Instead, I'd be left with a stonking debt, which is why I suppose my ex was so generous offloading the hotel on to me.

The realtor advised me to either give the place a spruce up and make it a blank canvas, bland and clean, the no-fuss low budget option; *or* customise the hotel with a particular theme to help it stand out when compared to thousands of accommodation options in Paris. The latter is a riskier option but has the potential to achieve a higher price upon sale, which is why I'm leaning towards that idea. She suggested building up clientele before putting it back on the market. How hard can it be? It's one of those 'you have to spend money to make money' scenarios, and I've got Manon's support when I wonder for the millionth time just what the hell I'm playing at. This is not in my wheelhouse; far from it.

What could go wrong? I have a lot of renovation experience as a... romance writer. *Gah!*

The idea is to revitalise this grand dame and have it at least partially opened by Christmas for all those last-minute holiday makers. An audacious plan, given that it's just clicked over to November. A mouse runs along the windowpane as I break out in noisy sobs that catch me unawares. Great big heaves that draw the eye of many a passerby.

'Don't let that fool win, Anais.' Manon isn't the tactile type, so she shoves me with her hip, which for her equates to a big squishy hug. 'Really, it could be worse—' Her words peter off when there's a grinding noise above us. We crane our necks upward and I let out a blood-curdling scream when the old L'Hotel du Parc sign comes crashing down, landing a whisper away from my feet.

I'm still screaming when I turn to Manon, who isn't the least bit concerned that I nearly lost my life in front of this neglected monstrosity. 'Can you knock it off?' she admonishes, holding her hands to her ears.

What can I say? It's been a fraught few months and I'm *feeling* all my feelings with an intensity that overwhelms me.

But, dammit, why is she so relaxed? 'I – I could have been kil—'

'You're looking at this all wrong. That was *literally* a sign from the universe! It could have pancaked you into the pavement, yet here you are still very much alive, with all your appendages intact.'

My cries grow more plaintive. 'I can't even be *killed* properly. I have to suffer this prolonged agony while Francois-Xavier is sunning his over-buff body' – a red flag in retrospect – 'with that woman who doesn't speak French. How do they even communicate?' Manon makes an obscene gesture to imply she knows exactly how they do it; and I let out a shaky sigh. 'You really don't need to paint me a graphic picture, Manon. I walked in on them, remember? Only a lifetime of therapy is going to remove that vision from my mind.'

'Sorry.' Manon twists her mouth into an apologetic moue.

My cousin lacks any filter and often drops truth bombs, but it's done without malice on her part.

'That woman is now stuck with him, which is payback in itself,' I say. 'He's a pig, a swine, a no-good lying cheating exhibitionist, with very little going on upstairs.'

'That husband-snatcher did you a *favour*.'

Did she though? 'I suppose, if not her, it would have been one of the others.' Turns out Francois-Xavier didn't comprehend what 'forsaking all others' meant when he boldly claimed such a thing in his wedding vows.

'Actually,' Manon says, with a mischievous twinkle in her eye, 'rumour has it *that woman* has been exiled from paradise, replaced with a certain socialite who goes by the name Ceecee.'

My jaw drops. 'He ditched Helga already?' Although, I'm not sure why I'm surprised; it's his modus operandi when it comes to flings, all while being married to yours truly.

'*Oui*, he switched her out with a fully paid-up member of the glitterati. I only hope that Ceecee's family will delve into his past and see he's a gold-digging, money-grabbing social climber.'

Unlike stupid me, who didn't put two and two together. There I'd been doing book launches all over Paris, my name up on billboards, when he happened along. I'd been so sure it was a chance meeting of two souls. Not the calculations of a con man.

'Who told you about this?' Why does part of me feel bad for my former housekeeper Helga, for crying out loud? I should have no sympathy, and yet I do, because I know just how charming that silver-tongued devil can be. While she did the wrong thing, my anger is directed solely at him, the person I exchanged wedding rings with.

'I read all about the new woman on his Facebook account. The guy is an over sharer of the finest order.'

Betrayal hits me square in the gut. 'You're still friends with him on Facebook?' I outlawed such a thing when we broke up. Demanded every family member block him in solidarity with me.

She snickers. 'Under a fake name to keep tabs on the slimy weasel.'

I slap my forehead. 'Manon! I bet you've toyed with him too for your own amusement.'

'*Oui*. I catfished the hell out of him, had the fool running all over Paris to meet his date "Lola". And *quelle* surprise, she had one disaster after another and didn't turn up.' She lets out an evil cackle.

I bite down on my lip to stem laughter because I really shouldn't encourage Manon. Next minute she'll make a hundred fake profiles and make it her mission to ruin his dating life. 'You shouldn't engage with him; he'll find out it's you and then I'll never hear the end of it.'

The grin she slides my way is a cunning one. 'He'll never find out. Firstly, he's as dumb as a broom, and secondly, I always use a VPN to hide my IP address. He's not the only person on my hit list, you know.'

Merde! Manon's probably got a revenge list taped to the underside of her laptop. It wouldn't surprise me. Still, she doesn't need to fight my battles.

I sigh. 'He has the IQ of an oyster.'

'That's being unkind to oysters.'

I give her a watery smile. 'Even if it kills me, which I'm certain is on the cards after the near-miss from above, I will get through this.' Francois-Xavier probably loosened the bolts on the L'Hotel du Parc sign and hoped for the best. Another worrying thought flutters through my mind and I gasp. 'I have to change my will! He's still the beneficiary. That's just what I need, me to be crushed to death and him to inherit the piddly amount I've got left. I'd have to figure out how to haunt him from the afterlife.'

'Are you suggesting...?' Her face twists with awe. Only Manon could get excited about a possible murder plot even if the intended victim is me, her favourite cousin. What can I say? She's got a grisly bloodlust side to her.

I tut. All I seem to do is cry, sigh or tut these days. 'I'm suggesting no such thing. Francois-Xavier wouldn't risk climbing on a roof in case he fell and disfigured his face.' The man is vain, no two ways about it. Originally, I'd thought it was a good thing, a man who put self-care as a priority, but I clearly had my rose-tinted glasses on. Now I see my ex is just a vapid attention seeker with wandering eyes.

'True, but I would have relaunched the podcast for that. Do a deep dive into your marriage and his web of lies and call it *Plot Twist: The End of the Story*. Ooh la la, as much as I love you, doesn't that sound enticing, what with you being an author?'

I frown. It should be no surprise that Manon is a true crime aficionado and once had a podcast where she investigated cases. Like almost everything with Manon, she grew bored and let it slip away even though she was doing well, helping families shine a light on cold cases. To me, it seemed gruesome, combing over case files featuring the worst of humanity, but none of that bothered Manon; she only wanted to help catch the bad guys.

We're as different as can be, but those differences are why we've always been close. I'm more measured, while Manon is spontaneous. She will blurt out every thought that flutters through her mind, appropriate or not, while I'll consider how every word will land. I'm her safe space when the world comes crashing down, or so I thought. Right now, she's that person for me. Who knew that I'd need to find solace such as this from my wayward cousin?

Light rain begins to fall as I push my hands deeper into my coat. 'I'll turn this relic into a vibrant hotel catering to festive holiday makers visiting for Christmas all while penning my novel: *How to Kill Your Husband and Where to Dump the Body.*'

OK, that might be the anger talking. I write heart-warming romantic comedies, but that's off for the foreseeable future, because I'm not exactly feeling lovey-dovey these days. Each draft of my new book devolves into a massacre – often a scorned wife who exacts revenge on her traitorous spouse and bludgeons him to death. Huh, maybe I'm more like my cousin than I first thought. But there's simply no way my British literary agent Margaret will let that sort of thing slide. Writing *is* cathartic though, so I figure bashing out murder-y plots will help me heal, even if all I do is send them all to the recycle bin. That's what I tell myself anyway...

Perhaps I need to pivot into the feminist serial killer genre, where I can gleefully dismember cheating men a hundred at a time? The tears start again in earnest. Honestly, what is happening to me? I'm not usually such an emotional blub- bering *mess*.

'This feels like pep-talk time,' Manon says, giving me one of her long looks that implies she's uncomfortable with my constant outbursts. Manon is a straightforward sarcastic type who finds feelings difficult to translate and even harder to understand, so my constant state of flux is probably grating on her. I've never been able to have those sorts of intense, deep and meaningful conversations with Manon, because she's unable to hide her complete lack of disinterest and just cannot relate. She's always curious why I get so hung up on discussing the minutiae of life and love, and frequently tells me it's an enormous waste of time worrying over such trivialities.

Even now, with my disaster of a marriage behind me, she treats it as a simple mistake that's not worth dwelling on. But I just can't help but hold on to the pain. The humiliation. I'm hoping Manon's no-nonsense approach will eventually rub off on me though, and I'll be able to let go and move forward with my life.

'Francois-Xavier *will* get sunburned and wrinkle like a prune in the tropical heat. He'll dehydrate and prematurely age. Long, coarse white hairs will grow out of his ears and possibly his nose from excessive sun exposure. The future looks *bleak* for the runaway husband.'

I have no words.

As the Parisian temperature drops, Manon shuffles on her feet and continues her so-called pep-talk. 'From the get-go we *knew* he was bad news, but would you listen, Anais? *Non.*' Almost every family member, from the coast of Britain to the south of France, put in their two cents, telling me he wasn't genuine, he was playing a part. I'd brushed their negativity off, figuring they'd all gone a little mad. They couldn't see what we had. They were swept up in the whispers that were passed along the family grapevine. I'm not usually spontaneous, that's Manon's department, so they were taken aback that my relationship and subsequent marriage happened so fast.

I choke back sobs. 'Love is blind.'

'And hard of hearing.'

She's right. I didn't heed any of their warnings. I was love-struck, in a daze, hypnotised by this man who seemed too good to be true. Spoiler alert: he was.

I'd been searching for my own real-life hero after writing romances for so long, and then he stepped into my life, dashing and debonair, a book-smart bibliophile who wasn't shy in admitting that he read romance novels because he enjoyed happy ever afters. The man said all the right things. He checked every box and then some. It felt like I magicked the perfect hero to my heroine – finally! A sweeping romance off the pages, starring me, the then thirty-two-year-old dreamer, with a dreamboat by her side forevermore. One month into our relationship, he proposed, and insisted on a quickie wedding, much to the alarm of my friends and family. But not to me. I'd been enraptured by him and certain he was my soulmate. Our marriage lasted five years and was not the fairytale I expected it would be. Well, five and a half if you want to count how long it took to divorce him and get him out of my life for good.

'How did I believe in the fantasy?' Honestly, love-drunk should be outlawed.

Manon shakes her head. 'Swindlers like that always find a weak spot, and he found yours. And phonies *always* have a double-barrelled name; that should have been your first clue.' She pulls the sucked lemon face – an expression Manon uses most, as if life is always a touch distasteful for her liking. 'Doesn't it just scream ego? "Bonjour, I'm Francois-Xavier Giradot."' She postures up as if she's my ex, and with a deep voice says, 'I'm a fake, a phony and a flop between the sheets.'

Gloom settles in my poor, bruised heart. I don't mention that, as far as pep-talks go, this isn't exactly helping. But Manon is using everything in her toolbox to draw me out of myself and, really, her impersonation is spot on. So why does it still hurt so much?

I'd had a huge amount of success with my books right around the time Francois-Xavier appeared in my life – coincidence, I think not. What I should have done was get a prenup, but stupid me in love-bubble land didn't feel it was necessary. He got the apartment in Le Marais and I got this rundown mess. Really, I should have done my due diligence when I found out early on that he came from a family of lawyers, although he didn't work at the firm – or at all, it turns out. Their legal team buried me, creating so much paperwork for my own lawyer I had no choice but to settle or end up penniless from fees alone. For a smart woman, I really dropped the ball. That stabby rage returns and my fingers itch to write him into a book and torture him. I'm not sure if this is a healthy response or if I'm losing touch with reality.

Silent tears stream down my face, catching me unawares. This lack of control over my own bodily functions is alarming, but there's not much I can do about it. Surely tears aren't a never-ending resource? I'm hoping eventually the waterworks will dry up. The man doesn't *deserve* my tears, but for the life of me I can't control these visceral reactions. Perhaps it's humiliation driving the engine. Who knows?

I swipe uselessly at my face, my fingers coming away blackened with mascara. I must look a fright.

'*Bonjour, bonjour.*' A man wearing a beanie approaches. He's got a whiff of a young Ernest Hemingway about him, with his intense masculinity and cheeks ruddy from the cold. There's a wild robustness to the guy, as he speaks in American-accented French. When he smiles, his eyes sparkle as if he's about to impart a secret. I get a jolt at his sudden appearance. It could be that he reminds me of the long-dead charismatic author. That or it's his disarming rugged good looks; either way I'm intrigued, and an alert goes off in my brain. He's main-character material and I've learned my lesson the hard way when a man like that comes along not to fall for it. I must remain on guard.

'You must be the new hotelier?'

'*Oui*.' Hotelier. Me. The idea is preposterous, yet here we are. 'I'm Anais and this is my cousin Manon.' I hold out a hand to shake, but he either doesn't see it or is uncertain about what might have discoloured my fingers black and doesn't want to risk transfer onto his big man hands. Once more I surreptitiously wipe my mascara tears and pull my coat in tight.

'I'm Noah.' He motions to the property next door to the hotel. 'I own La Génération Purdue Wine Bar.' The Lost Generation Wine Bar; how apt.

We have ourselves a literature fan.

American men have a different intensity to their French counterparts. Or maybe it's just this man who speaks French well but has a fervency with his body language as he does so. Like he's coiled, ready to spring into action to get his point across. I wonder if that's due to not being understood when he originally started learning French. That or he's got a chip on his shoulder and is ready to battle. I laugh at my mad musings. The man is just here to welcome us and here I am catastrophising that he's some evil villain!

Still sniffling, and unable to get a handle on it, I survey the dark façade of my neighbour's bar. It features an indulgent art deco black and gold aesthetic with geometric ornamentation. Behind the window there are sepia-toned framed pictures of Ezra Pound, Sylvia Beach and T. S. Eliot.

The Lost Generation – a term named for the period of time those literary greats reached adulthood after the war – was almost like rebellion, a coming-of-age for creatives. Expat

American writers, readers and poets threw off the shackles of the past in a post-World War One era and lived bohemian Parisian literary lives on their own terms. The phrase was coined by Gertrude Stein and included famous faces such as Hemingway, F. Scott and Zelda Fitzgerald, and Sylvia Beach.

'Your bar is lovely,' I say, meaning it. I'm about to compliment it further and tell him I'm a literature fan too when he gets in first.

'The thing is, rubbish like this drives my customers away.' He points to the shattered pieces of the L'Hotel du Parc sign littering the pavement. Ah, now his coiled intensity makes sense. He *was* readying himself to reprimand me. My instincts were correct! 'It's not a good look for the neighbourhood. Not to mention the hotel itself, which is unsightly and getting worse by the day with it being so... desolate.'

Just like me. Maybe this hotel and I are a good match, after all.

Still, who does this stranger think he is, admonishing me when I've been here all of five minutes? Noah doesn't stop there though. His monologue continues as he harps on about a range of hotel maintenance issues that impinge on his business. For a hot guy he's really annoyingly verbose. 'While it's only the beginning of November, Christmas will soon be here, and with that comes many tourists, whose custom keeps us going. Rue de Vaugirard must look its best for the festive season.'

With every sullen word, my leaky eyes dry up. His voice becomes white noise that matches my white-hot rage. What the hell *is* it with men lately?

'*Excusez moi.*' I hold up a hand to stop his rambling and give him a sweet, deadly smile that belies my inner fury. 'Do you make a habit of approaching a clearly upset woman and making demands upon her? Can you not see this isn't the right time?'

Confusion dashes across his face. He surveys me closely as if he's only really seeing me now. 'I ah—'

I fill my lungs, readying myself to retaliate. 'A few moments ago, this sign almost killed me, and you have the audacity to stomp over here and tell me it needs to be cleaned up. I haven't had a chance yet to put my key in the lock and you're complaining that my hotel is bringing down the look of the entire 6th arrondissement?' My voice rises as I continue my own tirade. 'How dare you call it desolate, as if there's no hope!' Manon presses my shoulder as if to quieten me, but I will not be silenced any more. 'And to imply I'm going to ruin *Christmas*? That's insulting.' A Parisian Christmas is like no other. It's a winter wonderland for young and old and happens to be my favourite time of year, but this Grinch is trying to stop my sleigh bells from jingling. 'Who made you the boss anyway?'

Noah grimaces and, with his hands up in surrender, he takes a tentative step back, like he's afraid I'm a wild reindeer gone rogue and about to attack. And maybe I am. Blitzen goes berserk! 'I've clearly picked the wrong time for this... ah, discussion, so I'll leave you for now. In fact, I can clean up the sign; will that help?'

Oh, he is the limit! 'What, because I'm a woman I can't do manual labour, is that it?'

His eyes widen and I *think* he lets out a yelp. Hard to tell when there's a storm raging in my head making it difficult to hear the world around me. Manon pulls so hard on my arm, I nearly fall over. 'What!' I screech, facing her.

'You know I love a good rage-fest, but, seriously, take a breath. It's Francois-Xavier you're mad at, not Noah.' If Manon is telling me to calm down, my behaviour must be bad.

My cousin turns to Noah and blurts, 'Anais isn't quite herself at the moment. Her husband had an affair, so now she sees all men as the enemy.'

'*Manon!*' Her frank admission is mortifying. But is she right? Am I looking at all men like they're the antagonist in my own story? Surely that's a normal part of the process when you've had an upset like this?

My writer's brain whirs into action.

Hilary loved everything about Christmas. More so when she conked her obnoxious neighbour on the head with a life-size candy cane and bound his prone body in Christmas lights, tight, the same way she wrapped pork loin to roast for Christmas dinner. There was the smallest of splashes as she rolled him into the Seine. He would remonstrate her no more.

The rage dissipates as quickly as it came. Am I being melodramatic? It's like I've had a personality change. The old me would never have bellowed like that. But, then again, the old me chose a man like my ex-husband, so perhaps this new ragey version is for the best. Still, I have to work in close proximity to this guy, so I'd better attempt to smooth things over even if I don't want to.

I turn to find him gone though. Typical. Men take one look at me and then vamoose.

Manon lets out a surprised bark of laughter. 'I never imagined my role would be peacemaker. That's usually more your speed.'

I cup my face in my hands. 'Have I done irreparable damage?' The last thing I need is a grumpy neighbour complaining every two minutes when renovations begin.

She scoffs. 'Hardly. Yeah, sure, you scared him off at the end. He looked like he could *taste* fear and he was deciding whether it was palatable or not. Before your outburst, he had love hearts for eyes. *And* he's a literary nerd, like you! Have we found the new hero in your next love story? A Christmas romance for my heartbroken cousin, *non*?'

Merde, she's picked up on it too. Noah is exactly the type I'd normally go for. Rugged, hot, literary nerd. But not any more.

I will not admit the man has me intrigued. 'Haven't you got the memo? Romance is DEAD.'

L'affair took care of that.

2

L'AFFAIR – SIX MONTHS AGO

'Darling,' my literary agent Margaret drawls, using a term of affection only when she's in the very best of moods. 'I have the most wonderful offer for you to consider. LA production company Kiss Films want to option your novel, *The French Billionaire's Secret*. They focus solely on romances, so it's a great fit. And the money, well, if the project is greenlit, will be a very nice boost, not to mention a resurgence in book sales for the title.'

I stifle a scream as I walk across the Pont Neuf, the oldest bridge in Paris, which translated ironically means New Bridge even though it was constructed in the early seventeenth century. I continue on towards the Bibliothèque Mazarine, the library I often write in even though the main librarian is a harridan who follows me around to harangue me.

'You're kidding me!' We've had bites from production companies before, vague offers and interest, but nothing has ever eventuated into signing on the dotted line.

'I'm not kidding. I got a call from them last night.' Margaret goes on to tell me more about Kiss Films and other developments they're currently working on. It's a no brainer but I try to tamp down my excitement. 'Are they really keen or just putting-the-feelers-out keen?'

'They're *really* keen. As in already talking figures and percentages keen. As in, it's-time-to-buy-a-bottle-of-bubbles keen. What do you say? Should we get into negotiations?'

'*Oui*, start negotiations!' I turn around, back in the direction of home in Le Marais. News this exciting has to be shared immediately with Francois-Xavier, who I left curled up in bed, with the beginnings of a migraine. When he's like that, I do my best to stay out of the apartment so he can sleep it off in total darkness. Instead, I usually work in the library, often finding I'm more productive surrounded by books. Words. Fictional worlds.

'I'll get the ball rolling. You start celebrating with that delicious French husband of yours. How's it all going with him anyway?'

I take a moment to contemplate the question. 'Uh – it's going well! It's just... Francois-Xavier is between jobs at the moment. He's not sure whether to pursue his dream of studying law like everyone in his family or to do up the rundown hotel he... sorry, *we* recently purchased in the 6th arrondissement. Things are a little up in the air, I guess you could say.' Maybe he's just a late bloomer. He often says he's the odd one out in his family, so I try and be supportive, knowing it must be hard on him feeling like he doesn't fit in as easily as his siblings do, who all practise law and have wildly successful careers.

'You bought a *hotel*?' Margaret's voice rises.

I slap my forehead. Why did I bring this up? 'Yes, we bought a boutique hotel. It only has eighteen rooms. His dream is to do it up himself and become a hotelier. But...'

'You can afford *that*?'

Margaret knows what I earn to the penny, so I don't bother lying. 'Barely. I'd hoped he'd have started the renovation work by now, but it seems he's lost interest. It's not his fault,' I quickly reassure her. 'He keeps getting these terrible migraines that knock him out for a full day at a time. Then there's the issue with his back that pops up every now and then...' To be honest, the mortgage for the hotel is so steep it keeps me from sleeping at night and it's eating away at the funds I have squirrelled away. The only solution I have is to write faster and release an extra book per year, to help keep us from sinking entirely. So, if this movie offer goes ahead, it'll give me some much-needed breathing space. But I know how these things work; it can be years before the film is greenlit and, until then, the option payments are just a small slice of the pie, nowhere near enough to assure me of a good night's slumber.

'Anais, is he a dud? You've been married a while now and he still hasn't found his mojo. Be honest with me.'

I smile. Margaret is, and always will be, forthright. 'No, no, it's just temporary.' That's what I tell myself every morning anyway. The thing is, Francois-Xavier won't even see a doctor about his headaches or back pain, in that typical manly man way where they pretend to be stoic. Really, I should just make the appointment for him, but I'm already under so much pressure to meet extra deadlines and the added publicity that goes with it. '*In sickness and in health*, I made that vow and I plan to honour it.'

'This is why you're writing more! I thought you were inspired by being in love in the city of love!'

'Well, there's that too. Paris is the most romantic city in the world. And I don't want you to get me wrong. While Francois-Xavier isn't working now, and, ah, hasn't found his calling yet, it's just a blip. Our relationship is stronger than ever. We're still totally besotted!' Why does the brightness in my voice have such a desperate air to it, as if I'm trying to convince Margaret *and* myself? 'Actually, today is our fifth wedding anniversary!'

'A double celebration then! Go share the good news with him and keep your eyes peeled for an incoming offer by email.'

'Will do. Thanks, Margaret.'

With a spring in my step, I make the thirty-minute trek back to our apartment off the Rue des Blancs Manteaux in twenty because I'm so excited to surprise my husband with the news. Sure, Francois-Xavier might not be in the best state to hear it suffering through a migraine, but it is our wedding anniversary, and we should at least acknowledge both bits of good fortune.

I take the elevator up to our floor, wishing I'd stopped for a bottle of champagne. Maybe the news will miraculously cure his aching head and we can go to one of our favourite bistros, La Tablier Rouge, for a long lunch instead. They have the most charming wine cave where customers can select natural or biodynamic wine to have with their meals. It's cosy, unpretentious and serves hearty French fare.

When I exit the elevator on our floor, I take my keys from my handbag. As I go to open the apartment door, I hear a burst of laughter. How can that be? Ah, I'd forgotten it's Helga's day. She's our new perky young housekeeper. Admittedly she barely speaks an iota of French or English so we use charades to communicate, which often makes us double over with laughter when things are misunderstood. That said, I've been meaning to cancel the cleaning service until our finances are back on track, but I haven't had the heart to do it. Helga usually stays longer than necessary, as if the job is important to her. I'd hate to take away part of her income while the cost of living is so exorbitant these days.

If they're laughing, that must mean Francois-Xavier feels

better, so a double celebration might be imminent. The idea makes me smile as I push open the door, frowning when I don't see either of them in the living room.

I throw the keys in the trinket bowl and follow the sound, not so much laughter now, as more of a... moan? My heart hammers, hoping they're moving a heavy piece of furniture and not the alternative. But, when I push open the bedroom door, I'm met with a sight that is so disturbing I freeze. Unable to take my eyes away, and unable to run. Worse, they don't notice me for a full minute. When they do, he pushes her away and yanks the sheet up to his chin, like that's going to help matters. She's left abandoned on the bed, *my side of the bed,* completely naked.

I blink and blink and still the vision doesn't clear. I wait for Francois-Xavier to speak. For Helga to offer me an excuse in her native language, but nothing comes except a blinding rage that builds inside me and shoots upwards to my mouth. 'YOU LIAR! YOU PIG!'

All his previous excuses flash in my mind as I put the timeline together. Every 'migraine' was on a day Helga 'cleaned'. How did I not see that?

Did she even clean? Have I been *paying* her to sleep with my husband? For some reason that makes the duplicity even worse.

'Get out, both of you!' I scream. Right now, Helga doesn't need charades or translation; she picks up her discarded clothes from the floor and dashes past me.

Francois-Xavier puts his hands up in surrender and says slowly, 'I'm not going anywhere. Let's have an adult conversation about this.'

My eyes widen so far I worry my eyeballs will fall clean out of their sockets. 'An adult conversation about you sleeping with our housekeeper, while you're supposedly bedridden with a "migraine"?'

How could I be so stupid? It's been right under my nose this entire time and I had no clue.

He has the audacity to give me a lopsided smile. 'It didn't mean anything. She's just a distraction.' I have the urge to pummel him until I picture myself in a jail cell. I weigh up the satisfaction of such a deed that will result in me living on poor quality jail food for a decade or more and decide it's probably not worth it.

'How can you be so *laissez-faire* about this?' The anger slowly recedes and is replaced by sadness. Heartbreak. My dream man is just that. A dream. A fairytale.

'I'm not, I'm just being honest.' Francois-Xavier slides the sheet down, exposing his chest, and taps the side of the bed Helga just exited.

'You cannot be serious?' Is he for real? 'How long has it been going on?'

My husband shrugs as if I'm asking a question as mundane as what the weather is like. 'A few weeks.'

'A few? How many?' He gets a cagey look in his eyes. 'Since she started?' Three months! Everyone warned me about Francois-Xavier's flirtatious side but I insisted it was just his playful French personality. I'd found my Prince Charming. More like Prince *Harming*.

He twists his lips into a petulant pout. 'You're always working; writing and worrying.'

Shock builds inside my brain, making it hard to focus. 'This is *my* fault?' Do I even know this man? Did I ever? 'The migraines, the back spasms; they were a fiction the entire time?' He has the grace to blush, at least. It's unnerving how convincing he'd been about his pain. If he could lie so easily about that, *and* Helga, what else has he lied about? I don't wait for an answer from him. 'You need to leave.'

He takes his time untangling his body from the sheet. They'll need to be burnt. A hot wash won't be enough to remove infidelity from the thread count. Will I ever get the scent of betrayal out of the mattress? That can go.

'Did you lie about reading romance novels too?' That confession sealed the deal for me, a man who loved reading about love. *Romantique!*

He squirms like the snivelling snake he is but stays quiet.

I blink back tears, not wanting to give him the satisfaction of seeing me cry, and instead make my voice icy. 'I'll give you an hour to pack your things. Leave your key on the kitchen counter.'

I rush from the apartment, stumbling blind down the avenue as tears finally fall. My mind spins as I try to process everything. Hadn't we been blissfully happy? Didn't we have it all: the romance, the intimacy, the mutual respect? The support, even when he acted on impulse recently and bought a rundown hotel in the 6th arrondissement without discussing the purchase with me. I'd hidden my shock and told him I'd help. It was my money he was spending, after all. My windfall from a few books that took off into the stratosphere. Even that I could forgive because he was a dreamer, a visionary, or so I'd thought.

In the cold light of day, the truth hits me with a force that almost bowls me over. He sold me a lie. He isn't the man he claimed to be. Did he ever intend to work, to renovate the hotel that was bought by all those extra hours I sat stuck at a desk, bashing away at my laptop, trying to keep our heads above water? I'd wanted to stash my windfall for the future because what if my next book flopped? What if the earlier success was a fluke? And I let him talk me into all those bad ideas... because he bamboozled me with bedroom eyes and his Machiavellian ways. The devil!

What happens now? There are too many happy faces about, too many people rushing towards me, chitchatting excitedly while inside I die a little more. I duck into a café and find a secluded table at the back where I can regroup in peace. I hastily swipe at my face before the waiter appears and takes my order. He soon returns with a café crème and a carafe of water. I nod my thanks, not trusting my voice to speak. If he asks how I am, I'll probably burst into messy tears and confess my husband is a scheming, lying heartbreaker of the finest order. Not quite the done thing in a Parisian café.

I sip my coffee and regain my equilibrium. One thing is for certain: I can never forgive Francois-Xavier, so any chance of reconciliation is out. For him not to have one iota of concern about his actions is tough to fathom; or was it a ploy to downplay it? Either way, it's killed the marriage. I can't love a man like that.

Having never been married before, I'm not sure what the next best course of action is. Do I hire a lawyer, start divorce proceedings? Surely he'll be fair when the time comes to divide our assets. After all, Francois-Xavier came to the marriage with very little, despite telling me otherwise in the beginning. We purchased our apartment just after our wedding, but he's never paid anything towards the deposit or the mortgage itself. My savings are fast depleting too, with steep payments towards the hotel that's been forgotten by him. I need to get my name off that mortgage as a matter of urgency and leave him to figure out how to finance it.

I cup my head as I remember some of the most fantastical career opportunities Francois-Xavier toyed with over our time together. He was going to work in the family firm – until admitting later he hadn't actually studied law, so his role would be more in the public relations department. When that didn't pan out, he admitted he found nine-to-five stifling. And I'd been understanding; working in a stuffy environment like a law firm did seem rather staid and not suited to my debonair, creatively minded husband. There was the art gallery idea after a spell of him pursuing a career as a painter. The rent for the gallery had been steep and the lease contract vague, so luckily the deal fell over before he tied us up in another expensive venture.

And most recently came the attempt at writing his own book, an espionage thriller. He managed one chapter before deciding he needed a change of scenery and complete quiet to write, even though he had no experience with such a thing. He took off for a month to the south of France and came back with the book scrapped and the grand idea of being a hotelier. And naïve me had been so happy to see him back wearing his cheeky smile that I'd encouraged him to investigate boutique hotels, presuming it wouldn't pan out just like everything else.

Within a month, he'd put the offer in and somehow had me co-sign, though I don't remember ever seeing any contract of sale, or recall signing any important paperwork. When I questioned him about this, he'd put my forgetfulness down to being distracted by a writing deadline. I do often live inside my imagination towards the end of a deadline; the real world becomes hazy as my fictional world becomes front and centre of my mind.

Now, musing about the nuts and bolts of our marriage, I can't see a divorce being an issue. I can sign the hotel and its eyewatering mortgage over to him, he can repay the hefty deposit I paid for it, and I'll keep the apartment. It's only fair, since he's never worked a day in all the time we've been married.

The vision of them coupled on my bed suddenly flashes in my mind and it's all I can do to keep my emotions at bay. How could he do this to me? I'd never suspected a thing. I get the attention of the waiter. 'A bottle of champagne, *s'il vous plaît*.'

'Celebrating?' he asks and lifts a brow.

Commiserating? 'Something like that.' When he returns and pops the cork, I toast myself. I toast Kiss Films. I toast endings. And new beginnings. I'll do what I always do and throw myself into my work. Writing sweeping epic romances. With that, I finally burst into messy tears.

After Noah, the Ernest Hemingway wannabe, vanishes, I put the key in the lock of my very own hotel. Me, a hotelier; who'd have thought? Despite my misgivings, it's sort of exciting to finally explore the place in person. All I've seen previously is some rather grainy photos online and on the hotel's website gallery itself, which painted the place in a much better light, if you're into seventies décor, that is. Francois-Xavier had invited me to visit the hotel many times, but I always refused, telling him I'd take a tour once he'd done it up. Deep down, I sensed that I'd panic if I found the place derelict and would've felt trapped by it, by him, by a marriage that clearly wasn't working, but at that point I wasn't even being honest with *myself* about the wheels falling off around me.

We step into the lobby with its sunshine-yellow walls that are so bright it's headache inducing. 'Oh god, look at that cobweb,' Manon says. 'It's like a portal into another world. How big do you think the spider is that made it?'

The web is abnormally large and sends shivers down my spine. 'Get rid of it.'

'*Moi*?'

'*Toi*,' I confirm. 'Not only are you here for moral support, heavy lifting, painting the high bits and the low bits, and being the cheerleader and shoulder to cry on, you're also the chief spider wrangler.'

Her jaw drops. 'And so, what, you get to paint the easy middle bits?'

'No, I'll be writing a sparkly shiny Christmas romantic comedy for release next year.' Or staring at a blank screen. Or having my heroine Mrs Claus lace the gingerbread with laxatives because she's sick of her husband's lies. Wait. Maybe that's me inserting myself inside my own stories again, dammit. 'You can do the middle too, but you have to cut in the top and bottom first,' I joke. It will be all hands on deck to get this hotel up and running on the budget we have. The quicker we open – even a few rooms – the better for the monthly mortgage repayments that eat away at my savings at an alarming rate.

Right now, the place is quiet, not a backpacker in sight. They must exit onto the back lane and come and go that way, rather than through the lobby, because the wooden parquetry is dusty with disuse.

Manon sighs. 'I thought I was doing the fun stuff like the website, and now I'm the painter and the spider relocator?'

'Relocator? I think you mean remover.' I make a stabbing gesture.

'You want me to *kill* it?'

How is she not understanding this? One arachnid can easily become two and on it goes. '*Oui*, or we run the risk of it coming straight back to its home. Look at the size of that web. You're going to need a chainsaw to cut through it.'

'But look at those diaphanous strings catching the light...'

'Christmas garlands are just as glittery in the muted light

and much prettier to look at, *non*? We can go wild and decorate as soon as the renovations are done.' What I don't say is we'll show that guy next door that I am not going to ruin Christmas; far from it. I'll deck the halls, all right.

'Fine. I'll rehome the spider, far *far* away. You deal with the web.'

'I suppose that's fair.'

Manon pings the web with an index finger and the spider comes running from its hidden hellscape. It makes my skin crawl. I don't want to see her pick up the beast, so I go looking for a broom and find one in a utility closet. I swipe at the web and pray that's the only portal-size example we're going to run into.

When Manon returns, she dusts her hands on her jean-clad legs. 'Right, let the tour commence!'

The lobby has a curved reception desk and large mirror, reflecting my startled face back at me. Is that how I always look? Like I'm slightly shellshocked.

To the left of the lobby is a guest lounge. It's spacious and would be full of light if the windows weren't so grimy. Bottle-green velour sofas sit in the centre of the room and all but one are laden with boxes and stacks of old newspapers and magazines. There's a mound of broken-down flatpack furniture dumped haphazardly in a corner.

While the guest lounge is a mess, there are redeeming features: the polished wood parquetry is in good condition, the ceiling roses are ornate, and the thick gold cornicing is intricate, like something you'd see in a chateau. 'This French baroque style' – I point upwards – 'is stunning. Perhaps we can work with that? Go backwards in time and present the hotel in a more luxe manner. Navy blues, creams and golds, marble table-tops, that kind of thing.'

'Very Versailles.'

'Doesn't everyone wish to live in a palace? If we can recreate the look with the existing features, it would be quite an achievement. We'd be preserving what's here. The ceiling itself is magnificent and the gold cornicing will look so much better once we lose the yellow walls. What were they *thinking*?'

'I guess in the seventies it was groundbreaking.'

I laugh. 'We'll keep this lobby and guest lounge for its intended purpose and spruce up the reception desk. While the sofas are ugly, they've held up well. We can find some fabric and reupholster them.'

Manon throws herself on the only sofa not littered with junk, making dust motes dance around her. 'I can confirm the sofas are comfortable and worth recovering. We can shop for fabrics at Place Saint Pierre at the foot of Montmartre. It's the heart of discount fabrics. A textile heaven with all sorts, from silks, linens, cashmere, to buttons, ribbons.'

'I love that idea.' I make a note on my phone. 'I'll watch some tutorials on how to reupholster sofas. But drapes.' I gaze at the ones hanging by the windows, that are ruched and gathered like an old ball dress. It's nice in theory, but the avocado-green is grey with dust in all the folds. 'Something simple, sheer perhaps would be a better alternative. How handy are you with a sewing machine?'

'I'll only stitch my fingers together. We can buy ready-made sheer sets in Montmartre at Marché Saint Pierre, for a fraction of the cost of custom-made drapery.'

'*Parfait.*' I survey the room once more. 'The flimsy retro wall prints can be ditched. Lights can stay. According to the inspection report done at the conclusion of the sale, all the electrics in the hotel are in good working order and up to code.' The lighting is surprisingly pretty. A golden crystal chandelier hangs charmingly in the middle of the room and the wall sconces only need a clean and polish. 'We can repaint the walls in a rich cream and add some bookshelves. All in all, not *too* much work in this area.' From the outside, it looked a lot worse.

'Not *too* much work? Says you, with her delicate writer hands who won't be doing most of the manual labour.'

I'll have to help even though my deadline looms. 'Manual labour just might cure my writer's block.'

Never in my fifteen-year career have I suffered with a block like this. Suddenly I can't write happy ever afters. When I envisage my characters, they're knife-wielding maniacs. I *should* reach out to my literary agent Margaret and get her advice, but I'm terrified she'll be disappointed and potentially drop me as a client. I don't think I can suffer losing another relationship, even if it's a professional one.

I'm hoping the problem magically restores itself and the words pour out of me, but so far that hasn't happened. My deadline is a week away, so that's not good either. While I'm a prolific writer, I'm not quite *that* fast. I swallow down the dread of having to tell Margaret my words have frozen for the foreseeable and turn back to the matter at hand.

'There's a salon off to the right of the lobby. I thought we could make it into a guest relaxation area, a space for aperitifs and cocktails. If we keep with the gold baroque theme from the reception area, we could make this room slightly moodier: dark paint, luxe velvet drapes, Louis XVI replica furniture.'

Manon lifts a brow. 'Sounds *very* Gatsby.'

'And? It will be a boutique hotel, after all. It has to be a little bit bourgeois.' Manon stares hard at me like I'm missing the point. I guess I am because what's wrong with wanting the place to feel luxurious?

'Only the hot guy next door might take offence if the hotel décor is the same as his bar.'

I wave her concerns away. 'Hardly. It's a Parisian aesthetic that's been around forever. Noah can't lay claim to an interior design style just because he did it first. Besides, Gatsby is more Roaring Twenties with all those geometric patterns and art deco touches. This will be more... refined, elegant.'

'Where are you getting all the money for this *elegance*? Last I checked, the budget was so tiny, I figured you'd missed a couple of zeroes.'

'*Merde.* I know. We'll have to scour flea markets or repurpose what we've got here for now.'

'You could finish your book. That would help.'

'That means I'd have to start it.'

'You haven't started it?' Her thick black brows shoot up.

'I have eleven thousand first chapters, but they're no good unless I am indeed a thriller writer, which I am not.' I pinch the bridge of my nose. Why can't I bloody get over this hurdle? 'I've been a little busy what with falling apart and sewing voodoo dolls and all.'

'You told me you were halfway through the manuscript!'

'I lied.'

She cups her face. 'Margaret is going to *kill* you.'

My agent is well known in my family for her fiery temperament. 'I wonder if there's another unscrewed sign I can stand under? Maybe I can hold a streetlamp and hope for a bolt of lightning to strike?'

Manon rolls her eyes. 'Sounds like a very grown-up way to deal with your problems. Let's finish having a look around and then you can get writing.'

'What's the point?' These swings in mood are intense! I'm stuck in a real-life rut. 'It's all so hopeless.'

'That's the spirit.' Manon is not one to let me get maudlin. 'Keep holding on to the negatives, Anais.'

'You're right.' I shake away the fear, the angst. I'm being insufferable and even *I'm* tired of hearing myself whine. 'So back to the salon. I'm envisaging it as a bar area but stacked with books as far as the eye can see. A plush and warm... Oh my god... A *library* for our guests!'

'A library?' Manon raises a thick brow.

'*Oui.*' I gaze around the spacious room. 'A literary sanctuary.'

'Uh, but what about the bar idea?'

'It can be both. Look at the size of this room with those big picture windows with a pretty view out to the busy street and the gates of Jardin du Luxembourg. The realtor suggested a theme and I think we've just discovered it!'

'We have?'

I clap my hands together. 'We'll make this place a haven for book lovers! We can provide a wide range of literature to suit every taste...' My mind spins with ideas to add bookish elements throughout the hotel itself.

Manon considers it before saying, 'It's not exactly Paris-centric though, is it? Isn't that what guests want? The full Parisian experience?'

'Well...' I tap my chin, considering it. 'We'll make the hotel an ode to Paris, highlighting books set here. We'll be spoilt for choice as we build our library. From classic tomes, romances, memoirs, travel guides; the list is endless. So many Christmas books are set in Paris!'

Manon's expression is animated as she comprehends the vision. 'And not just French authors. It'll be a nod to all the literary greats who made France their home! Instead of room numbers, the suites could be named after authors. The library too. What about "The F Scott and Zelda Fitzgerald Library"? His book *Tender is the Night* is set in the French Riviera.'

I consider it. 'Or we could name it after Zelda? Forget Scott.' I smile, loving the idea. Zelda was a writer too, but that's often overlooked in the history books. I take my phone from my pocket and google Zelda's name, looking for details about her. 'What about a direct quote from the woman herself made from one of those warm gauzy neon light word signs: "Nobody has ever measured, not even poets, how much the human heart can hold."'

Manon's eyes sparkle. '*Magnifique*.'

'We can stock her book for guests, memoirs written about her too. Hang photographs of her. Make this space an ode to Zelda and the jazz age. Although... maybe we should feature a French writer for the library rather than an American? If this room is to be our *pièce de résistance*, it should be Paris-centric like you suggested.' I bite down on a smile, excited by the prospect of making this room a showstopper and having a theme we can carry throughout the hotel.

Manon nods. '*Oui*, a French-born author is best to give the library the flair we're after.'

And just like that we've hit on an idea that's sure to appeal. 'We're bibliophiles who often shut the door on the outside world to sink into a book that transports us away from reality and the mundanity of real life. Paris is a popular tourist hotspot, but bookworms, like us, also enjoy time to relax and read on holidays. After a long, manic day taking in the sights of Paris, our book-loving guests will return with aching feet and can enjoy perusing the many novels on display around the hotel before sprawling on a chaise in front of a roaring fire, or reading in the comfort of their suites, blocking out the noise and the chaos of the city for a few hours. We can offer charcuterie and dessert boards. Bottles of wine. Each suite will have a coffee station for those who prefer coffee, tea, and hot chocolate. For our Christmas soft launch, we'll offer gingerbread coffee, pumpkin-spiced lattes. Mulled wine and eggnog in the library. I want them to feel like this place is a cosy retreat. They can escape into fictional worlds with all the creature comforts they desire.'

'Can I be a guest instead of your helper? I want to sink into my suite with a good book, a glass of wine and a dessert board.'

I laugh and shake my head as I try and keep up with the ideas flashing in my mind. 'We can hang bookish artwork that we print ourselves. Make bookmarks. Find literary mugs for the coffee stations. Reading pillows for Kindles. Bamboo bath caddies to rest books and wine. Annotation sets. We can wrap books in butcher paper and feature "Blind date with a book". The list is endless, and most of those things are inexpensive but will really highlight the literary aspect of the hotel.'

'Uh-huh. And you're just doing the place up to sell.' Manon's voice is laced with sarcasm, but even she seems swept away by the idea of what the hotel *could* become. How can she not get carried away by the dream of designing a space for word nerds, like us? While Manon and I are bookworms, we read different genres. My cousin prefers gritty true crime or terrifying horror stories, and when she's had her fill of those she switches back to classics, whereas I enjoy a comforting romance, memoirs, or a historical saga. A classic or two every now and then.

'I *am* going to sell. And I'm hoping the literary theme is enough to make that sale happen so I can get back to my normal night owl writerly life, where the only thing I have to worry about is *fictional* broken hearts. They're so much easier to mend.'

We continue our tour into the dining room. It's as bold as the other areas with a brown, green and yellow colour scheme, but the mahogany furniture is sturdy and in good repair. 'Paint and new drapes in here. Not much really, aside from a deep clean.' The closer I look the more my enthusiasm grows. It's not as bad as it first appeared. The kitchen itself is practical and updated, all stainless-steel functionality. The inspection report cleared all electrics and appliances so that's one less thing to worry about.

'Are you going to run this as a restaurant?'

'*Oui*. I suppose we'll have to interview for a chef, since I have no experience with the restaurant side of things, and let's be honest, I'm not going to be all that cheerful for a seven a.m. breakfast service.'

I write better at night and, if I'm in the zone, I don't stop until the early hours of the morning. I'm hoping that zest, that passion, for what I do soon returns. 'As we discussed before, I like the idea of offering simple fare too, like charcuterie and dessert boards for guests who want to graze while they read. For the opening, we can offer festive Christmas platters with fruit mince pies, *Bûche de Noël,* chocolate truffles, baked camembert and baguette. Simple stuff that you and I can prepare that won't have us in a tizzy.'

'Stop, you're making me hungry.'

We leave the first floor and head upstairs to the suites. There are eighteen rooms in total. Twelve on the second floor and six on the third floor, which, according to the website, are slightly bigger, catering to larger groups or families.

'Is it just me or does it feel kind of eerie wandering around a closed hotel?' Manon asks. 'I'd have thought the backpackers would be blaring their music, knocking back cheap wine and congregating here somewhere.'

'Not that you're into stereotyping or anything, Manon. Perhaps they're working or out sightseeing?' I expected we'd run into them too. I've spoken on the phone a few times with one of them named Juliette, when she had concerns about a broken window from a late-night reveller. But aside from that I don't know a lot about them, only that the previous owner trusted them implicitly and I felt comfortable knowing the hotel wasn't entirely abandoned while we sorted out who got what in the divorce.

With the gloomy lighting and piles of junk, it is a touch eerie in the hotel, but that will all be fixed when we commence work and brighten the place up with fresh paint and clean windows. 'We should enjoy the quiet while it lasts, I suppose.'

Soon enough, these halls will be filled with the sound of suitcases being trundled along, the chitchat of guests as they plan their Parisian days. It's so strange to think of myself in this situation, having been tucked away in the quiet, writing for so long, where the only daily concerns I usually deal with is my word count and how to thread my stories together to provide satisfying endings. This new me, hotelier, seems so wildly foreign, but I remind myself it's not forever.

I open the door to the first of the suites on the second floor. The dusty drapes and grimy windows stop most of the natural light entering the space, making the room dim and uninviting, but that's easily fixed. Most repairs seem cosmetic, but, really, how would I know? Paint, drapes and bedding. Crockery and a kettle and pod machine for the coffee stations. While the furniture is old, it's durable. 'We can get away with painting some of this furniture and updating the chest of drawers with new handles and hardware we can find at flea markets.' There's a lot we can do with little money if we're inventive enough. 'I'm most nervous about the bathrooms. If they need a full renovation, we're doomed.'

According to the inspection report, the bathrooms were functional and up to code but dated and would need modification in the future. I hope that means the very *distant* future and that we can make some tweaks to dress them up a bit without having to remodel them entirely.

'Plumber I am not.' Manon crosses her fingers as if hoping we're not going to be met with a disaster.

'How can you say that if you haven't tried?' I can't help but tease.

'*Anais.*'

From memory, the photos on the website showed the bathrooms were all the same colour, but I struggle to recall what that was. I send a prayer up that they're not avocado-green or sunshine-yellow.

I open the bathroom door and am greeted with an explosion of salmon. Salmon-coloured ceilings, walls, tiles, bath and floor.

'Wow... Salmon was *not* on my bingo card.'

'It could be worse,' Manon says cheerfully.

'*Oui*, it makes a nice change from avocado-green. At least it's sort of... calming. And while it's not super chic, they're clean and tidy so we can get away without having to fully overhaul the bathrooms if they're all like this one, which is a relief.'

I close the bathroom door and we turn back to the suite itself. The rooms are a modest size, but big by Paris standards. The bed is heaped with pillows and linens. I rifle through to find they're mostly ripped and frayed and can't be salvaged. So why they've been dumped here is a head scratcher.

'The balcony is nice,' Manon says.

It's just the right size for a table and chairs for two, for those who want to breakfast in fresh air, although the wrought iron is bent out of shape and will need repairs.

'I'll take this suite,' Manon says, her tone brooking no argument.

'Why this one?' I ask.

'It's close to the stairs, which are close to the kitchen if I want to go down for a late-night snack.'

'Good plan. I'll take the suite opposite for now.' Really, it makes sense being close to the lobby end of things in case our guests need us on short notice. Manon's suite has a view of the Jardin du Luxembourg, the high black gates with golden spears and a canopy of bushy green trees.

We check out the remaining suites on the second floor, which are largely identical, save a few different wardrobes and bureaus, and are laid out dependant on where the windows are situated. However, some suites are cluttered with broken furniture: odd legs of chairs lie marooned, and various-sized drawer inserts are stacked as if someone kept a junk pile hoping one day these bits and pieces would come in handy. In one suite there are a heap of overflowing rubbish bags, whereas a few are relatively neat as if waiting for guests.

Inexplicably, suite eight is home to an avalanche of old kettles and toasters. The room is fragrant with the smell of burnt toast. Why not ditch them if they don't work? We peek into the two remaining rooms at the end of the hallway, which the backpacker couples have claimed as their own. We quickly check their bathrooms to make sure no extra repairs are needed and leave their suites, one of which is pristine while the other looks like a tornado has whipped through and no piece of clothing was left unscathed.

'Why don't we unpack our things and tidy our suites? We can check out the third floor tomorrow.'

'Unpack?' Manon scrunches her nose in distaste.

'I'll unpack, you throw your suitcase in a corner.' My suite needs a deep clean if there's going to be any chance for me to relax into this new life. My space has to be organised so I feel like I've got a handle on things, whereas Manon will most likely change her bed linen and that's it. Oh, to be free of hang ups like she is, able to assimilate into a new environment easily.

'Right,' she says. 'But what about all the stuff that's been dumped on my bed? Do you want to keep any of it?'

'*Non*, not for guests, but perhaps we can use some of it for cleaning rags or something. Throw them in the laundry for now. Meet back for dinner later?'

'*Oui.*'

Once I've dragged my suitcase upstairs, I light a peppermint Christmas candle and place it on the shelf of the window. The minty scent helps disguise the stuffiness in the air and makes the place feel more like home as I clean and make the space my own.

4

2 NOVEMBER

After breakfast, we dispose of the rubbish we cleared from our suites the day before and tidy up the entrance to the lobby so there's no trip hazards and we can get in and out without having to navigate trails of junk.

A few hours later, we walk up the winding staircase to the third floor to explore the six deluxe suites. The staircase itself could be a showstopper with its ornate balustrading once we rejuvenate it and bring the gold back to life. The stairs are covered in a muddy brown carpet that peels away at the edges and is damp with the distinctive smell of mould. I bend down to pull at it to see what's underneath.

'Manon, look! There's marble under this brown monstrosity!'

'*Ooh la la*, why would they cover up such pretty flooring?'

'I suppose the hotel has been through many a refurbishment and had many different faces over the years. If only the walls could talk...'

'We'd hear some juicy tales.'

I make another note in my phone. 'We can pull the carpet

up and find a navy stair runner with a gold trim, keeping the edges of the marble exposed.'

'Very regal,' Manon says. 'Or we could do everything in black and make a statement that way.'

I roll my eyes. Manon wears only black. Black jeans and jumpers. Black eyeliner. Black boots. Even in summer, but she'll swap to black form-fitting dresses. What can I say? She's edgy. I tend to wear bright colours and have a capsule wardrobe that can be easily mixed and matched. My clothes are already hung neatly in the closet, whereas Manon's clothing is still in her suitcase and will eventually be discarded in messy heaps around her room as time goes on, much like one of the backpacking couples, who no doubt Manon will gel with.

'How much will a fancy stair runner cost though?'

'I'll research.' I jot that into my notes app.

At the top of the stairs is an ornate wrought-iron double door with gold accents, but it's marred by touches of rust. I'm not quite sure how to spruce up wrought iron but I'm sure it can be done. We check out two of the suites as we go down the hallway. They're a lot bigger but still have the same colour scheme. The furniture is of a higher quality, although slightly shabby and scuffed from age. 'These are more sumptuous and definitely deluxe. We need to be mindful how much it will take to refurb these bigger spaces.' The photos on the website hadn't shown the width and breadth of just how generous the third-floor suites are. The hotel doesn't have an elevator, which is more common in Paris than people think, so I'm glad we can avoid having to carry heavy pieces like wardrobes and sofas up and down stairs, and instead we can make the best with what we've got and dress the rooms with some extra bits and pieces like rugs, artwork and lamps if we can find them on the cheap.

'*Oui*,' Manon says. 'Why don't we makeover one deluxe suite for the soft launch and do the other five at a later date?'

'Great idea, Manon. We can decorate each suite for Christmas too, which can distract from the fact they're not as fancy as we'd like right now.'

The last suites we peer into are even bigger, apartment-sized with kitchenettes for large groups or families. My mind whirls with how we'll manage scheduling the renovations and which suites to complete first to appeal to our Christmas holiday guests.

The suites that have the view onto Rue de Vaugirard and the gardens are probably the ideal candidates, rather than the opposite side, which has a view to the buildings behind. I shut the door and wipe my hands on the front of my jeans. Dust has taken up residency on every surface, especially on the third floor where the backpackers clearly haven't explored and disturbed it, as it clings to our clothes, our hands.

'That mirror is gorgeous,' Manon says, pointing to a gold floor-length arched mirror that hangs on the wall at the end of the hallway. 'But it looks like it's going to fall off.'

I check behind the mirror. It's secured only by a thin bolt that bends under the weight of the baroque gilded frame. 'We'll have to rehang it with a stronger fixture.'

We need a professional for the renovation work but I hope we can teach ourselves DIY for jobs like securing the mirror. 'We'll have to hire a builder for the more laborious aspects and see how much we can save by doing some things ourselves. Then we'll have to tally figures for each room, even if we only keep three or four suites for the soft launch. At a minimum, rooms will need fresh bedding, mattresses, bath towels, bedside tables, lamps, Christmas decorations...'

I don't have the budget for such luxuries; I've only budgeted for the builder, so even the bare necessities might be a stretch. I guess part of me was hoping to find a neat, clean hotel ready to add a magic touch to elevate it and *voilà*. My ex-husband has really put me in a bind with the hotel, and that same wave of panic washes over me. How can I manage this and not lose everything?

'I'll have to consider increasing the loan, even though that's the last thing I want to do.'

'Or you could borrow from your parents? Or mine? They'll loan you money, me not so much. They're still upset about me totalling their Audi. They think the wild boar story was a lie.'

'It *was* a lie.'

'That's beside the point. Anyway, all I'm saying is your parents aren't holding a grudge against you so will most likely be amenable to a loan.'

I sigh. 'But I'd never hear the end of it, would I?' Nothing is sacrosanct in our family. Gossip runs hot and with the advent of WhatsApp family group chats, there's no avoiding it. It'll be splashed online and dissected by every family member. I'm still recovering from the Francois-Xavier chat, where the conversation descended into talk of revenge, and for a moment I was truly suspicious of my family, recalling that we'd never seen or heard from Aunt Odette's husband after it was discovered he'd been selling off our family heirlooms to fund his gambling habit and had a woman half his age stashed in a Parisian pied-à-terre. I'm *still* suspicious. Even if their hearts are in the right place. I'm not brave enough to ask Manon about her involvement in a possible missing person's case, because, let's be honest, if someone had to do the disappearing, the job would be given to her.

'*Non*. You'd never hear the end of it.' Manon blows out a breath. 'But is the payoff worth it? Probably.'

I throw up my hands, surrendering to this feeling of fear. Fear I'll lose everything. Fear I'm not experienced enough. All I can do is face those fears head on and keep the faith. 'We'll do as much as humanly possible, and I'll avoid borrowing money unless there's no other option. Maybe the builder will be remarkably affordable, and all this worry will be for nothing.'

'I can see blisters in my future. Scrubbing, painting, cleaning, backbreaking labour. Why did I ever agree to this plan? I was happy working three menial jobs so I could afford my rent in the 20th arrondissement.'

'You hated all three jobs, and you love me and know this is a good plan.'

She cocks her head as she surveys me. 'Is it love though or just a familial bond? And how strong is that bond? That's the debate raging inside my head right now.'

I laugh, the first proper laugh I've had in ages. I moved in with Manon after negotiations turned sour in the divorce and Francois-Xavier was granted permission to live in our apartment in Le Marais while we finalised everything. There was no way I was going to cohabit with him again, no matter how they spun the benefits of such a preposterous notion. And really, that was probably their game plan, to ensure I'd move out. My cousin welcomed me with open arms and gave me a place to stay until we were able to move into the hotel. Once the sale of the hotel is complete, we plan to rent an apartment together. Although living in close proximity with Manon has its challenges, it's preferable to living alone, and, despite our differences, we're a good team.

'Everywhere I look there's a wall to paint, and if I have to do the high bits, the low bits and the middle...'

'Let's break for lunch. You'll feel more inspired after that. We've got to come up with a new hotel name... something liter-

ary. Something that all bookworms will recognise and then you
can get onto the branding side of things.'

'*Ooh la la,* what will the name be?'

* * *

Later that night, I slip into my freshly made bed, prop my
laptop on a pillow and open my Word document. It's been a
long, tiring day and my nerves are shot, but I must write, even
though every part of me wants to sleep.

> Outside, night fell, and stars flashed in the inky sky as Hilary
> congratulated herself on the way she'd handled the devas-
> tating end of her marriage. Now, all she had to do was figure
> out where to hide the body.

> Hide the body?

I close the laptop. Tomorrow is another day.

5

3 NOVEMBER

The next morning, I'm rifling through the kitchen, wishing I'd thought to bring basic supplies like a French press and ground coffee. We stored our belongings at Manon's *maman*'s house without putting much thought into what we'd need here.

I search the cupboards but don't find anything resembling a French press or even a kettle. Maybe they're upstairs in the kettle graveyard, languishing under layers of dust.

'*Bonjour?*' A red-headed woman in her mid-twenties wanders in with a wave. 'I'm Juliette, one of the backpackers from Avignon. The others have already left for breakfast, but I heard you in here and wanted to say good morning and thanks for letting us stay.'

'*Bonjour!* I'm Anais. It's lovely to meet you in person. I'm sorry, I don't have any coffee to offer you. I'll get some today.'

She waves me away as if it doesn't matter. 'Around the corner is Café Madame where we have café et croissant for only five euros.' An espresso coffee and buttery croissant sounds good right about now. 'Would you like to join us for petit déjeuner? We can walk there in only a few minutes.'

'Breakfast would be great. I'll grab my scarf.'

I hurry back to my suite and don a jacket and woollen scarf. We meet in the lobby a few minutes later and head out into the dark of the dawn. There's something magical about Paris so early in the morning, where there are very few souls in sight. The air is foggy and the streets deserted as if even the city itself is sleeping.

'What do you all do for work?' I ask as I push my hands deeper into my coat pockets and blink against light drizzle.

She tucks an errant strand of red hair behind her ear. 'We do walking tours for tourists. It's slowing down now as the cold weather creeps in so we're just hoping there'll still be enough tourists who are willing to brave the elements so we keep some money coming in. Some days we do really well, other days we do tours but don't get tipped at all.'

'Ah, I see. The weather would really factor into your work.' Walking tours are plentiful in Paris, and a great way to learn the history of the place for a minor cost. Most tours offer a 'pay what you wish' tip system, so their income can fluctuate wildly, especially if people take advantage of that. 'You must know a lot about Paris.'

She grins. 'I do now. There was a lot of cramming in the beginning and, while I've learned a thousand facts about the city, there's always more to learn. At first, I was terrified, having to speak to the groups like I'm an authority on such things, but now I really enjoy it. We aim to make it fun and throw in unique and silly titbits as well as the history about each sight.'

I smile at Juliette. There's a real warmth to her and I love that she's made her tours memorable for visitors. 'I bet it's fun. So where to next?'

She shakes her head. 'We're going to stay for Christmas and

then we'll move on to the Netherlands, Belgium, Germany and beyond. It'll depend on where we can find work.'

'What an adventure.'

'It will be. Although we were supposed to leave Paris a couple of months ago.' She laughs. 'None of us factored in that we'd fall in love with the first city we stopped at, in our own country. We made a pact we'd stay until we'd explored every part of Paris. Will we have the same issue everywhere we go? I didn't know you could fall in love with a place. It can capture your heart just like a person.'

'*Oui*, Paris is like that.' I should know. After I finished university in Bristol around sixteen years ago, I came to visit Manon for a holiday and never left. I can't see myself ever returning to Britain long term. 'So which suite are you staying in?' I can't help but wonder if Juliette is the tidier of two couples, or if she lives more like Manon, where chaos reigns supreme.

'My boyfriend Timothee and I are in suite eleven. And Zac and Kiki are in twelve.' As suspected, Juliette is in the tidier suite.

'I hope it's OK – we had a quick peek in to see what work needed to be done.'

'For sure. We're grateful to be able to stay in such a central location.'

'*Merci.*'

We arrive at Café Madame and introductions are made with Juliette's fellow backpackers. There's her boyfriend Timothee and their friends, the other couple Zac and Kiki. They're a jovial bunch and energetic despite the early morning. Kiki talks a mile a minute and has a machine-gun laugh that is contagious. She's animated and speaks fast compared to a quieter and more softly spoken Juliette. The strong friendship is evident in the way they complement each other and offer a squeeze of an arm or a tap on the hand when slinging words back and forth.

'Have you got a tour lined up early?' I ask after placing my order for café et croissant. The sun is slowly rising but it won't be light for another hour or so.

'*Oui*, the first one is at eight thirty. We run the tours twice a day and also offer private guided outings for tourists who want the privilege of an exclusive one-to-one experience.'

Kiki says, 'And what about you, Anais? Are you planning to renovate the hotel yourself? I can see you wielding a hammer for some reason, as if you've got a lot of pent-up emotions that need to be expressed.'

My eyebrows shoot up. 'Uh – well, how do you...?' Am I sitting Nutcracker stiff? Shoulders up around my ears? Wearing that resting *kill* face I can't seem to dislodge, no matter how much I massage my cheeks?

Kiki breaks into a loud cackle that makes the birds flee from the horse chestnut trees. '*Désolée*, I read about your divorce in *Paris Scandale*, and if it were me who suffered through a marriage with a man like that, I'd become a hammer-wielding, revenge-seeking, *je ne sais pas*, maniac.'

I take a moment to process Kiki's words, not sure at first whether I feel offended or completely understood and decide it's the latter, and that she's quite possibly my spirit animal.

'The thought has crossed my mind once or twice, Kiki. In fact, I'm having a little trouble writing romance after his many infidelities, and I must admit there are times when I do have murder on my mind.' Juliette's eyes widen in fright while Kiki gives me a slow nod of understanding. '*Fictionally*, at least. But isn't living well the best revenge?' I quickly add and give Juliette what I hope is a reassuring smile and a pat on the hand. Would a killer do that? *Non*, they'd delight in their audience being uncomfortable.

Our breakfast arrives and I take a much-needed sip of coffee before I fill them in on our plans for the hotel, including that we aim to do as much of the work ourselves; well, as much as our capabilities allow. 'The hotel will be designed around a literary theme.'

Juliette dances in her seat. 'Ooh, perfect for the 6th arrondissement, which I've found to be the most literary of all!'

'*Oui*,' I say, my mind going to all the magnificent libraries and bookshops in the vicinity. 'Maybe I should make a literary map for guests...' I muse as the idea takes shape. Not only can we offer a literary haven inside the hotel, but we could provide a detailed map of all those hidden gems that most people miss because they don't know to go looking for it.

Juliette clicks her fingers. 'I can take you to a couple of special places for your literary map that are very close by and are the best-kept secrets.'

'I'd love that.'

'I'll have a look at our bookings and let you know what day I'm free.'

'*Parfait*.'

'Soo...' Kiki says, smirk at the ready. 'How are you finding your new neighbour, Noah? He had quite the list of complaints when we moved into the hotel. We had to explain many times we weren't there for maintenance.'

That man! Just what is his problem? How exactly does the hotel impinge on his business aside from the fact it's a little rough around the edges? Is he bored?

6

5 NOVEMBER

After yet another fruitless evening of killing my darlings, and by that I mean literally murdering my fictional heroes, I awake groggily in the musty confines of my suite and know it's time. I've put off the call as long as I can. If my literary agent Margaret's frantic voicemails are anything to go by, I'd say our telephone call ping pong days are over.

If I don't return her call, there's every chance she'll arrive on my doorstep, and I'd like to avoid a face-to-face meeting if I can. When there's bad news afoot, Margaret can be domineering and terrifying in equal measure, which is great when it comes to her negotiating my contracts, but not so good when I'm not meeting my end of the bargain.

I dread the thought of telling her I'm not going to meet the imposed deadline. I've already spent the advance on some over-priced divorce lawyers, and I've got no book to hand in. No book means no chance of royalties once I've earned out the advance. And, worse still, it could also mean a lawsuit for breaking the terms of my contract.

In my suite, I sit at a desk that's past its prime with a scratched surface and a wonky leg that I'm growing to love. Every scar and scrape is part of its story and evidence of a long, rich life. Who else sat at this desk over its tenure in suite two? Did they write postcards to family at home? Or long sweeping letters trying to capture the vibrancy of the city and all they'd seen and done? Now I'm taking comfort by the marred and rickety desk, trying to pull my life back together one word at a time. In these quiet, reflective moments I see beauty in these abandoned belongings throughout the hotel.

But... musing time is over. There's no avoiding the dreaded call to Margaret. I've got three building contractors arriving this week to quote for the reno job and, if I don't sort my writing life out, I won't be able to fully focus on the hotel.

I brace myself and dial the number. '*Bonjour*, Margaret!' I say, forcing brightness into my voice.

'Cut the crap, Anais. What's going on? You've been avoiding my calls.' Margaret is old-school publishing ilk. You'll find her sitting at a desk littered with manuscripts, by an open window that overlooks the Shard, smoking a raspberry-flavoured vape and screeching at staff. It's not exactly PC but she is lauded enough to get away with it.

'I'm glad you asked. You see—' There's a crash from below and a blood-curdling scream soon follows.

'What on earth was that?' Margaret says, her voice laced with suspicion as if I'm creating a diversion in the hopes of ending the call. And, truthfully, I wish I'd thought of that.

'It's Manon!' I take flight, picturing the worst. She's fallen through a ceiling. She's tripped down the laundry chute. Who even has laundry chutes these days? Well, L'Hotel du Parc sure does. I've had to pull the hood of Manon's jumper many a time to stop her attempting to slide down it, 'to see where it leads', imagining my poor cousin stuck bent and twisted in a pipe for all eternity.

'Where is she?' I yell as I race down the brown carpeted steps, dust dancing as I go.

Sweet relief hits me as I find Manon in the room we've picked to be the future library. It's mostly empty except for a row of bookshelves, some with dusty leatherbound editions abandoned on the shelves higher up and out of reach. Well… I find her feet. She's stuck under a fallen bookshelf with only her Doc Martens on display like she's the Wicked Witch of the West. I'm still holding my phone, so I inform Margaret, 'I have a medical emergency on my hands! I'll call you back.'

'No, you won't. I'm invested in this now. Put me on speaker.'

I sigh and press the speaker button, dropping the phone to the parquetry floor. 'Manon, are you OK?' My chest tightens at the thought Manon might be seriously hurt. There's a faint groan. I say, 'I'm going to lift the bookshelf up.'

'Noadajldk,' comes her muffled reply. I give the old bookshelf a great big heave but it doesn't budge. I'd previously marked these shelves for the bin because they appeared somewhat flimsy, but it turns out they're surprisingly heavy.

'*Merde*! It's impossible! Can you breathe under there?'

'You need another pair of hands to help, Anais. Get to it,' Margaret says in her usual brusque way.

'NOAJDAJLDK!' Manon says, her voice raspy but strong as if she's using every ounce of lung capacity to talk.

'What? Conserve your energy, Manon.'

Margaret says, 'Is she asking for someone?'

'Who would she ask for? The backpackers are all at work.' I give the bookshelf another shove. Nothing. 'I'm going to need assistance. Someone with muscles. A dependable, solid—'

'Noajkh.'

'Noah!' Margaret shrieks. 'Who's Noah?'

'The next-door neighbour! Margaret, you keep talking to her and I'll get Noah.' I move my mobile phone closer to Manon so she can hear my agent and dash outside into the drizzly day.

I race to The Lost Generation Wine Bar, as fast as my out-of-shape romance writer body can take me, and bang on Noah's door. What if he's not here? My heart gallops as I screen my hands against the darkened glass to peek in. I let out a shuddery breath when I see his purposeful strides coming towards me.

When he opens the door a crack, I say, 'Noah, we've got an emergency! Manon is stuck under a heavy bookshelf and I can't lift it off.'

Thankfully, Noah understands the urgency and follows my quick steps. He doesn't seem to be holding a grudge about my unleashing on him the other day when I went a little off script. Still, best he knows I'm not going to allow a man to boss me about.

We rush back to find Margaret telling Manon all about a new author of hers who's single and has an upcoming book tour in Paris and would love a native French friend to help guide him during his stay. 'Margaret! Now is clearly not the time for matchmaking!'

Noah assesses the situation and in a matter of moments lifts the shelf from Manon's frame as easily as if it's made of ply. I really must work on my upper body strength. Either that, or Noah is deceptively strong. While he's got that robust alpine man swagger, I didn't think a man who owns a bar would be that athletic, what with being in close proximity to wine, whisky and cocktails serving and imbibing. Am I buying into the stereotype? He probably spends his days off trekking up mountains, hunkering in humble cabins with no electricity just to prove he can, like Hemingway used to do with his first wife Hadley. Again, probably a stereotype but I am a writer and that's where my mind goes.

I put Noah out of my mind and focus on Manon, who sits up, her face darkened with dust. 'You're alive to tell the tale!' I drop to my knees and pull her in tight. She yelps.

Noah inspects the shelf as if it might offer up a clue as to why it fell over. He's bent at the waist like he's Poirot or something.

'I'm alive – just. I might claim compensation. I haven't decided yet.'

'You'd make me, your favourite cousin, pay compensation?' The patient looks remarkably well despite a heavy piece of furniture having landed smack bang atop her. Still, injuries can be internal and that is a worrying thought. 'We should get you to the hospital to get checked.'

Manon scoots to the side of the room and leans against the wall. She's clutching her midsection, which is a concern. 'No, I don't need to go to hospital. It's not that serious.'

'I'm sure she's fine,' Noah says breezily.

And really, how would he know? 'Are you medically trained, Noah?' I narrow my eyes. 'With X-Ray vision?'

A frown mars his brow. 'Well, no. It's just that the bookshelf itself is—'

'—made from solid wood and must have fallen on her with some velocity!' I butt in. 'For all we know, my poor cousin could be internally bleeding, or worse.'

Manon's eyes widen.

'She might fall asleep and never wake up again.' I twist my

mouth into an apologetic pucker. 'Sorry to speak so bluntly, Manon. Your *maman* would kill me if you died on my watch.'

She gasps. 'You're more concerned about my *maman* than me waking up dead?'

I nod gravely. 'She's rather intimidating.' Let's just say, Aunt Josephine would give Margaret a run for her money. My school holiday visits were always fun with Manon by my side, but Aunt Josephine ran a tight ship, and I behaved because I was terrified of getting into trouble, and also because my younger cousin *did not*.

'Maman is the reason I have so many issues. Do you know she threatened me every Christmas that Père Noël wouldn't be coming to deliver presents because of my behaviour, and instead I'd be paid a visit by Père Fouettard, who would whack me instead? What kind of a mother does that?' Manon shakes her head at the memory. When we were children, all French parents threatened such a thing. Fairytales about 'Father Whipper' were enough to keep most of us well behaved as we imagined this old, stooped stranger arriving to dole out punishment instead of the jovial Père Noël, who'd deliver our presents while we slept.

'Well, it didn't stop you, did it? You still wouldn't do as told.'

'Where's the fun in that.' There's a wicked gleam in her eye as if she's right back there baiting her poor mother. 'You just need to understand how to handle her, and playing by the rules is not the right way. Help me up, would you?' I lift her up and she wipes her hands on her black jeans. 'I only hope... I'll recover in time for the festive season.' She hugs herself tight and I get the first inkling all is not what it seems.

'That's, like, seven weeks away, Manon.' My shoulders relax. If she's exaggerating, she's healthy. 'You're fine. You probably pulled the bookshelf on top of yourself so you didn't have to help me sort the kitchen cupboards today.' There is all sorts of detritus in the cupboards: canned food that goes back decades, mismatched crockery and broken appliances that need to be relegated to the scrap heap. All that, and I still haven't found a French press, but have managed to buy one at a local market so at least our mornings start with the required jolt of caffeine.

'It did cross my mind.'

I'd almost forgotten Noah is still here when he says, 'How could you not lift such a light shelf?' Suspicion flits across his features.

Light shelf? Is this some kind of macho man thing? He wants to be fawned over for his big, strong, wild-man muscles? 'The shelf is so heavy I couldn't even get it to budge! I don't think you need to highlight the fact my upper body strength is somewhat lacking to feel better about yourself, Noah.' The ego on the man is astounding!

Manon shrugs. 'Anais might have very strong phalanxes from all that typing but that's where it ends.' I go to argue, but she's probably right. If I didn't force myself to walk the streets of Paris for sustenance or at least a baguette to go with a home-cooked meal, I dread to think what shape I'd be in.

I survey the books that lay scattered on the carpet and suddenly the jig is up. 'You climbed the bookshelf like a tree to get to the hardbacks on the top shelf in case they were first editions you could smuggle out and sell, Manon?'

My devious cousin has the grace to blush. 'I would have gone halves with you.'

'Please, do keep nattering,' Margaret says. 'It's not like I have other authors who need my attention.'

Oh god, my life has devolved into a comedy of errors! 'Sorry,

Margaret.' I pick up the phone and take off the speaker function. 'I'll get Manon settled and call you back.'

'No, you'll make another excuse to avoid me. Get that man to watch Manon while you and I have a *serious* talk.' There's no avoiding it, I guess. The brief reprieve is over.

'Fine.' I turn to Noah. 'Would you be able to keep an eye on Manon while I talk to my literary agent who doesn't take medical emergencies into account?'

'*I can hear you!*'

'Sure.' He folds his arms. 'Your literary agent, eh?'

'*Oui*, I'm a novelist.'

He raises a brow as if impressed. 'What do you write?'

'Romantic comedies.'

His face falls. Typical. He's probably one of those men who get off denigrating romance novels as trashy when they're anything but. 'Oh, uh, I see,' he eventually manages.

'Not literary enough for you, Noah?' He wears his judgement like a cloak, apparently. Not a surprise, but still.

'*Still waiting!*' Margaret says just as I'm about to educate the ignorance out of him. Romance is the highest-earning genre of fiction for a reason and it riles me up when people (men typically) frown upon it, as if it isn't literary enough because the books end in a happy ever after or a happy for now, so get labelled as predictable. Formulaic. It makes my blood boil. Trust Noah to fall into that category, with his love of the literary authors from the Roaring Twenties. He's got that hot-guy scowl perfected too, as judgement lines his masculine features. Men – who needs them! I'll stick to my misunderstood fictional heroes, *merci beaucoup*!

'I'd better take this,' I say and turn to Manon. 'Will you be all right?'

'I don't need a babysitter.' Manon wears the expression of a petulant child.

'Let me put out this fire before I return to yours. *Please.*'

Manon rolls her eyes dramatically before wincing. 'Fine.'

I turn to Noah and grudgingly thank him for his help. 'Sure, sure. I've got nothing better to do.'

Sarcasm? I don't tell him that's the lowest form of wit; instead, I express my contempt with a cool gaze, just like one of my heroines would do, and hope it cuts him to the quick.

I return to my suite when there's a commotion down the phone line.

'Ah, damn it all to hell,' Margaret says. 'I've got another client here. Some two-bit celebrity who has written yet another cosy mystery. I'll have to go and dance attendance on him, which irks me no end. I'll call you back, probably not until tomorrow since I'll have to be the one who wines and dines him.'

We say our goodbyes and I return to the library room to check on Manon and find that Noah is nowhere to be found. So much for keeping an eye on my poor cousin, who could very well be concussed. It says a lot about the guy, just vanishing like that. Comes to our rescue, tells us how strong he is, and then leaves with no care or concern for Manon's possible collapsed lung, or worse.

'Are you OK?' I ask, finding her leaning against the wall, reading a book.

'I'll need a few days to recuperate,' she says, twisting her features. She's clearly in pain. What if she's broken some ribs? Or is bleeding internally? Is it possible that she will really fall asleep and never wake up? Maybe her earlier stoic reaction was for Noah's benefit.

'Manon, maybe we should get you looked at?'

'A nap will suffice.' Her words are clipped, as if she's really hurting.

'OK. Do you want to move to the sofa in the guest lounge? I can bring a rug and pillow or...?' She shakes her head, so I survey the spacious room and what will be our raison d'être, the library. Right now, it's soulless but soon it will be magnificent. I sigh. There's so much to do but right now I need to make sure Manon is comfortable and not concussed.

Noah left the offending bookshelf standing in the middle of the room, but I don't want to risk it falling over again. There's no chance I can shift it since I couldn't budge it before. 'I need to move this out of the way. But how?' I say, almost to myself.

'*Non!* It's fine there! Leave it!'

Hands on hips, I study my cousin. What's with the sharp outburst? Is she worried it might topple over on her again? This must be some kind of trauma response!

I hurry to reassure her. 'I'll be careful. If I lift an edge, I can pop a rug under it and slide it across the parquetry.'

'Now you mention it, I am rather woozy. Get me *une demi bouteille* of Chablis, will you?'

'What! No. You can't drink alcohol with a concussion!'

There's a shifty look in her eyes that takes but a mere moment to translate. To test my theory, I go to the bookshelf and push it. It moves easily as if it's made of plywood, which upon further inspection, I suspect it is. No wonder Noah made those comments about me not being able to move the thing.

'Manon! Were you *holding* the bookshelf so I couldn't lift it off you?'

Her face dissolves into a grin. '*Oui.*'

'To get out of working today or—' I slap my forehead when I figure it out. 'To get knight in shining armour Noah over here? How transparent! He would have known it was a farce as soon as he lifted the very light shelf off your poor, prone body!' This is why she's doesn't have any external injuries; it was all a set up. 'You planned this? Why?'

'He came running just when you needed him, did he not?'

Her heart is in the right place but what Manon doesn't seem to understand is that, when I say romance is dead, I *really* mean it. 'One day, in the future, when my battered heart is healed over, I might consider dating again, but the nasty divorce proceedings where all our dirty laundry had been aired really did a number on me. And Noah, he's a walking cliché and I happen to know a lot about men like that.'

'How is Noah a walking cliché?'

'Can't you see it simply from the swagger? The literary nerd sartorial choices? The whole broody, robust, I'm a wild mountain man who can lift heavy things who marches home to the little lady and slugs back a glass of whisky, neat *of course*, and smokes an imported cigar, while analysing and dissecting nineteenth-century literature as if he knows what he's talking about? I mean, it's *obvious*, right?'

Manon gapes at me like I've got two heads. At least now I'm certain it's not concussion causing that. '*La vache*. Not that *you're* into stereotyping, Anais, you hypocrite!'

Am I wrong? Men like him are the love-and-leave-them type and I don't care what anyone says, I know it to be true. It's why these over-thirty and -forty macho men are still single. Because they're not the commitment types. 'I'm calling it like I see it, so can we agree our focus should be on the hotel, not on men? Especially not on men who live and work next door?'

'I cannot.'

I let out a frustrated sigh. '*Manon*. I've got very little time to write a first draft, and to renovate and open a hotel. Adding a love interest into the mix is just asking for trouble. Been there, done that, got the writer's block.'

'I'm not going to join your pity party, if that's what you're hoping for, but let me say this: have you ever thought your writer's block might be cured by a new love interest? It makes perfect sense.'

I can only shake my head. Manon and Margaret both think a man is the answer. How can they not see a man caused all these problems?! 'Back to work.'

7

6 NOVEMBER

An almighty crash wakes me from a dead sleep. Did it come from upstairs? There's no one staying on the third floor though. I sit up and strain to listen. Could someone have broken into the hotel? I fumble for my phone and swipe it to life to see it's just gone three. I pull the covers back and contemplate investigating. What would I do if faced with an intruder?

Scanning the room, I can't see one single thing I could use as a weapon to protect myself. What sort of hotelier am I? I jump out of my skin when my door creaks open and I let out a scream when a head appears.

'Would you stop?' Manon says, swiping at her sleepy eyes. 'If there's a criminal on the loose inside the hotel you've just alerted them to our whereabouts.'

'So you heard it too?'

'*Oui*, obviously. I'm not here to read you a bedtime story.' She yawns as if not concerned at all there could be a villain roaming the hotel.

'Should we check? What if there is someone out there?' I ask, slightly panicked. 'Then what?'

'I'll handle it.'

Manon does jujitsu and is very good at it, so I trust we'd have a fighting chance if she felt the need to put life and limb on the line. But that's all well and good if it's one person. What if there are two? What if there's a whole gang?

I slide on my robe and then pick up my phone, activating the torch function.

'*Non!*' she hisses. 'He'll see us coming a mile away.'

'*He?*'

'Statistically speaking, he.'

'Right. Right. I'm not very good at this. I have no true crime experience and I'd like to keep it that way.'

I creep behind Manon, holding on to the corner of her jumper so I don't fall behind. She keeps brushing my hand off and I keep replacing it. I don't know jujitsu so I'm not losing sight of my only hope of survival if we do run into a bad guy or three with an ulterior motive.

We check the hallway and find it clear. 'Didn't the sound come from above?' I ask.

Manon grimaces. '*Oui*, I thought so too, but it seems so much more dangerous going up another level *away* from the exit, you know?'

I cock my head. I've never seen Manon scared. It's jarring. 'Are you... frightened?'

'A little,' she admits.

I reel back, surprised at her frank admission. 'How can you be when you read about this sort of thing for fun? You listen to hours of podcasts. To *relax*, for crying out loud!'

She lifts a shoulder. 'Well, that's because I usually feel very safe in my own world and not at all threatened there's a serial killer lurking about, lying in wait for me.'

'Serial killer?' I hold my breath and hope she doesn't give me one of those 'statistically speaking' answers again.

'It's best I keep some things to myself. Knowledge is power and all that, but not in every case.'

Mon Dieu! My skin breaks out in goose bumps.

'We should at least get a knife from the kitchen!' I hiss.

'Rookie mistake, Anais. It would take but a moment for him to overpower you, and then guess what? He's got the knife, and you're not exactly a fast runner. Boom, he catches you and...' She makes the horror movie slasher sound.

'Let's wake up the backpackers! There's safety in numbers!' I march ahead and am suddenly flung backwards as Manon grabs the belt on my dressing gown.

'No, don't disturb them.'

'Why? They're in danger too!'

She activates the torch on her phone and shines it under her chin, which is a frightening sight to say the least. When she gives me a maniacal grin, I know I've been had.

'You're the worst cousin in the world, Manon!'

'This again?'

I shake my head. 'Revenge will be sweet. My next book will feature a side character named Manon who wears only pink, has a girlish giggle and listens to Mariah Carey's Christmas album on repeat.'

'*You wouldn't!*'

'Polka-dotted pink!'

'Fine, I'm sorry!'

'Good. You are inherently evil, Manon.'

'Aww, thanks. Look, I'm no Miss Marple but I'd hazard a guess the crashing sound from above was the heavy mirror sitting on the flimsy screw finally falling down.'

I slap my forehead. It's so obvious in retrospect. We go

upstairs to investigate and sure enough at the end of the hallway is the once beautiful mirror face-down on the parquetry.

'I'll get a dustpan and broom,' Manon says and disappears. I lift the heavy frame up and inspect it. The mirror is smashed to smithereens but the frame hasn't suffered much damage. There are a few nicks and chips but, for an antique mirror, that's bound to be the case anyway.

Manon jogs back and sweeps up the mess.

'We can get this fixed. It's too beautiful not to rescue.'

I stand and stretch, looking at the big hole where the mirror once was. 'The mirror took a fair chunk of wall with it when it toppled down.'

'Let me see,' Manon says, handing me the dustpan and broom. 'I think I can fit my whole head in there!' Before I can stop her, her head disappears into the hole.

'Manon! Who knows what's hiding in that wall! There could be toxic dust or a build-up of... ah, toxins for all you know!'

'*Ooh la la!*'

'What is it?' I'm not about to believe her again, not after her last attempt at fooling me.

Her head pops out, dusted with plaster crumbs. 'Anais! Stick your head in there and tell me I'm not seeing things!'

'Nice try.'

'I'm not joking this time! Have a look.'

I lean close to the hole and peer through. 'Is that part of Noah's property?'

'*Non*, look at the doors.'

My jaw drops when I see the exact same brass numerals that are on each door of L'Hotel du Parc. 'Suites nineteen and twenty! But – how can that be? Why would they be blocked off with a wall like this?'

Manon considers it for a moment. 'They must be special? That or they're derelict.'

I shiver in the cold of the unheated third floor. 'It's a little too early in the morning to use a sledgehammer to break down this wall.' We'd wake up not only the backpackers but probably Noah next door and nothing is worth hearing him harp on about broken sleep and bad manners.

Manon's shoulders slump. 'Oui, we don't want to disrupt the backpackers.'

'Tomorrow then?' I glance at the time on my phone. 'Technically that is today. Let's try and get some sleep. Not that I'm going to be able to. I'll be wondering about what's behind the doors of suites nineteen and twenty.'

Did a family maybe hide in there during the war? Or could it be as simple as Manon suggests, that the rooms are a mess? But surely then just locking the doors would suffice?

It's more than that. I can feel the secret pulse like a heartbeat as I make my way back to bed.

8
7 NOVEMBER

After an interrupted sleep I'm startled awake when my phone rings. The caller display shows it's Margaret. I'd completely forgotten about everything except the mystery upstairs as I tossed and turned, unable to fully get back to sleep after our witching-hour wakeup. I mentally prepare and formulate how to break the news to her, all without the benefit of my first morning coffee.

'*Bonjour*, Margaret!' I say faux sunnily, before a yawn gets the better of me.

'We did all that yesterday, Anais. Get to the point. Why haven't I had an update about your manuscript that's due imminently? And I warn you, I'm in a foul mood after meeting that ghastly celebrity yesterday. Some of the things he said – completely inappropriate. Guaranteed to be the sort of client who will end up being cancelled. Anyway, don't get me started on privileged men in publishing. We're here to talk about your writing. So. You... spill.'

'Ah, well, as you can appreciate, things are a bit hectic at the moment, so I haven't been in the right frame of mind to – uh, write romance.' She gasps, not a good sign, so I hurry on. 'You know I've *never* once missed a deadline but...' My stomach twists in knots and I can't quite get the rest of the words out.

'And you're just telling me this when your book is about due?'

I screw up my face. 'Upon reflection, I should have mentioned it sooner.'

I hear a string of expletives and then she says in a surprisingly gentle tone, 'Start at the beginning, Anais. Where are you?'

'I'm at L'Hotel du Parc.'

'That's the hotel your husband bought on a whim?'

'The very same.'

'And where is Francois-Xavier? Why did a neighbour have to rescue Manon yesterday?'

The trashy tabloid *Paris Scandale* reported on the dissolution of my marriage recently but evidently the news hasn't travelled across the English Channel, so none of my British colleagues have any idea. I inhale, filling up my lungs with the requisite oxygen needed to catch her up.

I haven't confessed about the divorce to anyone outside the family. It's not exactly a fun subject matter. And only Manon really knows the true extent of it. When I booted my husband out of our apartment for good, he posted on Facebook about our split, playing the woe-is-me card. Shortly after that, I received a torrent of messages from loads of other women who he'd had... tête-à-têtes with. Some he'd brazenly invited to our apartment while I was writing at the library; others he'd met at theirs. They all believed he was in the throes of a divorce, or worse, single, as if I never existed. To say I was blindsided is an understatement. Who knew heartbreak and humiliation could feel like a death?

And while all that was happening, I had to pretend to Margaret everything was super, and I was ecstatic when we were negotiating the Kiss Films deal. What should have been one of the happiest moments of my career was marred by despair.

'Francois-Xavier slept with our housekeeper.' I go into great detail about catching them entwined together on our fifth wedding anniversary so Margaret knows just how fragile I am right now. 'We've since divorced; he got the apartment, I got his rundown disaster of a hotel in the 6th. Manon is here to help me after giving up her true crime podcast and three jobs. I convinced her to join me in case I snapped and killed my ex-husband. With her experience with grisly murders, I figure she'd know how to dispose of the body so it would never be found. All that aside, we'd like to soft launch the hotel by Christmas because I need the income pronto and I want to be swept up in the festive season and start the New Year with a clean slate.'

'Focusing on a Christmas launch makes sense. But as for the rest... just, *wow*. This is a lot to process, Anais. No wonder you can't write. I *knew* Francois-Xavier was a phony. No one has a tan like that all year round, and why was his skin *orange*? And those too-tight shirts he wears, surely they cut off his circulation?' Margaret met Francois-Xavier a few times, including at the British Romantic Novelists Awards. He flirted up a storm with my fellow nominees, which I'd put down to him trying to charm them in his innocent French way. The writing has always been on the wall, and I just didn't translate it.

I swallow a sigh. 'I was the last to see, so it seems.' Of all the clichés. Gah.

'Look, it's not ideal but this sort of thing happens every day. How many heroines have you written that go through the same sort of conflicts and come out the other end shinier, happier versions of themselves, complete with a new man who worships them?'

I groan. 'But they're fictional! I'm going to die alone in a hotel, possibly crushed by a falling chandelier or when I tumble down the stairs because the banister falls off clean in my hands.' OK, I'm exaggerating because that seems to be my new default setting.

'Anais, you're overwrought. This isn't *like* you. Perhaps you need your own *amour-affaire* to put your past to bed, eh? That Noah guy any good? His voice was certainly alluring. Wish we'd video called now.'

I roll my eyes at the thought of an *amour-affaire*. 'Noah is a literary nerd with a side of buff brawny mountain man about him. All he needs is to wear a woollen turtleneck and have a stag head on the wall to complete the persona. Wait, he probably does have a stag head on the wall. I wouldn't put it past him.'

'Who doesn't love one of those rugged, good-with-their-hands types?'

'*Moi*, that's who.'

She groans as if I'm a disappointment. 'Think of a brief dalliance as good old-fashioned research for your book, eh? No harm, no foul.'

'No way. The warning bells clang whenever he appears. So can we talk biz for a moment?' While I don't want to draw her attention to the fact my words have dried up unless they're about bludgeoning, I want to talk about men even less.

'Right, so what's the problem exactly? You've got the rejuvenation to contend with and...?'

'And, I can't write about love. I just cannot. It makes me wail. Or stare in a semi-catatonic state at the wall while I replay all my failures with men, and how I rushed into marrying the king of idiots when everyone warned me about him. Even the little fluffy dog in the apartment next door in Le Marais used to bark aggressively and flash its teeth whenever Francois-Xavier appeared, and *still* I brushed it off. Dogs always *know*.'

Margaret tuts. 'You write fiction, not memoirs. Can't you use that great big imagination of yours? Your fans are expecting your Christmas romcom to come out next September. Get your jingle on, girl!'

'All I've got so far is the red Rudolph nose.'

'Perfect! You're halfway there!'

'That's from crying though.'

'Oh.'

'This state of... flux is just temporary,' I rally. I need to pump those Christmas carols and turn my mood around for good. 'In terms of writing a romantic comedy, my heart isn't in it. I don't want to lose my fanbase writing subpar love stories and, as much as I try to avoid it, the hero always ends up dead. First his fingers and toes are blowtorched off and it descends into madness from there and that's just the first chapter.' Sharing this is really a tonic; I feel lighter already.

'It descends into madness from *there*?' I can almost hear her shuddering. 'OK, here's what we're going to do. I'm going to call in a favour with your publisher and ask they give you two more months. It's almost unheard of, I know, but they can rush things through when necessary. But that's it, Anais. I'm empathetic to your plight, I really am, but we've got your 2025 Christmas book scheduled across all territories and all formats. We're risking future deals if you don't meet the timelines. I'm sorry, that's just the way the beast works with traditional publishing.'

I'm grateful at this unexpected stay of execution; alas, there's still that niggle deep inside. 'But... but what if this latest block is permanent? What then?' What if my career is over after all this time? What if I never get over it?

'Nothing is permanent, not even marriage, remember that. Use it as fodder for your book. We can always publish a gripping serial killer thriller under a pseudonym later, if that's where your heart lies. But first, get this Christmas romcom done. *Please*. The LA production company has the first right of refusal for it, after they optioned *The French Billionaire's Secret*. Progress has been slow on the movie front but that's the film industry. They're keen to read your latest offering, so make it good.'

So no pressure then? 'OK. Two months though, Margaret. It doesn't seem like enough time, not with the hotel renovations and...' I really should shut my trap because there's every chance Margaret will change her mind and, really, she's being more generous than I expected.

'I'm not asking you to write a bible-length book, I'm asking you to write a first draft. Make it messy but make it happen. Don't overthink it but *do* get that word count up each and every day.'

I sigh, but I'm glad for the reprieve no matter how impossible it sounds. I'm lucky really. Margaret has dropped clients for a whole lot less than missing deadlines. 'So what is the official deadline date then?'

'December thirty-first. Ho. Ho. Ho.' And with that, she screeches at someone and hangs up.

That's less than two months, being that today is 7 November, but I know Margaret is being more than fair.

Coffee. Everything will be better once I've had coffee.

In the kitchen I bump into Juliette. '*Bonjour*,' she says.

'*Bonjour*. You look bright-eyed today.'

She grins. 'We've got a private tour booked and paid. It's a relief. It's been far too quiet of late, and I'm worried we're going to burn through our savings if things don't pick up.'

'If only you were staying for good once the hotel was open and at capacity; you could offer tours to our guests.'

'Ah!' She holds up a finger. 'That's a great idea, Anais! Perhaps I could make some brochures and drop them into hotels?'

'Why not?'

'*Merci!*' She goes to the fridge and holds up a carton of orange juice.

I shake my head. 'Only caffeine can fix what ails me this morning.'

'You didn't sleep? Ooh, was it that loud crash in the middle of the night? I heard it but fell back asleep because I couldn't rouse Timothee to go and check.'

'*Oui*, a mirror on the third floor fell down.'

'I hope you're not superstitious!'

I laugh as Kiki comes to join us. '*Non*, but I'm very happy I wasn't the one who broke it, therefore my luck remains intact.' And just in case, I tap on wood.

9

---

7 NOVEMBER

Once the backpackers leave to meet their tour client, Manon and I dash upstairs to the third floor. For some reason, I wasn't yet ready to share with Juliette what we found. It feels like a delicious mystery that I want to preserve until we know what lies beyond those doors.

'You just wanted to wield a sledgehammer, didn't you?' I say to Manon, who is dressed in black overalls and has a plastic visor covering her face as she holds the hammer over a shoulder, body vibrating like she can't wait a moment longer to swing it.

'*Oui!* But because I'm a considerate cousin, I'll allow you to do the honours. It's your hotel, after all.'

'That's generous of you but it's best if I protect my so-called delicate writer hands, *non?*'

She shrugs and turns to the wall, throwing the hammer with all her might, taking out large swathes as she goes, all the while screaming bloody murder as if she's a rage-fuelled beast.

'*Manon!*' I admonish, but she can't hear me over her own animalistic caterwauling. Next minute, Noah's going to stomp over and let us know we're breaking yet another cardinal rule – making too much noise. And, I mean, I'd probably have to reluctantly agree with him because Manon's screaming loud enough that I worry my hearing will be permanently damaged.

A few minutes later, the wall and support beams are demolished – nay, disintegrated. Gone from this world.

'Are… you all right, Manon?'

She drops the sledgehammer by her side. 'I've never felt so ALIVE! What else needs to come down? WOO!'

I prise the weapon from her hands. 'Ah – that's enough destruction for one day.'

She wipes her brow. 'I've never felt so powerful. So in control.'

'So lost to the dark side, even. Could we perhaps investigate now?'

'*Oui, oui.* Sorry.'

The parquetry floor is the same on the other side but pristine, not as dull and bowed as our side is from years of foot traffic.

Manon and I exchange a glance. 'Let's hope there's a very good reason these rooms have been hidden for so long.'

The doors to the suites are painted the same creamy colour as the others in the hotel, but are in much better condition. The brass number plates are also the same, but the door handles are different, more traditional perhaps from the Belle Époque era.

A hush falls between us. I hold my breath and grab the cool of the brass handle of suite nineteen and push, but the door is firmly locked.

'*La vache.* I wasn't expecting that.' Disappointment flutters through me but it makes sense the rooms would be inaccessible since a former owner went to the trouble to build a wall to hide them from view.

Manon sighs. 'I can pick the locks.'

'With what?'

'A bobby pin, a pen? A coat hanger!' It's probably the only time Manon *would* use a coat hanger.

'I don't want to risk damaging anything. The realtor gave me a huge bunch of master keys that I stashed behind the reception desk without any thought because none of the suites were locked when we arrived. Why don't we check those first?'

'I doubt we'll find an antique master key to fit but we can try.'

I put my ear to the door of room nineteen. 'What could be inside?'

'A mystery. Try suite twenty, just in case.'

I turn and try the handle of suite twenty and it swings open. '*Voilà!*'

We squish together in the doorway and survey the contents of the musty room. Under the window is a neatly made bed with a white lace coverlet. The pillows bear an imprint still. Who slept here?

There is a pile of vintage Christmas decorations, including a 'creche', which is what the French call a nativity scene, except they go one step further and make an entire village. Just before midnight on Christmas Eve, children get the honour of putting baby Jesus to bed before the family traditionally go to midnight mass.

'Who are those by?' Manon asks, her voice awed. 'Anyone famous?'

I take a tentative step inside the suite and lift one of the many paintings leaning in a neat pile against a wall. 'Impressionist style?' I muse. 'Signed by an L. L. Toussaint.'

Manon whips out her phone and investigates. 'I don't think

L. L. Toussaint is the next Monet. No record of any notable paintings by that name.'

I gently place it down and go through the others. They're all by the same painter. 'Aren't they lovely, though, Manon? No matter whether the artist is famous or not. This one particularly so.' It's of a woman lying on a bed, similar to the one in this room, a sheet strategically placed to protect her modesty. She has long wavy hair and sharp-angled cheekbones, but it's her eyes that are mesmerising; they sparkle, even through the dulled colours of the canvas, like there's untold secrets within. Her cheeks are blushed pink – from the heat of the day, or something else? I have the strangest sensation, like I know this woman. Maybe this woman is all of us, with her vulnerability on display, yet it's obvious she feels safe, comfortable. 'We should hang these around the hotel. That would save us buying new artwork.'

We spend the next few hours digging through the treasure trove of belongings in suite twenty. 'Why does this room feel different?' I ask Manon. 'We've found suites full of all sorts of odds and ends, but this one...'

Manon rocks back on her heels, as she squats in front of a Louis Vuitton travelling trunk that's full of petticoats and linens. 'These are someone's cherished possessions,' she says. 'This room houses a whole life, and luckily for us it's been sealed up and preserved.'

We find the most beautiful collection of nostalgic items. A jewel box. Delicate music books with tissue-thin paper, ravaged by time. Vintage perfume bottles that still carry a lingering scent even though the liquid is long gone. Opera gloves. Hat boxes with intricately styled head pieces. A velvet pouch with smelling salts! Embroidery hoops with colourful stitching and balls of wool. 'Whoever owned these things seems well off, don't you think? So why would they be here in the hotel? Abandoned like this?'

Manon considers it. 'Once upon a time, L'Hotel du Parc would have been the height of sophistication. A prestigious place to stay. The grandeur is evident by the baroque elements that have survived. Perhaps these are the belongings of a former owner?'

'Could be.' It makes sense that whoever owned the hotel would store their things neatly away if they lived at the hotel rather than at another location. In the wardrobe are gowns and dresses of varying sizes. Some are more formal and some very plain, as if the wearer didn't care much for fashion. Or perhaps they were her day-to-day clothes and she only frocked up in the fancier attire on occasion.

'But then why is suite nineteen locked?' Manon asks. 'And why was there a wall to hide them both? That's a large undertaking to hide a room full of seemingly innocuous belongings.'

A trail of goosebumps breaks out along my arms. 'Suite nineteen is locked because there's something special inside.' I feel it in my bones as I sit in the middle of a room full of beautiful objects whose owner remains a mystery. For now.

'One thing is certain: a person went to a lot of trouble to disguise the fact these rooms ever existed... and I'd really like to find out why.'

* * *

Manon's busy drawing a design for the library layout when I go to the reception desk to look for the set of master keys the realtor gave us. The keys are various sizes and shapes and none of them are marked or numbered.

I head up to the third floor and down the long skinny

hallway to the locked door. I peer into the keyhole as if I can discern on sight what kind of key it might be. Which it turns out, I cannot. There's no other choice except to try each one and see which fits.

Ten minutes later, I get to the last key and still no luck.

I head back to my office and email the realtor to ask if she knows if there's any other spare keys lying around on the off chance she was given an antique bunch and popped them in a drawer or something. A girl can dream! I don't mention the secret suites; after all, how do I know she won't report back to Francois-Xavier?

She replies a few minutes later telling me there is a key safe cabinet behind the reception desk. When I find it, I smile. It's so old fashioned. These days most hotels have electronic keys, but not L'Hotel du Parc. In a way it's charming, although perhaps I'll have to make sure there are plenty of spares in case of any losses. There are keys hooked for suites one to eighteen. A dead end. I crank Christmas carols on my phone and spend the afternoon singing as I sort behind the counter, ditching old paperwork and tidying up, but I don't come across any extra keys.

Why is suite nineteen locked? What's behind that door?

10

---

8 NOVEMBER

The next day, the first building contractor, a big burly thirty-
something man named JP, arrives to quote. He wears a bright
yellow hard hat and reflective vest. Probably sensible, what with
the falling objects around L'Hotel du Parc. With clipboard in
hand, he scribbles notes as we go from room to room.

He assures me the lobby, library and other shared guests'
spaces are mostly cosmetic to fix at first glance. The idea puts a
spring in my step. Maybe the renovations will come in under
budget? I motion for him to head upstairs to the suites. 'This is
the first of eighteen guest rooms?' JP asks, tapping the clipboard
with his pen.

It's on the tip of my tongue to tell him about the secret suites
nineteen and twenty, knowing he'll have to fix the damage we
did bringing the wall down, but as we've been unable to locate
keys, I want to keep the discovery of those rooms quiet for now.
I send Manon a warning look, to keep her mouth closed.

'*Oui*, eighteen in total. For our soft launch we're hoping to
get three or four suites completed to start with, plus the ones
we're staying in, but ours don't need the full treatment. Perhaps

you can advise us as to which suites need the least amount of work and we can focus on those for our Christmas opening?'

'*Bein sûr.*' He pushes the door open to Manon's suite to find her lacy underwear strewn from one side to the other, including a pink G-string that hangs from the bedside lamp. *My* pink G-string. I take stock of the lingerie on display and blush when I realise it's all mine and she's staged this scene to embarrass the poor guy. Manon gives me a wicked grin. 'Ahem. Ah.' His cheeks pink as he drops his gaze, as if willing himself away.

'Sorry, Manon is a slob.' My cousin has never grown out of these sorts of high jinks.

'It's not *my* underwear,' she says faux innocently. 'Personally, I don't understand the practicality of wearing a piece of material so thin it disappears up your...'

'Anyway,' I say, giving him a bright smile. 'If you look past the, erm, clutter, we were hoping to get our rooms done first so we can settle in more comfortably. The bathrooms will need a little updating, perhaps new sinks, new tapware, as I'm hoping the budget' – the very mediocre budget, I might add – 'will mostly be to cover a few suites, lobby and guest lounge with a focus on the library. Manon and I can pitch in wherever you see fit, so we can save money.'

He does his best to swallow a sigh but fails. I guess us pitching in is more of a headache than helpful to him. 'Right, but you've got mould on the ceiling here, which means there's a leak of some kind. We'll have to investigate and determine the cause. Repair and replace, and paint.'

I grimace. 'Sounds... expensive.'

He shrugs as he jots notes. 'It can be.'

I survey the ceiling, looking for mould, and can't see any black or green spots. There are just some small swirls of discolouration where the crumbling cornice meets the ceiling.

Surely that's easy to fix? 'OK, let's continue.' We go from suite to suite and JP examines every room up close like he's a detective hunting for clues. I respect a man with an eye for detail – it's a tick in the box for JP – but as usual Manon finds the pace tedious and lets out numerous exaggerated yawns. I shoot her a glare, but it bounces right off her.

We get to suite seven and I go to open the bathroom door with JP a step behind me and Manon trailing after. 'So what do you—' The words die in my throat, truly die, as we tumble backward and bang into one another in our hasty attempt to retreat while we're hit with a stench so malodorous that it will outlast time.

'*Mon Dieu,*' JP says, his eyes bulging like he's been poisoned as he covers his mouth with his clipboard and coughs and splutters like a man possessed.

Even Manon grimaces and doesn't burst forth with any sarcastic comments. I rally, giving him a sunny smile, implying all is well. I don't want him scared off. 'I hope it's easily fixed!' In my mind my budget explodes and is replaced with all those zeroes Manon thought were missing.

'The only thing that could fix this would be an *exorcism,*' Manon unhelpfully adds, recovering. The poor guy flinches at her comment and I fire her my best cease-and-desist glare, which she duly ignores.

JP peeks behind the shower curtain and gasps. That can't be good.

'I know salmon-coloured... everything can be a little overwhelming at first, but you get used to it.'

What *is* that smell? To say it's overpowering would be an understatement, but the bathroom appears just the same as the others. Mostly neat and tidy with a layer of dust from being empty for so long.

'It's not the design per se, it's the *reek*. Whatever's causing it, it can't be good.'

Manon takes a great big sniff and nods to herself. 'Is someone buried under the bath itself?' she asks. 'I mean, it's possible. With my wealth of experience as a true crime podcaster, I hate to say but these things happen all the time and are often unearthed during renovations.'

'It *could* be a dead body, I can't rule it out,' JP says. 'But, in all likelihood, it's probably decades worth of mould. Bacteria growing faster than inflation ever could.'

'*Pas possible!*' Why I react more violently to a mould infestation than a potential hidden body, I'm not quite sure. The pressure must be getting to me.

'It's very possible!' JP assures me.

I throw my hands in the air. 'Great, more mould!' Moralistically, I would prefer no one died and got buried here, but, from a fiscal standpoint, well, it would possibly be cheaper to remove human remains *if* authorities weren't involved. What am I even *saying*? I shake the craziness away.

'From a health and safety perspective' – JP wiggles his hard hat – 'we need to get on top of this first.'

'*Oui*, of course.' Renovation is clearly not for the faint of heart. By my calculations, a big chunk of the budget is going to be spent on mould removal. Will there be enough left in the coffers for furniture, beds, bedding? More importantly, books? A few Christmas decorations? Although, those beautiful vintage Christmas decorations we found in suite twenty would outshine anything we could buy. Perhaps we can set up the nativity village in the guest lounge window?

I lead him to the third floor and go through each room until we get to the last two at the end of the hallway. We've cleaned up the mess from the obliterated wall but we weren't able to hide the jagged edges where the sheeting came off with Manon's galactic-force swinging. 'If you could tidy up this area.' I point to the damage where the wall once was.

'What happened here?'

'Oh.' I wave him away as if it's nothing. 'Not sure, it was like this when we arrived.'

Manon rolls her eyes.

'And these suites? Wait. There're twenty rooms in total?' He checks his notes with a frown.

I managed to keep that secret for all of thirty minutes. 'We can't find a key for this door, so at this stage we're just going to leave them as is. Maybe they'll become an office or something down the track but they're not important right now.'

JP leans down and sticks a finger on the keyhole as if it will magically open. 'Have you called a locksmith?'

'It's on my list to do today.' I'd been hoping to save the funds and find the key, but every search has proved fruitless.

'OK, so I'll quote to fix these edges where there must have been a dividing wall or something...' He's stuck frozen to the spot, running a finger along the messy join. '...But why would those two rooms have been blocked off?'

'It was probably a doorway?' I say, pivoting away in the hopes he'll follow me. 'The owners probably wanted some privacy from guests...' A doorway to two more doorways doesn't make much sense, so I let out a trilling laugh as if to say, *What can you do?*, but it must sound too forced because JP's forehead furrows. 'You know, extra sound protection, and erm—'

'Ignore my cousin,' Manon says. 'She's imbibed a little too much, if you know what I mean.' She gives him a salacious wink.

'Coffee, she means coffee. *Oui*, I'm a little jittery from too much caffeine, but can you blame me?'

The man looks from me to Manon as if he's landed in the twilight zone. And maybe he has. 'Where were we?' I'm officially losing it.

After our walkthrough is complete, JP says, 'I'll get the quote to you in a week or so. If you'd like to go ahead, I'll need a deposit and then weekly progress payments.'

'Sure. Anything we can do to cut costs will be appreciated. And anything we can do to make the process go faster would also be ideal. As mentioned, we'd like to soft launch before Christmas if we can, welcome some guests for the festive season and iron out any crinkles. And then, long term, work on renovating suites two at a time, funds depending.'

'You and all of Paris,' he grumbles, shaking his head. 'We'll do our best but old buildings like this, things crop up. Leaks, mould, electric issues, plumbing mishaps.' That does not sound good. 'It's best to rectify those things fast so the damage doesn't spread.'

I want to stick my fingers in my ears and block out all those expensive-sounding worst-case scenarios. 'Of course, if there's a serious issue we'll have to fix it, but, for now, we're just doing a gentle makeover.'

'If you'd like things done rapidly I can hire more tradespeople, but the price will increase. How about I quote for both scenarios?'

'*Merci,* I'll crunch the numbers when I get your quote and go from there.' The expense of paying for more tradespeople would be offset by being able to open earlier and have paying guests.

Back in the lobby we say our *au revoirs* and he leaves. Once he's out of sight, I throw a cushion at Manon. I'm thrilled she doesn't sense the surprise attack as it hits her square in the face and springs off her nose. '*Pourquoi...?*' she screeches.

I sit on the arm of the green sofa. 'Nice trick with the lingerie, Manon. Seriously. The poor man didn't know where to look.'

She gives me a sly smile and slides onto the sofa beside me. 'Genius, wasn't it?'

'Not genius. He'll probably up the quote now or never return.'

'*Or* he might lower it.' She gives me an exaggerated wink.

I take the elastic from my hair and redo my loose ponytail. 'Right. With that and the whole spiel about the dead guy buried under the bath?'

'How do you know it's a *guy* buried there?' Manon asks, suspicion heavy in her voice.

I rub my temples. 'There's no corpse, Manon! You have to stop saying that or the hotel will get a reputation as some kind of burial ground and then I'll have no chance of selling it.'

'*Or* ghost hunters from all over the world will visit and set up those recording devices and those temperature things and we'll become famous. *In*famous!'

'Why are you so macabre?' Only Manon would hope there's a body there, and *not* because it will save on renovation costs.

'I'm dark because the world is dark.'

I laugh at her dramatics. 'I'm worried we're going to blow the budget before we've even really begun what with all that talk of mould removal, not to mention if there's an issue with plumbing and whatever else he warned about. Then what? We're stuck here forever.'

I'm worried that sinking my savings into the hotel might be yet another misstep. 'Back when Francois-Xavier did the deal, I paid a hefty deposit and if I lose that and more, I'd feel like I've taken a giant leap backwards. I'm at the pointy end of my thirties...'

'Thirty-eight to be exact,' Manon chimes in. 'But what does age matter?'

I sigh. 'It matters because I've worked so hard, and I lost so much in the divorce. The windfall I had from my last few books has been chewed up by this place and whatever's left will go to mortgage repayments and renovations. And what if it fails? Then what?' My lungs compress, making it hard to breathe.

'What if it doesn't?' Manon gives my arm a pat, but her eyes shine with determination. Sometimes I wish I could have blind faith like she does. 'It's going to work out. The bad guy never wins in your books, so how could this be any different? You'll rise like a phoenix and life will be sunshine and roses.'

I sit on the sofa, a green velour outrage that has somehow stood the test of time and is still structurally sound. 'If only my life was as simple as a mixed metaphor, like a sweet, happy romantic comedy where the heroine prevails despite all the obstacles in her way.'

'You need to write again, Anais.' Manon's voice is soft. 'Writing is your happy place and—'

'Ooh, the Tin Man does have a heart.'

'—without it you're lapsing into this maudlin version of yourself. Next you'll be wandering the hallways in your full-length nightgown at midnight, screaming for your lost love, and it can only go downhill from there.'

'Wow, Manon, you really do know how to bring me back to earth with a thud.' I need to shake the gloom away once and for all, but it's easier said than done.

I gaze outside to the busy street. Most passersby walk in the direction of Luxembourg gardens because there's so much to see and do inside the *jardin*. There are beehives near the Rue de Fleuris entrance, and an apple and orange orchard in the south-west corner. A pétanque field and tennis courts. A pond to sail model boats. There are busts of many a writer and poet, like Verlaine. There's a statue of Gustave Flaubert, who wrote *Madame Bovary*. But what I like even more than all the beauty as far as the eye can see is walking in the footsteps of all those writers who came before. James, Faulkner, Stein, Hemingway and Wilde were all known to wander these very same gravel paths. So, as far as locations go, the hotel is well situated, especially with our literary theme.

And, personally, the 6th arrondissement is my favourite. There's so much to see and do and there's plenty for literature lovers, including the San Francisco Book Company, on Rue Monsieur le Prince, a cute-as-a-button English language bookshop that's often overlooked in favour of the more famous shops like Shakespeare and Co. or the Abbey Bookshop. All three shops have an eclectic mix of used books and are a joy to spend an hour or two thumbing through, looking for treasure. We've got a lot to offer, not just at the hotel but in Paris as a whole, and I just need to focus on that and all the positives.

'You're right, Manon. I need to stop making excuses and write,' I say. 'It *is* my happy place and if I don't find my way back there, then he's won again, hasn't he? By snatching away not only my income, but the work I love doing.' It feels like a balancing act, and at the minute I'm teetering on the edge of the tightrope, looking down instead of looking ahead. That has to change. 'And we'll give this place the facelift it deserves. Soon enough we'll be welcoming guests with big smiles and we'll make them feel at home. We'll build the business up, show potential buyers this is a great investment and then we can resume our normal lives.'

'I don't know,' Manon says, gazing around the lobby. 'This place, it's growing on me.'

'That's probably the mould – you should get that looked at.' Manon's laughter follows me out of the room.

I go to the reception desk in the lobby and call a locksmith who says they'll be out in the next day or two. Our next builder arrives to quote and this time I send Manon into the kitchen to prepare lunch so she can't scare the guy off or pull any more pranks.

11

9 NOVEMBER

The day is grey and overcast, and big black clouds float above as if it's about to rain hard. I've been waiting for a break in the weather to clean the front windows of the hotel, so I hurry to gather what I need. You'd think the incessant rain would do the job for me, but the windows need a decent scrub more than anything.

I slip on my raincoat and take my cleaning supplies outside. I'm keen to see how much brighter the lobby and guest lounge will be once the build-up of grime is washed away. Even though it's a little early for Christmas decorations, I'm going to string tinsel and Christmas lights up. Later, once renovations are done, I'll decorate the wooden ledge inside with the 'creche' nativity scene, but I don't want to do that now and risk the stunning vintage set getting damaged or dusty.

Outside, I slide on rubber gloves and dunk my cloth into the soapy water, marvelling at how menial work such as this is really quite satisfying. Perhaps it's because I'm avoiding writing, and even chores I usually despise like vacuuming or mopping are a delight when each word I type feels weighted, like an insurmountable effort that goes nowhere.

Once I soap and scrub down each window, I refill my bucket with clean, clear water and use my squeegee to wipe the suds off, the mindless task allowing me to ponder about my writer's block and possible solutions.

This late in the game it's probably best to write anything, no matter how clunky the sentences are. Get those words on the page with the knowledge that I can shine it up later, because I can't edit a blank page and if I don't stop deleting what I write every evening then that's all I *will* have; a white, blank, page. How hard can it be to write a light-hearted festive romance? So, my own love life went up in a big ball of flames, but that doesn't mean I don't remember how love *feels*. All I need to do is forget about my own woes and get into the head of my heroine Hilary...

While I have the satisfaction of washing these windows, I picture my heroine and what she yearns for. A Parisian romance? Parisian Christmas romance. What's so hard about clearing the mind and getting into the zone? Nothing. I dream of a hero for Hilary who woos his *amour*, whispering sweet nothings... as he gently—

'It's nice to see a cleanup finally happening but what about the windows above those?'

And just like that I'm pulled from my fictitious romantic meanderings with a bang in the shape of my surly American neighbour. '*Bonjour*, Noah. Was there something you needed from me?' I arch a brow while my heart hammers at his intrusion. I won't let him know I'm ruffled by his constant *man*terrupting, and I certainly won't acknowledge his advice on cleaning my windows, for pity's sake.

Noah shoves his hands deep in his pockets and rocks back

and forth on his feet with that same coiled energy, like he's trying very hard not to take over and do the upper windows himself, or at least tell me in great detail how to do it better.

If I stay silent, will he stay or will he go? *One, two, three—*

'It's only that I don't see the point of cleaning the lower windows if you're not going to do the ones above. It looks worse that way.'

'How do you know I'm not going to do the ones above?' Which I am not.

The ones above are too high for me to reach unless I dig out a ladder, but therein lies another problem. I can safely step up two rungs of a common household ladder; any higher than that, flight mode is activated and fear sets in. I don't want to have to pay someone to do such an easy job though. And surely this is a good start. Maybe I can rope Manon into doing the higher windows another time?

Although, I'm not going to tell Noah any of this.

'I know you're not going to do the ones above because no one in their right mind would do the windows below first because the drips would run down the windows from higher up and ruin all that hard work.'

I give him a cool stare. 'Do you always give unsolicited advice to women?'

His lips pull to one side as if the idea amuses him. 'Is that a trick question?'

I bristle. 'Was there anything else, Noah? The suds are drying and soon you'll be complaining of streaky windows even though I have no idea how it affects you, yet here you are.'

'I've already explain—'

'*Oui, oui*, this ugly hotel is impacting your bar. I got the memo.' I hope he hears the sarcasm in every single syllable.

He folds his arms and surveys the façade as if seeing it for the first time. 'I wouldn't call it ugly, I'd call it... shabby.' I guess sarcasm is lost on Noah.

'Shabby?' I give him a stony glare.

He nods enthusiastically as if he can finally get his point through my clearly thick head. 'A little... decrepit. But now you're here so I'm hoping things will improve, *non*? If you'd like a ladder, I can bring mine so you can do the windows properly.'

'That won't be necessary.'

Manon wanders outside with a yawn just as rain starts falling. 'Ooh, that looks great but what about the higher windows? It looks shabby without them done too.'

Noah gives me a triumphant smile as if to say, *See?* 'I'll bring my ladder over so you can reach.'

'A ladder, great!' Manon says. 'But Anais is afraid of heights. She has a two-rung limit. That's why I always have to paint the high bits.'

'Oh!' I say, needing to escape. 'That's my phone ringing. I'll be back.'

Never. Why is he so irritating? It's not just me, in my misandry era, is it? Although Manon seems to get along with him just fine, but I suppose he's not correcting her every five minutes, is he? And with steam coming out of my ears, a story forms as I storm off in a huff.

The man wore a woollen beanie that had seen better days. But it was of no concern to Hilary, as she folded away the ladder and stepped over the motionless form on the pavement. He wouldn't need it where he was going...

When I'm mad, I clean. I march into a storage room at the back of the hotel and pull out all of the plastic tubs. In a huff, I sort what can stay and what can go. There are stacks of newspapers and magazines. Tubs of old rotary telephones from the sixties. I startle when I open a box full of porcelain dolls with painted glass eyes. Their faces are crazed and cracked with age. As I rummage through oddities, my blood pressure slowly lowers and I manage to push thoughts about my interfering neighbour from my mind and focus on the task. I unearth a box of brown medicinal apothecary jars that are so pretty we can repurpose to them use around the hotel as vases.

I keep going until I've sorted every box, finding all sorts of weird and wonderful bric-a-brac. Old-fashioned board games, French prayer books, and two bottles of wine that look like a rare vintage to my untrained eye. I hope they haven't turned into vinegar. I put the lid back on one of the tubs of newspapers and use it as a seat and take my phone and google '1949 Chateau Latour Bordeaux blend'. I scroll through results until I find a wine searcher site that offers up varying prices for the vintage, ranging from €2,000 and above. My eyebrows shoot up.

Perhaps all these quirky curiosities around the hotel can be sold? Even the creepy porcelain dolls might hold value for the right buyer. I keep going. Behind a stack of tubs, I find a set of four antique armchairs that can be saved if we replace the cushion inserts. There are frames in all sorts of styles and colours.

I pull out one of the armchairs to sit on while I look up antique traders and land on the website of a local vintage shop in the 5th arrondissement that buys from the public. I spend the next little while cataloguing what I've found and take photos so I can reach out and garner any interest.

Maybe the hotel is already beginning to pay for itself? I leave the storage room much happier than when I went in. My eye is drawn to the light pooling into the lobby, and I catch sight of Noah leaving with a ladder tucked under his arm.

'Well played,' Manon says from her perch on the sofa in the guest lounge, laptop next to her.

'What do you mean?'

'The whole getting mad at him thing because you're afraid of heights *and* feel a spark towards him so you storm off and *voilà*, Noah returns with his trusty ladder to get the windows clean to his exacting standards, thus leaving you with another job completed. If I didn't know better, I'd say you're turning out more and more like me every day.' She waggles a brow.

My mouth falls open. How can she get this so wrong? 'It's infuriating that he's taken it upon himself to clean the windows when I specifically told him we didn't need or want his help. I can't believe you'd think this is a good thing, Manon! What gives him the right...?'

She holds up a hand. 'Save it, please. Let's plan what job we want him to save us from next. The painting? Shall we tell him we have no idea how to cut in the high bits and it's a little scary being a whole *four* rungs up the ladder?'

I fight a smile because Manon is wrong, but she is funny. 'You're single-handedly going to set feminism back a hundred years, Manon, with that nonsense.'

'If I don't have to paint the high bits then I'm totally OK with that.'

I plonk down on the sofa next to her. 'You're a liar too. Please don't encourage Noah. I can't handle any more of his condescending *him*pathy. I swear he thinks it's still the Roaring Twenties for crying out loud and us little women are best hidden away in the kitchen making batch food and leaving the heavy lifting to the men.'

She shakes her head. 'You're crazy not to accept his help.'

'We don't need his help!' I cry. 'But then he goes ahead and does it anyway.'

She averts her gaze but not before I detect a guilty look in her eyes. 'I told him he could do the windows.'

'Manon!'

'What?' She lifts her palms into the air. 'Look at this room now bathed in natural light, even though the skies are moody today, just like *some* people who shall remain nameless. *Anais.*'

'Ugrh, there's no getting through to you. Come and see what I found.'

'Now?'

'Now.' I grab her hands and pull her from the sofa.

In the storage room, I show Manon all of the items that we can either sell or use around the hotel, like the four armchairs that will be our next DIY project.

'Do we really have to sell the wine? I've never tried a vintage from 1949. What if it's the best thing we ever tasted?'

'Think of it this way. It'll be the best thing we *never* tasted.'

'How did I know you'd say that?'

'Help me take these chairs to the guest lounge. We'll see about finding new cushion inserts and hopefully we can save the velvet blue fabric. And the frames, we can paint those.'

12

10 NOVEMBER

The next afternoon, the backpackers return earlier than usual,
bringing in with them an icy wind.

It's cold for November and I hope it means we'll have snow
for Christmas. There's just something about snowy wintry
weather when you catch a snowflake and make a Christmas
wish. They join us in the guest lounge, where we've set up a
makeshift workshop, layering newspaper to protect the
parquetry to paint bedside tables from the four suites we've
chosen to redo first. I'm just putting the finishing touches on the
last one. For such small pieces of furniture, it's surprisingly
time-intensive to paint.

We've gone for a dark navy chalk paint that hides most of
the battle scars. 'These are gorgeous,' Kiki says, pointing to our
row of freshly painted bedsides.

'*Merci*. We're going to replace the standard silver drawer
pulls with some brass or gold ones to give them a more luxe
look.'

'*Magnifique*.'

'Do you want me to light the fire in the library room?' I ask.

I found a stack of firewood earlier when I was out the back washing paintbrushes. Another cost saved, and we'll be long gone by next winter so won't need to worry about another wood delivery.

'*Non,* it's OK,' Juliette says. 'I wanted to show you a couple of literary places that we spoke about! No one turned up for our second tour today, so I have time, if you do too?'

'*Oui*, I have time. I'm sorry about your tour. Does that happen often?'

'Almost every day, lately. It's to be expected. Tourists get held up in queues for the Louvre, or Sainte-Chapelle, many of the popular sights. Or they get lost and lose track of time. It's part of the job but still stings when a big group is a no show, which is what happened today. *C'est la vie.*'

'I'm sorry, that really is disappointing.'

'I'll make gingerbread coffee if anyone wants some?' Manon says, standing to arch the crick in her back. 'Let me quickly clean up first. Give me your brushes, Anais. I'll wash them.'

Manon wanders off with Kiki, both talking over the top of each other without any concern for who's saying what. In the short time we've been here, they've become firm friends, often staying up late watching true crime documentaries on Netflix together on Manon's laptop.

'Where are Timothee and Zac?' I ask as Juliette falls into step next to me. In the laundry, I soap my paint-splattered hands while she rubs her palms together to stave off the cold. There's a real chill in the air – I'll light the fire in the library room when we return so we'll have a warm place to congregate. I'm not a Grinch by nature, but I don't want to turn on the central heating in the hotel until absolutely necessary, although we each have a little electrical radiator in our suites that we turn on at night.

'Tim and Zac have an interview for a job at the Marché de Noël Notre Dame.'

'Ooh, the one on the Left Bank?'

'That's the one. I hadn't heard of it. You know it?'

I dry my hands on a towel. 'It's one of the most popular Christmas markets in Paris. In late November they set up tiny Swiss-style chalets around the square and they offer all sorts: *vin chaud*, gourmet food like foie gras, thick German-style sausages, roasted chestnuts and every cheese you can imagine. There are gift stalls; last year I bought the most beautiful mohair scarf there. There's handmade jewellery, toys, ceramics. Musicians play as you wander around. Even Père Noël makes an appearance!'

She breaks into giggles, but I'm not sure what's provoked such a reaction. 'That's what they're interviewing for. The part of Père Noël! They want two Santas – one for the crowd and one for a photo booth.'

I laugh, imagining the two of them dressed up in padded Santa suits. 'I'm sure it'll be fun. Hectic but fun.'

'Let's hope they get the job then. I'm going to freshen up and then we'll head out?'

'Sure.'

13

10 NOVEMBER

Christmas lights are twinkling up and down the avenues as the afternoon darkens. Each year, Parisians seem to decorate earlier, and I get swept away by the sight of so many festive window displays. I itch to do more Christmas decorating in the hotel but can't until the messy work has been completed.

We chatter as we walk, sidestepping around people who walk at a slower pace.

'Where are we headed?'

Juliette throws me a wide smile. 'To the wall of The Drunken Boat. Have you heard of the poet Rimbaud?'

'*Non,* I don't think so.'

Juliette's eyes twinkle with excitement. 'You're in for a treat. Rimbaud was a genius who was way ahead of his time, although he's sometimes called *l'enfant terrible* of poetry, probably because of his age and precociousness. He was a libertine who had a rather disreputable private life. It's rumoured that he had an affair with the married poet Paul Verlaine, who later shot him! It was all very scandalous for the nineteenth century.'

'He shot him?' I gape at her, as this true story has taken an unexpected twist.

'*Oui*, in the wrist. But that all came later. Rimbaud was a literary prodigy. Well educated and widely read. He wrote 'The Drunken Boat' in 1871 when he was still a teenager. Here we are.'

We stop at Rue Ferou. A poem is inscribed in French along the length of wall down the block. I read as we slowly walk. It's beautiful. It's about a sea voyage and a sinking boat, a metaphor for torment perhaps? It's dark, haunting.

'It's believed he first recited the poem near this location, which is why they chose to display it here.'

We shuffle slowly as I continue to absorb the words written on the wall. 'At seventeen, Rimbaud had what he described as a "visionary experience" that inspired him to write mystical, almost hallucinatory poems that broke the traditional rules of rhyme and meter. He was known for his experimental way of writing, which I'm sure ruffled a few feathers.'

Juliette goes on ahead as I take my time to finish reading. 'After much success and at the young age of twenty, he abandoned his gift and never wrote another word.'

'Never? Not one more poem?'

'Never. He never wrote another poem. He left France and travelled the world. At one point he enlisted in the Dutch army, but later went MIA in Sumatra. On his many travels he landed in Ethiopia where he became a trader and an explorer. Sadly, in 1891 he discovered a tumour on his knee, so he returned to France where his leg was amputated. He died the same year from bone cancer. He was thirty-seven. And, sadder still, his work went on to become much lauded, studied by other greats, gaining him much recognition... after his death. Not only were poets influenced by his style, but singers were too, like Jim Morrison and Bob Dylan.'

My eyes are wide as I try and process these fascinating snippets of the poet's life. 'It sounds so fanciful, as if it couldn't all be true.'

'There's so much more to it. Arthur Rimbaud led an interesting life even though he died so young.'

'*Oui.*' I blow out a breath. 'I'd love to read more about him, include his works in the hotel library.'

'"A Season in Hell" is another poem I think you'll like.'

I make notes in my phone to research more about Arthur Rimbaud and to find his books and biographies about the poet.

'Now for something lighter? I'll take you to 12 Rue de l'Odéon, where we'll find a very small plaque. It's the *original* site of the very first Shakespeare and Co. English bookshop, run by the American-born Sylvia Beach. She sold books and had a lending library that all the literary greats at the time borrowed books from, including Hemingway. Most people think George Whitman's Shakespeare and Co. on the Left Bank is the original site, but it is not. He named it in ode to Sylvia's bookshop. And here we have another fascinating life...'

Juliette goes into great detail about Sylvia Beach, who was more than a bookseller; she was a fierce cheerleader and confidante for her literary pals.

'Here it is.' Juliette points to an unassuming plaque on the wall that reads in French, *In this house Sylvia Beach published Ulysses by James Joyce.*

'It's lovely she's recognised like this. I only wish it was more about her than James Joyce, although I suppose without her there would be no *Ulysses.*'

'*Oui,* it's always about James Joyce.' Juliette laughs. 'Sylvia bankrolled and published it despite many obstacles of the time, her efforts leaving her in debt. Sylvia moved heaven and earth to help the struggling writer publish *Ulysses,* even though it was banned in many places for "obscenity" and was confiscated at customs in England and America as it was deemed a scandalous novel, when really it's nothing of the sort. But it was seen that way at the time. Not too bad for her first venture into publishing.'

'She was a visionary. And I'll have to stock biographies about her.'

Juliette smiles. 'And let's not forget Sylvia's dear friend and companion Adrienne Monnier, who had a French bookshop at 7 Rue de l'Odéon.'

We cross the street and find the second plaque for the bookshop La Maison des Amis des Livres, which translates to The House of Friends and Books. Even though these small plaques might seem insignificant to some, I find it special that these two women are recognised and honoured for their work in literature all those years ago.

14

11 NOVEMBER

I clutch my heart and fall back in my chair with a yelp.

Manon rushes over. 'What is it? Are you sick? I told you not to eat the whole box of macarons. I'm all for eating your feelings, but every single one, Anais?'

'They're Pierre Hermé limited edition Christmas-flavoured macarons, only the best you'll find in all of Paris, and I know, I've tried them all. Besides, consuming sugar is an effective coping mechanism, and I won't be stopping anytime soon. But it's not the sugar come down. It's... *that*.' I point to the laptop, opened to my email. The renovation quotes have arrived and the first one I opened is eye-wateringly large.

Manon grips the mouse and scrolls down the page and shrieks. 'Is this a typo? It must be a typo. How can it be so much?'

'There's a second page.'

'*Non!*'

'*Oui!*'

'He's a crook, a charlatan. A...! Let's cross that builder off the list.'

I pinch the bridge of my nose. 'Let's read the other quotes. Maybe they're better.'

She waggles a brow. 'I'm sure JP's quote won't be as steep.'

'It probably will be after you terrorised him with strewn lingerie and the dead-body-under-the-bath theory.'

'You're so naïve.'

I force a smile but have a sneaking suspicion the totals are all going to be similar. There's a lot of work I didn't factor in because my knowledge of such things is non-existent. The damp and the mould are the main costs, but we won't know how extensive the issue is until they investigate.

'Let me check.' Manon toggles through the inbox and finds the other quotes. 'How do these people sleep at night?'

'Probably remarkably well due to all that manual labour. And really, it's worth every penny, but what if they find more damage? Where will it end?'

Her lips twist into a grimace. 'OK, builder two is out. His quote is even higher and they can't start until *after* Christmas.'

'And JP?' Is our plan to partially open for the festive season a pipe dream?

Manon finds the email from JP and reads. 'Told you so.' She gives me a triumphant smile. 'It's less than the other quotes. But still far more than you budgeted.'

'Damn. And honestly, I'm not surprised, because how can I budget for such a thing when I have no idea what I'm doing!' My voice gets a little high as I wonder again if my life is really going to implode this time. What was I thinking? I shouldn't be renovating a hotel!

'He says he's had a cancellation and can start soon. He can do four suites before Christmas, plus a quick nip around ours, just swapping the sinks and taps. He will do the majority of the noisy, messy work before our soft launch. But, overall, the other more time-consuming work will take months but he'll stay on and do that alone, without the team.'

'OK.' I talk myself down.

'He's given us the option of saving even more if we do some of the painting ourselves. Although, he's said they'll paint the ceilings and cornices because they're fixing the damage on those.' Manon steps away from the computer and stretches her arms above her head. 'I'm so glad we don't need to do the ceilings; can you even imagine? I'd die.'

I pull the computer onto my lap and scroll down the list of work and the relevant costs. 'It's a reasonable quote considering, and the timeframe works, so we won't be disturbing our Christmas guests if he does most of the noisy work now.'

I take a breath. This is doable, if I had some more funds...

JP's also made copious notes of what we'll need to achieve down the line, including fixing the wrought-iron balconies that are damaged in a few of the suites. Let's hope that's a cost for the new owners.

'There's obviously going to be some noise and mess as we do up other parts of the hotel as we can afford to,' I say, 'but we'll make that up to our guests by reducing the rate somewhat and wowing them with our happy sunny dispositions.' I give Manon a toothy grin.

'Please don't smile at them like that. They'll run away screaming.'

'I'll work on my happy sunny smile.' Manon drags the computer back her way. 'He can do the lobby, guest lounge, library and four suites in about four weeks' time as long as nothing untoward crops up. Or, we also have the option of less trades but a longer completion time. February, March timeframe.'

'Let's go with the extra trades. When did he say they will start?'

'Monday November eighteenth. That means they'll be finished around December eighteenth. We could partially open a week before Christmas.'

'*Oui*. But with that quicker timeframe comes a heftier cost because of the extra tradespeople.'

'Right. And dipping into what's left of my savings is a huge risk. I need to keep a buffer for the monthly mortgage until we have a steady income when the hotel is fully open and paying its own way.'

'There's no getting around it, Anais. You're going to have to ask the bank or your parents to loan you the money.'

'Hmm. Let's take a visit to the vintage shop in the 5th and meet the vendor I emailed about the finds in the storage cupboard. They're especially keen to see what condition the two wine bottles are in.'

'That's avoiding the issue. You need to sort this first.'

I scrunch up my nose. 'I know, I know, I'll figure it out. We need to clear out as much as possible before JP and his team start anyway, and whatever money we raise can go towards buying books. I can't help but worry the library is going to look bare and not as appealing as I imagine it to be for a so-called boutique literary hotel.'

Look at me, avoiding my problems!

'There won't be a library if we can't pay for the renovations.'

'When did you get so sensible?'

'About ten minutes ago when I read those quotes.'

Manon is right. Not only do we need to come up with the money for the work, but we also have to do so much ourselves in a short amount of time if we're to make our goal of a

Christmas opening. 'We need a detailed list of jobs that are up to us, items we need to buy.'

'You and your lists. Do you want me to make a spreadsheet? We can keep track of expenses that way too.'

'You're so very handy, Manon. Really.' Often Manon's brilliance is overlooked in our family because she pivots from one thing to the next, and while I joke about her being fickle, I admire her for living life on her own terms.

'I'm actually enjoying this more than I imagined. But that's subject to change.'

'We better work fast then.' There's writing time to factor in too. I'll have to stick to a routine. Hotel work during the day, writing in the evenings.

'What about suite nineteen? There could be untold riches in there.'

'*Oui*, hopefully a treasure chest full of gold! The locksmith is coming today. Soon we'll know what lies behind that door.'

I flash her a dazzling smile. I'm happy for the first time in a while. Things are moving forward. Soon, this place will be a hive of productivity with the bang of hammers, the buzz of drills. The sound of progress. 'I'll call JP and tell him they can start immediately. And then we'll take those odds and ends from the storage room and sell them for whatever we can.'

'*Oui*, but the whole you-need-extra-money thing?'

Keep the faith. That's all I have to do.

'Urgh. I'll call my mum.' My British-born mother isn't as theatrical as my French family, but still, once she feeds the news back to my *père*, he'll inevitably post on the family group chat, asking for their advice, enquiring if everyone's grown child needs such support, and then they'll all chime in with complaints about their own children, not realising or not caring that WE CAN ALL SEE.

Manon gives me a mechanical pat on the shoulder. 'Sell her the dream.'

I steel myself and make the call. 'Mum, *bonjour!*'

'Hello, darling. How are you? I thought you'd dropped off the face of the earth!'

Mother guilt – there's nothing quite like it. I *have* been lax in calling as much but it's mostly because I get a lecture every time about why I haven't moved on and found another man so I can produce grandchildren. And when I gently rebuke them and remind them that men and babies aren't something I can simply order online, they accuse me of not trying hard enough. 'I sent you an email a few days ago, Mum. And you replied.'

She tuts. 'It's not the same as hearing your sweet voice now, is it? How's it all going there?'

'Fine. Fine. Better than fine.' I must sell her the dream. 'It's fabulous actually. Wonderful.'

'You hate it.'

I may have oversold it.

'No, it's not that. It's that the renovation costs are a little higher than first thought. To be expected when it's such an old, architecturally beautiful building like this.'

'I see,' she says guardedly.

'The thing is...' I send a prayer up to the heavens. 'I'm in need of a loan to tide me over. I could ask the bank, but the interest rates are appalling, and, well, you always say come to you first.'

She lets out a chiming little laugh. 'Come to me first when you need a shoulder to cry on, Anais, or when you need me to look over a manuscript for typos, or advice about a new man; now that I'd be keen to hear. Best colours for a nursery, that kind of thing.'

I sigh. This was a bad idea.

'How much do you need?'

I rattle off a figure and hold my breath.

'That much?'

'*Oui*. But it's only a short-term loan. Once this place is up and running, I'll sell it to an astute buyer who sees the value and pay you back, *with* interest.' With interest? I must be desperate.

'Darling, are you quite certain you're not throwing money into a sinking ship?'

'Quite certain,' I lie.

'Let me speak to your dad and I'll call you back.'

* * *

Manon and I load the car with all the odds and ends from the storage cupboard to take to the vintage shop in the 5th arrondissement.

We meet the owner, a sixty-something man who is genial and welcoming. 'Have a look around while I go through your items.'

We wander the quirky shop and, when we're out of earshot, Manon whispers, 'Have you got a figure in mind for everything?'

'*Non*, why? I know roughly what the wine is worth; the rest, no idea. I mean, who wants a box of sixties-style telephones? And those dolls, I would happily give those away because they have creepy nightmare-inducing eyes.'

'The reason these traders are happy and oh so sweet is because they're experienced negotiators. They kill you with kindness to fool you into thinking they're kind and generous when really they're looking at you like you're a dollar sign.'

I scoff. 'Manon, you're reaching. They're doing us a favour by taking all of this off our hands. Better than in the scrapheap.'

She cups her face. 'It's already working! Mind control is alive and well.'

'Seriously?'

'Just let me do the negotiating.'

'Fine,' I say, shaking my head as I peruse a stamp collection on display. My eyes almost fall out of my head when I see the price. Maybe they're rare? What would I know.

'OK,' he says from behind the counter. 'I'm happy to take the lot. Would three hundred euros suit?'

Manon was right! How does she know these things? 'Three. Hundred...' My sputtering comes to an abrupt halt when Manon digs an elbow into my ribs.

'Three hundred will get you the vintage magazines, and that's being generous. Now, are you going to make a serious offer or should we contact a professional who knows the real value of treasures such as these?'

The man gives her a slow, understanding smile. 'I see you've got some experience in the trade.'

'*Oui*. I also have experience in how to dissolve a bod—'

It's my turn to jab Manon in the ribs so she doesn't finish that particular sentence. Next minute we'll have the *gendarmes* knocking on our door. And really, we haven't figured out what the hell is buried in the bathroom of suite seven yet so it's best if we don't have an unexpected visit from the authorities.

We do a deal that is way more substantial than expected and I have a newfound respect for my cousin.

* * *

The locksmith arrives, a tall gangly man with spiky hair and a smile that almost swallows his face. 'I'm sorry it's taken so long to get here. Work has been hectic. It seems like most of Paris is being renovated and keys are nowhere to be found.' He takes brisk long strides as I struggle to keep pace with him.

'It's suite nineteen,' I say, attempting to mount the stairs three at a time like he easily does. 'Go ahead.' Doesn't he know I'm a romance writer, not a runner? Gah.

Manon pops up behind me. 'Who is that?'

'The locksmith.'

She rubs her hands together. 'Finally. All will be revealed.'

We catch up to the locksmith, whose smile has disappeared as he bends his tall frame to study the lock, and he makes tutting noises that imply this isn't going to be straight forward.

'*Pas possible.*'

Not possible? He hasn't even tried lock-picking tools!

'Should you try with a tool of some sort?' I mean, I don't want to tell the guy how to do his job, but if I were a locksmith I'd start there.

'I could, but I risk damaging the vintage locking cylinder. This one is rare indeed. I respect the design too much to interfere with it. Paris is full of antique locks like this and they need to be preserved. Protected. We don't know what techniques were used to make them, so I cannot pick it for fear I'll ruin the workmanship.'

'Erm...? I understand your reservations. As far as locks go, it's, uh – lovely? However, what's behind the lock is far more important to me. Can you at least have a gentle go at opening it?'

His aimable expression turns stony. 'I cannot! And no self-respecting locksmith would dare tamper with it.'

'I see,' I say, clearly not seeing. 'How do you propose we get into this room then?'

'Sledgehammer?' Manon says.

'*Without* causing further damage,' I clarify.

He slips his phone from his overall pocket and takes some pictures of the lock. 'I suppose I can investigate, look through some vintage lock blueprints, but I can't promise anything.'

I nod. 'OK, that would be great.'

He lopes off as fast as he arrived.

'So is that a no to the sledgehammer?' Manon asks.

I shrug. 'That's Plan B for now. Have you ever heard of a locksmith who respected a lock so much they refused to open it?'

'It feels fitting somehow. Like room nineteen isn't quite ready to give up its secrets just yet.'

15

14 NOVEMBER

Manon and I are shopping in Montmartre for discounted fabrics to recover the sofas in the guest lounge and looking for ready-made sheers for the hotel, when my phone rings.

I swallow a lump in my throat when I see the caller display. 'It's *mon père*.'

My cousin holds up some creamy fabric to the light. 'You knew he'd call, didn't you? Then he's going to have to share it on the group chat. By my calculations you're still a few days away from your parents agreeing to the loan. Answer it.'

'*Bonjour, bonjour.*' I leave Manon to it and stand outside under a concertinaed awning that doesn't do much to stop the rain.

'*Chouchou*, what's this I hear about you needing a loan?'

He manages to add just the right about of incredulity in his voice to make me wish I'd asked the bank instead. I go into the whole sorry saga, explaining what we're up against and how building clientele is a factor for the upcoming sale, but I can't have any guests if there are no renovated suites, and time is of the essence.

'This is all because of that man!' he bellows down the line just like always when he's reminded of Francois-Xavier.

'Well, yes, I wouldn't have the hotel if not for him, but I've moved on now and I want to focus on the positives from here on out.' As I say the words, I feel the truth in them. 'Can you help, Papa? If not, I can go to the bank but it's a matter of urgency so we can get a few suites ready for Christmas. Get some reviews online from our happy guests, all those things to show it's a viable business.'

'Let me get back to you.' He hangs up.

I join Manon who has draped herself in several lengths of material. 'What are you doing?'

'Nothing. How did it go?'

I sigh. 'He's going to get back to me.'

'Check the WhatsApp family group chat.'

'He won't post that fast. First he'll have to tell Mum every single word, then he'll have to pace around the kitchen for a bit. Wail about Francois-Xavier.'

'Check.'

I shake my head and swipe open my phone.

ARNAUD DE LA CROIX

> Anais has asked for a loan for the hotel renovations. The figure she requests is eye watering. Tell me, should I have to step in when that con man did this to her? I love the child, but she's almost forty years old. Have you ever had to bail your adult child out like this? What would you do?

Within seconds there's a reply from one of my uncles.

MAEL DE LA CROIX

As you know, my thirty-five-year-old married daughter still asks for money and it's not for something as grand as hotel renovations. Non, it's for holidays to the Riviera! And she can't holiday in last year's fashion, oh no, she must have a whole new wardrobe for that. Not to mention the beauty treatments she must have before the holiday even begins. At least Anais is doing something practical with the money. Mine is all gone to Chanel and Louis Vuitton! Lend her the money and count your blessings it's not going to Bulgari.

ARNAUD DE LA CROIX

Ah, but your daughter is married! At least you have a chance for grandchildren!

ODETTE LAMBERT

My thirty-year-old son still lives at home! At this rate I don't think he's ever going to leave. At least Anais has a stellar career. She's finding her feet again after that disaster of a marriage. Lend her the money. You can always take her earnings from the next book! And you will have a free place to stay while in Paris. Actually, do you think we can all stay there for free? We are family, after all.

ARNAUD DE LA CROIX

You son is just a late bloomer. Of course you can stay for free. I'll insist on it.

'Great, Papa is offering free hotel accommodation to the family.'

'Let me see!' I pass Manon my phone. 'Oh no, my own mother has chimed in. Have a read.'

JOSEPHINE ORVILLE

At least your children aren't obsessed with murderers! Did any of you listen to Manon's true crime podcast? My child thinks she's invincible. Would she listen when I warned her these criminals would come after her? Non, she did not. Lend her the money, Arnaud, but I'd ask for interest. Ten per cent should suffice.

ARNAUD DE LA CROIX

I enjoyed Manon's podcast. I wish she'd stuck with it. OK, thanks all. I'll consider it.

'OK, well it looks like they've given him the go-ahead. Let's hope he doesn't listen to your *maman*. Ten per cent interest!'

'Told you. She is merciless. But would you listen?'

'You made her that way.'

'*Oui*. I did. Now, what colour for the sofas? Navy blue or beige?' She holds up two fabric samples.

'Beige. It'll go nicely with the gold tones in the guest lounge.'

'Done. Let's get these and then we can go to Marché Saint Pierre for the sheer curtain sets.'

That afternoon, money magically appears in my bank account and so does a lengthy email about payment terms and conditions and a demand that, if any family members ask to stay for free, I'm to give my blessing.

That's one problem solved. For now.

16

18 NOVEMBER

JP and his team arrive and get straight to work. Every time I turn, I bump into a brawny chest or trip over a splayed set of legs. No matter where I go, I'm in the way. I find Manon in her suite, chatting the ear off a guy who's trying his best to detect the leak, his head somewhere up in the ceiling cavity while Manon rambles on, oblivious or unconcerned that he most likely can't hear her.

'Manon!' I hiss. 'Let him work.'

'You're no fun. I'm hungry but there's a group in the kitchen already checking some plumbing predicament, and where else am I supposed to go?'

Plumbing predicament? Please let it be a simple fix. Manon is right; we're in the way and the noise and dust makes it hard to focus on our other work. 'Ah, it sure is crowded in here now.'

'There's tradespeople, mostly men, spread out all over the hotel and usually that would be my dream but they're not the talkative sort.'

I can only shake my head. 'Good, the last thing we need is you breaking one of their hearts.'

She pouts. 'Why not?'

I lift a shoulder as I watch work unfold around me. They run like a well-oiled machine, and I can only see Manon's frustration increasing as the day wears on if she has to dodge them or stay out of their way. Patient she is not.

When JP mentioned he had extra hands, I didn't expect it to be quite this many extra. It bodes well for our timeline but makes it hard to navigate around them. 'JP has suggested we stay elsewhere for the week while the noisy, heavy-duty work is getting done. So, pack a bag! Giselle from my book club offered use of her apartment in the 7th when I split up with Francois-Xavier; I'm hoping the offer still stands. She's on holiday in Greece so I'm sure she'll be fine with it.'

'Giselle offered her apartment in the 7th and you chose to stay with me in the 20th? Are you *crazy*?'

I laugh. 'Lower your expectations. It was once the concierge's room but it's in a fantastic location and has a double bed and a sofa we can use. It's right by La tour Eiffel.'

'An adventure! You can have the sofa bed.'

'It's just a sofa.'

'Oh. My request still stands.'

'Fine.' I shake my head. 'I've sent Giselle a text to ask. If not, I'll call Aunt Odette.' Our aunt lives just outside of the Boulevard Périphérique, which is a ring road that circles the twenty arrondissements of Paris. When I try to describe the order of the arrondissements to people, I always think of it as a snail shell curling around from the 1st arrondissement in the middle all the way out to the 20th.

'Please not Aunt Odette!'

'Why? She's lovely.'

'She's still holding a grudge after that Christmas prank that went awry a few years ago.'

I slap my head. 'So she's out then. Anyway, let's see what Giselle says first. Let's get some lunch and we can make a plan in the quiet.'

'Music to my ears.'

'Don't forget your laptop.'

The backpackers have gone for the day, so I send Juliette a message:

> We'll be away until Friday. I hope the renovations and subsequent mess won't bother you too much.

Half an hour later we meet back in the lobby with our bags. I find JP to let him know we'll be staying locally, and he can contact me by phone if he needs to. 'Sure, sure. Probably for the best. The damaged ceilings will come down today and that's a messy, dusty job.'

'*Merci*. We're having lunch at La Closerie des Lilas first if you run into any problems.' Why am I suddenly protective of the hotel? As much as I want to escape the chaos, I also feel some sort of separation anxiety. What is that about?

'I'm sure we'll be fine. See you back here on Friday.'

While it's full steam ahead at the hotel, we can get started on the branding and the website remodel. There might even be time to write a solid first chapter. Which will lead to a second chapter...

I'm surprised to feel a pang leaving the hotel, but I know it's safe in JP's capable hands. In the short time we've been at L'Hotel du Parc, the place has grown on me, and that's not just the mould talking. While it might be a seventies horror story, it has the potential to be so much more. It's got good bones and is in a great location. If I shut my eyes, I can picture future guests dressed to impress in the library, champagne glasses held aloft, the tinkling of their laughter, the soft expressions of people on holidays where no alarm clocks are necessary.

'Why are we having lunch so far away? It's a fifteen-minute walk at least.' She flicks me an impatient look.

As always, Manon is ruled by her stomach. If she doesn't eat on schedule her grumbling gene is activated, and we've well and truly missed that deadline.

'That *is* nearby. It's just on the other side of Jardin du Luxembourg.' I hold my bag with one arm and link my elbow through Manon's to help drag her along. 'We're going there for research. La Closerie des Lilas was a well-known haunt for literary greats in the Roaring Twenties. Ernest Hemingway wrote about the restaurant in *A Moveable Feast*. It's rumoured to be the spot where F. Scott Fitzgerald showed Hemingway his manuscript for *The Great Gatsby*, and on it goes. So much literary history under one roof.'

'You and your literary history.' Cue the dramatic eye roll. Once her blood sugar has been evened out, I'll get the real Manon back.

We cut through the *jardin*, past la fontaine Médicis, one of the prettiest fountains in Paris with its cascading flora and vibrant colourful flowers. It's like something out of a storybook. Even the cold weather doesn't dissuade people from finding a spot to sit and chat, or to read while the water laps gently in the breeze.

'It's sort of crazy to think some of the suites are being stripped today,' I say. 'Stage one, a fresh start for the boutique literary hotel, for which we've yet to figure out a fitting name!'

'*Oui,* it has to be perfect. We can come up with a shortlist over the next few days. Most important is to figure out how to update the antiquated booking system on the website. But all that aside, it's going to be fun, spending Christmas in a hotel rather than at *maman*'s, getting bossed about and told to keep my elbows off the table.'

Growing up, I spent every second Christmas with Manon and her family when I visited on school holidays after we moved to Suffolk when I was a child. My *père* didn't want me to lose my French connection with family, language and culture, so it was agreed us cousins would be sent back and forth as much as possible over school breaks. Manon visited us every alternate year for Christmas so we've always been as close as sisters. 'You rile her up on purpose. Why can't you just keep your elbows off the table for the sake of peace?'

'Then what will we have to talk about?'

I shake my head at the memories of Manon, an only child, making merry hell on her mother. Aunt Josephine is reserved and a little aloof, but that's just her way. She's all about conduct and decorum and the universe gave her a daughter like Manon who pushed against rules and regulations and refused to play the part. While they've always bickered and remained stubborn in their convictions, there's no question they love each other.

We come to Boulevard Saint-Michel and cross at the busy corner to La Closerie des Lilas, one of the oldest restaurants in Paris. While it's a tourist hotspot because of its history, abundant greenery and its beautiful façade, it's also well known for its authentic French bistro food. I'll add this to the guide we make for our bibliophile guests, a literary map of Paris they can use to easily find all these hidden gems. While I've dined here a handful of times, I've never paid much attention to the literary aspect, hence the visit today.

We speak to a waiter, and I tell him I want to learn about the history of the place. He gives me a wide smile, as if he's used to being questioned this way. 'You'll want to sit at the bar, then?'

'Ah – *oui*?'

He leads us to the dark wood, leather-upholstered bar area. The moody aesthetic has that whole dark academia vibe that seems fitting for wintry days. 'Here is Hemingway,' he says, and I startle, expecting to turn around and find the author himself propped up at the bar. Instead, there's a golden plaque bearing the name 'E. Hemingway' bolted to the wood itself. 'Each table has a plaque. There's Oscar Wilde, Emile Zola, Honoré de Balzac, Ezra Pound, F. Scott Fitzgerald, Samuel Beckett, to name a few,' the waiter says. 'Their legacy lives on here at La Closerie, *non*?'

'*Magnifique*.' Literature is celebrated in Paris, revered like art and music.

The warmly lit piano bar with its moody aesthetic makes me feel like we've truly travelled back in time to the Roaring Twenties. Outside, rain patters down, blurring the windows. I have the strangest sensation as I pause at the bar in front of the plaque bearing Hemingway's name. It's as though they've been holding his spot for all these years, hoping one day he'll return with his cheeks ruddy from cold, extolling patrons about why he's been missing, what he's been writing, as he takes a drink at the bar, all eyes riveted to him.

Unless he never left. Maybe his lively spirit hovers here in the ether, in Paris, in La Closerie des Lilas where he wrote, read, swapped manuscripts and debated with fellow wordsmiths. Celebrated and commiserated with them on the long, blustery days inside, out of the rain, with a shot of his favourite tipple of rum to warm his body.

'You sit in Hemingway's spot,' Manon says. 'You're all starry eyed, as if he's really here.' She brings me back to the present with a bang. 'Why you're suddenly so rapt thinking about long-dead writers is mystifying, unless... it has something to do with a certain neighbour, who reminded you of a young Ernest.' She

waggles a brow suggestively. I should never have admitted that
to her. But Noah does remind me of Hemingway, not only in
looks. It's also his verve, his soulful eyes, the way he takes
charge. A man who knows his mind. It's a heady thing, and I
must avoid it at all costs.

I heave a sigh and order a Kir, a French aperitif of crème de
cassis and white wine, while I peruse lunch options. I don't
point out to Manon that even the menu has a nod to the writer
whose barstool I've taken, with a pan-fried fillet of beef cooked
'Hemingway' style. For an American, he's part of the fabric of
Paris, then and evermore.

Manon is waiting for a response, her hunger seemingly
forgotten, so I say, 'It's got nothing to do with Noah, and more
with the idea of helping future guests find these hidden gems
all over Paris. Really, we'll need to offer them more than just
stacked bookshelves if we're to call ourselves a boutique literary
hotel.'

'You keep telling yourself that. I don't believe a word of it.'
Manon takes the menu and we place an order for sea bream
tartare for me, and duck foie gras for my cousin.

'Isn't that Noah now? It's like you wished him here!' Manon
says, and she points to a man storming down the avenue, eyes
ablaze as our drinks are deposited on to the mahogany bar.

'Is he coming in here?' I ask as my phone beeps with a text
from JP.

> Your neighbour Noah is on his way to you.
> Says it's urgent. JP

17

18 NOVEMBER

'Ugh, JP told him where to find us.' Noah locks his eyes on mine through the rain-dashed window. By the set of his jaw, it's obvious he's not happy. He swaggers inside, as if he owns the place. No surprise there; it tracks with his massive ego. Noah points in our direction as the waiter gives a lackadaisical shrug, leaving him free to stomp towards us.

'You didn't think to tell me renovations were starting today!' Noah says, his voice tight. Just who does he think he is? He doesn't own the entirety of Rue de Vaugirard, so it's none of his business.

Not wanting to rush my retort, I take a sip of Kir, the alcohol instantly warming me. 'Oh? I didn't realise I had to run everything past you.' While it might be good manners to warn the neighbours, I didn't want to get into a slanging match with Noah about it. Looks like that avoidance tactic has backfired.

He sighs and gazes up to the heavens as if he needs guidance from above. 'They're already banging about, making enough noise to wake the dead.'

'I'm not sure if there's a way to bang noiselessly, but I can ask.' How else does he think I can change the 'desolate' hotel that's bringing down the entire 6th arrondissement without creating any noise?

'I have a literary event in the bar today. How are my patrons going to hear the guest author with that sort of carry on going on next door?'

I frown. 'Obviously renovations aren't silent for the most part.'

He huffs and puffs like the big bad wolf. 'Can you tell your builder to stop the noise between two and four p.m. at least?'

'I mean, I could, but isn't it best for all involved if we get the work done as fast as possible?'

Noah scrubs his face as impatience radiates off him. '*Oui*, faster is better, but there are so many of them. The place is heaving. There are trucks going up and down the length of the street. It cannot continue like this.'

I bristle at the way he talks to me, as if I should be conferring with him for permission like I'm some underling.

I'm about to retort when he says, 'And why would you get that huge industrial-size skip deposited right out the front of the hotel? It's an eyesore. Every time they throw something in it, a layer of dust coats my freshly washed windows.' This man is obsessed with clean windows!

I fold my arms across my chest to stop myself poking a finger in his face. I have to force myself to remain composed because I'm at my limit with men who think they're the supreme voice in every matter, even matters that aren't their concern. 'When you renovated your wine bar, where did your skip go?'

Noah has the grace to blush. 'How is that relevant?'

'How is it not? You know there's no room at the back of the building for the skip, Noah. If there was, we'd have put it there. It's double standards, is what this is.'

He unravels his woollen scarf as if he's overheating. I'm not sure if it's from his temper or the warmth in the restaurant. 'There's plenty of room out the back, further down the side street.'

I arch a brow. 'And your skip went all the way down there, did it?'

A muscle works in his jaw as if he's trying to stop the truth leaking out, but I can see right through that. Typical alpha-male behaviour. 'Well... *non*, but my renovations were on a smaller scale, and I discussed it with the previous hotelier first. We can work together, Anais, if you keep me informed.'

The hide of this man. The wannabe king of Rue de Vaugirard. 'I'm acting under accordance of city rules and regulations and with the guidance of my building supervisor. There's going to be some disruption, noise, and mess for a month or so, but we'll keep it to daytime hours as is standard practice. Your bar is usually closed during the day, so I can't see this being an ongoing issue for you.'

Another glass of Kir is deposited on the bar and Manon motions to Noah that it's for him. He gives her an easy smile and takes a sip, pressing his lips together. She's trying to drag this confrontation out for her own amusement.

Noah continues, in a softer tone, 'I often open the bar during the day for various literary events, so I'm not sure where you're getting your information from, but it's wrong.'

'I got the information from your website.'

His shoulders stiffen as if I've won a point. I could get used to one-upping him. And all men. 'I update the website when I can, but not every event is advertised on there. I'd prefer if you check in with me and ask what I've got on and we can come to an arrangement that way.'

My eyebrows shoot up. 'You want me to run our schedule past you every day? And then what? You'll tell my builder no? I'm on a timeline, and JP has other projects too. We can't delay simply because you say so.'

'We can compromise.' What Noah's saying by 'compromise' is me stopping all tradespeople whenever he sees fit. How is that fair?

'This is me compromising. I'll be mindful of your patrons when you have events, but you can't expect I'm going to kowtow every time you have an issue. I have to fix my desolate hotel, *non*?'

'Fine.' He lets out a long, weary gas-lighter sigh. 'I have something for you.'

'Oh?' A list of handwritten rules? An invoice for cleaning my windows?

He takes a key from his pocket. 'I found this behind the hotel a few months back. I presume it's for one of the rooms in L'Hotel du Parc?'

I gasp and take the rusty antique key from the palm of his hand. 'It could be for suite nineteen!'

Noah shrugs. It's a completely different shape from the other suite keys, which were updated at some point. While the patina of this key has suffered being exposed to the elements, it's also clearly from another era. It might just be a coincidence and not the missing key in question, but there's a weight, a heft, to it. Inexplicably, it feels special. What lies behind the door of suite nineteen?

'The secret room might finally be revealed!' Manon says.

'Secret room?' Noah queries.

I shoot Manon a warning look. Would Noah know anything about the room, or what it contains, from his friendship with the former owner? Do I dare tell him? I decide to risk it in case the previous hotelier shared anything with Noah that may be helpful to us.

'On the third floor, a heavy mirror fell, leaving a head-size hole in the plaster. Sealed behind that wall are two suites: nineteen, which is locked tight, and twenty, which is unlocked. The locksmith refused to toy with the lock itself in case he damaged it. Not being able to see what's in there adds to the intrigue, I guess.'

Noah scratches his chin. 'Ah. I take it you never heard the rumours then?'

Manon sits up straighter on her barstool. 'What rumours?'

'It might just be one of those stories that gets exaggerated with each retelling, but there have always been whispers that a famous writer once lived in L'Hotel du Parc, though no one could ever confirm who it was. The previous hotelier said he'd searched every inch of the place but couldn't find evidence of such a thing, though he still believed it.'

A rush of blood to the head makes me woozy, but I press him for more details. 'When did he think the writer lived there?'

'Oh, this is going back to the 1920s or '30s.'

My eyebrows shoot up. 'Really?' The timeline fits with the belongings we found in suite twenty, which were of that era.

Noah grins and it transforms his features from gruff to pleasant. 'Really.'

It's so strange to think of a mystery as great as this as I sit on Hemingway's barstool in a restaurant that it's rumoured he wrote part of *The Sun Also Rises* in.

'So, this writer holed up at L'Hotel du Parc? Like a Coco

Chanel situation?' It's well known that Coco Chanel moved into suite 302 in The Ritz in 1937 and lived there for over thirty years until her death. It's awe-inspiring to think of the sumptuous hotel being called home to a famous fashion designer for all that time. Now her suite costs around forty thousand euros per night, a price tag that puts most of us out of contention. Still, I'd love to see it one day.

'Well, Coco residing in The Ritz was never a secret. Whereas details about this mysterious writer staying at the hotel are sketchy. It's said she was a reclusive for some reason. It could be a rumour perpetuated over time, who knows, but I like to think that there must be some truth to it. The way the hotelier spun the story was that the writer assumed another name when they moved into the hotel, so perhaps no one knew their real identity.'

'But how did the previous hotelier know that but not any further details?'

'That's just it, it could all be gossip. But he believed it enough he searched his own hotel inside and out. L'Hotel du Parc was owned by generations of the same family until he bought it in the seventies and remodelled.'

'So he's to blame for the atrocious colour scheme,' Manon pipes up.

I ignore her jibe and ask, 'Were they an affluent family?' The belongings in suite twenty were rich and lustrous, with a few house clothes that had more humble origins.

'I'm not sure. Do you think these hidden suites have something to do with the writer?'

I think back to objects we sifted through in suite twenty. There was nothing that pointed to a writer: no books, no letter-writing paper, no typewriter; not even a fountain pen.

I drop my gaze to the key. I have the urge to run back to the hotel and, trust me, I don't get an urge to run very often. Noah's eyes twinkle; I sense he's feeling the same way too. 'There was nothing in suite twenty that would indicate a writer stayed there. Perhaps there could be in suite nineteen? It would make sense if they were reclusive to hide away in the rooms at the furthest point of the hotel, but why seal the suites up for all this time? What is it that they wanted to keep hidden?'

Noah lifts a shoulder. 'Only one way to find out.'

'*Oui.*' I pocket the key. 'We're staying elsewhere for a bit so it'll have to wait, but thanks for passing on the key, Noah.'

'You're welcome. I hope it fits.' He glances at his watch. 'So, two to four this afternoon. Can you ask them to keep the noise down just a little?'

I give him a solemn nod. 'I'll call JP now.'

He smiles and drinks the rest of his Kir and takes some euros from his pocket and places them on the bar.

'*Non*, it's—' But he's gone, back into the drizzly day.

Manon makes a show of pulling out her collar as if she's hot and bothered. 'Ouah, you two are sizzling together! It's like... Pow. Pow, pow – pow! Those sparks, like fireworks. I wonder if I caught them on camera.'

'What do you mean, caught them on camera?'

Manon takes her phone, zooms in on the photo and turns it to me. 'Sparks!' she says as if such a thing is tangible. I squint at the screen. She's managed to catch the moment we both looked up from the antique key with awed expressions at the possibility of a literary mystery to solve. Drops of rain on the windows are caught through flickering candlelight, making it look like sparks are flying between us.

'Those are candlelight rain drops.'

'Really?' she groans. 'The universe is still throwing signs

directly your way and yet you're still blind to them. What will it take?'

'For what? I told you romance is dead and buried. My heart is a no-go zone. Closed for business. And sure, Noah did the right thing sharing the key with us, but did you hear him before that? He's bossy and unyielding.'

Her eyebrows shoot up. 'Truth-bomb time: since the divorce, *you're* bossy and unyielding.'

'Exactly. So no man will ever get the better of me again. I'm sick to death of the opposite sex telling me what I can and can't do, like my divorce lawyers, who carried on the farce for so long draining me of money, knowing winning was futile but urging me to continue to fight a losing battle and increase their billable hours. Noah is no exception. Fine, he might be hot in that suave, cocktail-swilling, intense masculinity, broody way, but he's still a guy who is attempting to control me and that means he's going to learn the hard way that I'm no pushover.'

Manon's shoulders droop. 'What about his event today then?'

I sigh. 'I'll call JP and ask about minimising noise for the sake of his customers, but we can't stop altogether. Noah has to learn that he can't stomp around and expect the world to fall at his feet. I'm over men trying to orchestrate my life. Delete that photo.'

'*Non*, I will not. Let's eat or I will die.' Manon clocks the waiter returning with our meals, who motions to a nearby table for us to sit to eat more comfortably. The plaque on this table reads *S DE Beauvoir*, better known as Simone De Beauvoir, a French writer famous for her revolutionary ideas around feminism.

I make a note to research the plaques on each table for the literary map before I find JP's number and call to explain the situation about our surly neighbour. JP complains about time constraints and his scheduling, but agrees to try his best to reduce the noise between 2 and 4 p.m.

After I end the call, I say, 'Bon appétit.' But Manon is already digging into her lunch with great gusto. Once our plates are cleared, we order café crèmes and pull out our laptops. We chat for a while about a literary name for the hotel, but nothing sounds quite right.

'I'll start redesigning the website because that's going to be a big job, making the booking system more efficient,' Manon says. 'We'll also need to take photos but we can't do that now, and of course we need the new hotel name, but I can make a start at least.'

'*Oui.* I'll look for suppliers for the items we need, mattresses and linens specifically.' I spend an hour trawling through various websites and sending enquiries, but I'm distracted. The mystery of room nineteen is far too enticing to let go.

I google 'reclusive writer living at L'Hotel du Parc', but nothing comes up. Not one hit. Did Noah make it up? Surely not. If it's a mystery from the twenties, I presume there's not much online about it, but it's strange there's not a whisper. Not even an outrageous conspiracy theory to work with.

My phone beeps again with a text message from Giselle:

> Bonjour, Anais, of course you're always
> welcome to stay and so is your cousin. Key is
> in the lockbox by the door, the code is 9876.

'Giselle is happy for us to stay. We can return to the hotel on Friday afternoon to meet with JP before they finish work for the weekend.'

Finally, I open my Word document and promise myself I'm going to write one paragraph, then two and then a page.

Rain lashed the windows of the La Closerie des Lilas as Hilary sipped her café crème and considered the new man in her life. Or what was left of him.

I shake my head. I've killed my hero. Again. In the second sentence. What is wrong with me?

18

22 NOVEMBER

We give Giselle's apartment a quick tidy before we pack up our belongings ready to return to the noise and progress at L'Hotel du Parc. The brief reprieve has done wonders for us. Manon's figured out how to revamp the website for bookings, and despite us not having a new name yet, she restructured it, so it's inviting and modern. Guests can't book as yet, but if they click on the link there are posts about our progress and an expression-of-interest form they can fill in, to be informed when bookings become available for Christmas. We can't do much more with the site until we figure out the perfect name. No matter how much we brainstorm, nothing sounds quite right. Manon likes L'Hotel des Buveurs d'Encre, which translates to The Ink Drinker Hotel. It's another word used to describe a bookworm in French, but I feel it doesn't quite hit the mark.

I'm hoping the right name will appear, just like I hope the writing fairies will pay me a visit.

My romcom is still stubbornly refusing to write itself. Nevertheless, I'm hoping once I get back to my own space things will improve.

Back at the hotel, JP takes us through the work they've done, which is an incredible amount considering it's only been a week. The leaks have been detected and repaired and the mouldy ceilings replaced. The delicate cornice work he'll do later as it's not a noise-producing job. JP takes us right around, pointing out what they've accomplished and what's coming next. Without all the retro seventies décor, the place already appears cleaner, tidier, like a blank canvas.

'OK,' JP says. 'Follow me.' We walk to the second floor and stop by the door of suite three. 'Here's the first suite we've started on.'

'Ready?' I ask Manon. The idea of a clean slate and imagining what the suites *will* look like is a heady thing indeed. Be gone, avocado-green drapes!

'Ready,' Manon confirms, giving JP a salacious wink. He frowns as if confused by such an action. Honestly, the guy is handling her well, considering.

I open the door and gasp. While it's an empty shell, it's so much lighter and brighter without the dingy brown rug and dusty thick drapes. They've cleaned the windows, and the room is bathed in natural light and ready for us to paint. 'Manon, look how well the floors have shined up!' The herringbone-style parquetry has been sanded and polished.

'We could tap dance, it's so shiny.'

And she probably would. I can see Manon in a leotard and tap shoes for some reason.

I get the first inklings of happiness. Such a small rejuvenation has produced such dramatic results. JP and his team have replaced the mouldy ceiling and fixed the crumbling cornice in this guest room. There's still more to do but, for now, it's a great start. 'This is lovely!'

Even JP cracks a smile at our enthusiasm. 'Now to the bathroom,' he says.

And... back to reality. I scrunch my eyes closed as I open the door, not wanting to be disappointed, that the vision isn't quite what I hoped for. While the bathrooms are spacious, there's only so much salmon a person can handle. JP agreed on a simple fix of switching out the mirrors, sinks and tapware. The salmon tiles will stay for now, but I'm hoping they look more glamorous with golden hardware in the form of taps and soap and towel holders. Once we add thick fluffy white luxurious towels and bathmats, it should complete the look.

'*Mon Dieu!*' Manon says. 'Anais, look. The gold accents are just beautiful. It complements the salmon colour.'

I give her a wide smile. The new extra-wide mirrors hide the bulk of salmon tiling as you enter the bathroom, and the salmon ceiling has been painted a vibrant white, which helps to calm down the previous intensity. 'We just might make this renovation work.' It's a huge energy boost, expecting the worst and being pleasantly surprised. We shut the door and survey the bedroom area once more. 'What about drapes, bedlinen, rugs? We need to decide what colours are best. I like the sheers we got for the guest lounge, but the drapes in here will have to be a blackout type.'

Manon takes her phone from her pocket and opens the notes app. 'Well, we've painted the bedside tables navy, but we're yet to switch out the handles, so we should stick with whatever matches that.'

'Right.' We have so much on the go, my to-do list is pages long. 'What about simple white bed linen with a textured throw at the end of the bed, navy-blue blackout drapes with white sheers? We can go back to Marché Saint Pierre. Maybe you can use your haggling skills and do a deal with them for ready-made drapery?'

'*Oui*, easy.'

'But will those colours suit the salmon bathroom?'

'Let's check on Pinterest.' Manon brings up the website and a page of colour swatches appear. 'Those colours are great together.' She points to the photos on screen and, somehow, they do work. The overall effect is sophisticated.

'Gold bedside lamps. A curated selection of books.'

JP points to a space by the door. 'We've added electrics to that area for your coffee station. Did you want a shelf hung there, or...'

'A shelf would be great, and we can buy those inexpensive trolleys for mugs and coffee and tea.'

'Before I get back to it...' JP coughs clearing his throat. 'There's one other thing. Suite seven.'

'AKA the crime scene suite!' Manon says with a grin.

'*Manon!* It is not. Is it, JP?' Why does he stay silent?

He leads us down the hallway, and I can't help stiffening, preparing myself for bad news. Surely he'd have called me if there *was* indeed a dead body buried there. Wouldn't there be caution tape? Detectives? Reporters out the front? I shake myself back to reality. Manon's true crime chatter is obviously getting to me.

JP swings open the door and we take a tentative step inside. The suite smells... musty, like the rest of them. 'The smell that I thought would outlast humanity, it's gone! What was it?'

Manon's face falls, as if she's bitterly disappointed. 'Was it mould? How utterly boring.'

Is JP grinning? 'There *was* a body—'

I gasp and Manon claps a hand over her mouth, her eyes ablaze with hope.

'—A rat.' I can't help but shiver. The rats in Paris are rabbit sized. I'm not exaggerating. If you happen to walk along the edges of the garden surrounding the Eiffel Tower late at night, they have free rein, and you *will* step on one. They don't seem to fear humans under the cover of darkness as they search for food.

Manon deflates, as I smile. 'Where was it?'

'Behind the vanity, so we had to replace the shelving because – it's best if you don't know every detail.'

I exhale a pent-up breath. 'I'm *so* glad it wasn't human.'

JP nods. 'Me too. If there's nothing else you needed me for, I'll get back to work then? We're hoping to get a lot of the demolition rubbish downstairs today before the skip is picked up and replaced with a fresh one.'

'*Merci*, JP,' I say.

'*Oui, merci*,' Manon says as an afterthought.

The big broad-shouldered guy blushes and gives Manon a shy smile, which she frowns at, as if she can't translate the meaning of such a gesture. That or she's toying with the poor fool. You never can tell with my wily cousin. '*De rien. Au revoir.*' JP scratches the back of his neck as he backs away, his gaze firmly locked on Manon, who doesn't seem to pick up on it.

'*Au revoir*,' I say as he ducks out, and I put the weird pause down to him not quite knowing how to deal with Manon. It happens a lot.

'What about the literary aspect?' Manon asks, jumping straight into the next thing as if JP isn't a consideration at all. Perhaps I'm imagining the awkward atmosphere between the two of them. 'How should we incorporate that in every guest suite aside from a curated selection of books for each guest? Stocked bookshelves? Themed rooms?'

I tap my chin, considering what would work best. 'The Ritz

Paris has suites named after icons. There's Suite Coco Chanel. Charlie Chaplin, Windsor. Why don't we do the same, but each room is named after a memoir set in Paris or by those who made Paris their home? There are so many evocative novels that share different eras of life in Paris.'

'OK, throw me some titles.'

'I'll have to check my Goodreads list, but off the top of my head... um...' I struggle to name many of the books I've read over time that have all added to the experience of living in Paris. 'OK, how about *The Piano Shop on the Left Bank*. Such a great novel about discovering a dormant passion in a little atelier, that for the life of me I've never been able to find. He kept it secret so the shop wasn't bombarded.'

Manon pulls a face. 'I mean, I like it, but isn't it a little wordy for the name of a suite?'

I grin. 'It is, but the quirkiness of such a thing appeals. Book lovers will get it. What about *The French Ingredient*? An American woman who was so bold as to open a cooking school in Paris. It was unheard of!' Manon's brow furrows so I press on, becoming more taken with the idea as I remember other awe-inspiring memoirs. '*Time was Soft There* is a memoir about the author's time as a Tumbleweed, a name given to those itinerants who blew in on the wind and were permitted to live and work inside the bookshop Shakespeare and Co. In *Almost French*, the author navigates love in a new city in a language she doesn't speak.'

'You are *so* eccentric. Although I must admit, it does sound rather fun and frivolous. Let me make a note of these names and we can choose the strongest contenders.' She pulls her phone from a pocket and types in the book titles. 'What about our writer in residence? The incomparable Anais De la Croix?

Surely we get to name a suite after you, given all your best-selling romances?'

'*Non, merci.* Plus, mine aren't memoirs.' As a writer, I don't crave the limelight at all. In fact, I actively avoid it as much as I can and only do events like book tours, festivals and awards nights when Margaret demands it of me. Which is all the time. 'That would be a bit arrogant, don't you think?'

Manon shakes her head. 'It would be sweet.'

'*Non*, there are plenty of other books we can feature. There's *A Moveable Feast,* the classic. Or *My Paris Dream.* We'll gift a copy of "their" special suite book on check in. Each suite will have a notebook in the room, for guests to pen their thoughts about what they read during their stay with us. Sort of like a guest book... for books. They can read what the previous guest wrote. I've already ordered bath caddies for the four suites and old-book-scented candles.'

'Actually, some hotels offer a pillow menu, so why don't we offer a reading pillow menu? There are all sorts, like tablet holder cushions, or chunky pillows with arm rests and back support. There's full body-length pillows for those who sprawl when they read. Massaging neck pillows to relax those jetlagged readers. I'm sure we can find a selection and offer them to our guests upon check in.'

'Great idea, Manon! We can advertise our very own reading pillow menu on social media closer to the time.'

'*Oui,* there's a few other things on our spreadsheet we need to get too. Let's see if we can find some bookish décor at the markets, *non*? We need literary mugs for the coffee stations, cute library-card stamped cushions. Anyway, we've still got plenty of time for finessing. Let's get back to work.'

'Real work, as in manual labour?'

I nod. '*Oui!* Time to start painting!'

We've chosen a creamy white because of the golden cornicing, and I'd rather highlight that feature and keep the rooms light and bright, clean.

'We have to paint so many walls.' Manon has an air of defeat in her tone. Us painting saves a huge amount of money and while it'll be tedious, it's not hard, even though it does seem like a mammoth task. One step at a time. Painting seems so much easier than facing a blank screen on my laptop. The clock is ticking, and my word count is exactly two. And those two words are: Chapter One.

'I know it feels endless, and having to do so many coats to hide the bright colours is a kick in the teeth.' I rummage in my jacket pocket and produce the antique key. 'First, we need to see if this fits suite nineteen.'

Manon slaps her forehead. 'I'd forgotten all about it.'

There's a sense of excitement about discovering what's inside. I only hope that excitement isn't extinguished if we open the door to find a basic hotel room with a horrific colour scheme just like the rest.

'Wait!' She holds up a hand. 'I'll be back in a moment.'

She dashes out before I can ask her where she's going. I wait a few minutes and then give up, making my way up to the third floor when there's a commotion on the stairs behind me. I turn to see Manon dragging a very reluctant Noah behind her, blithely ignoring his protestations. It's like she's taken him prisoner.

'Manon! What are you *doing*?' I turn and hold on to the banister for support as tradespeople slip up and down the stairs, surefooted like mountain goats. I'm definitely going to improve my own fitness here traipsing up and down.

'I'd like to know that too,' Noah says, wrenching his arm from hers. 'I was in the middle of a meeting with a supplier, but she wouldn't take no for an answer. Can you tell me what's so urgent that I have to be here? Let me guess: another bookshelf has toppled over?'

'We're opening the secret room, but I didn't want your supplier to find out. What if it's full of gold, or the hidden corpse of your reclusive writer? Best we keep this *petit* mystery to ourselves for now.'

I'm rankled she's roped Noah into this. While it was nice of him to offer us the key he found, we don't even know if it fits the lock. And whatever is in that suite is ours to explore. Alone.

'Sorry for the disturbance, Noah. Manon took leave of her senses temporarily. You'll come to learn this happens quite a bit where my cousin is concerned. You can leave.'

'Perhaps I've been a little hasty. Manon is only doing the neighbourly thing by inviting me here. I'll stay, just let me text my supplier.' He loses his gruff countenance, which irks me even more. How fickle he is!

My brain won't compute an excuse fast enough to get rid of him, and Manon doesn't help when she pushes him in the back to get moving. 'We don't have all day.'

Part of me is furious with her; the other part just prays the key fits. If it's another dead end, we're back to square one and will have to try another locksmith, or the sledgehammer option. Both unappealing. Last night, locksmith *numero uno* sent me a terse email saying he didn't discover any details about the internals of the lock and, if I forced entry and damaged it, I'd be bringing down a lot of bad juju on myself and every guest who ever deigned to stay here. Who knew locksmiths could be so threatening. He topped off his stroppy email with a rather large invoice for his call-out fee. Hence, I'm a little reluctant about calling in any other 'experts'.

We find JP at the top of the stairs in deep conversation with one of his workers. We sidestep him and Manon calls out, 'If you hear a scream, don't panic.'

JP frowns. Honestly, the guy is going to prematurely age working in close proximity to Manon. While he seems intrigued, he also spends a fair amount of time perplexed by her. Such is the Manon effect.

When we get to the end of the hallway, I take a series of deep breaths. I wish I could say it's from the adrenaline pumping, but that would be a lie. *So many stairs. So often.* While Noah and Manon are conversing about what we might find behind the door, seemingly not affected at all by physical exertion, I'm struggling to stay alive.

'Anais,' Manon says, hands in a prayer gesture. 'Do you want a drum roll?'

I roll my eyes. 'I want no such thing.' In Noah's presence, I act a little haughtier than usual. I'm not sure why.

'Do the honours, then.'

I stand in front of the door and briefly close my eyes, readying myself for any disappointment that may come. We've beat this so-called mystery up and there's not one solid bit of proof there is any truth to it.

'I hope this works,' I say, and I put the key in the lock and turn it.

19

22 NOVEMBER

The key turns and I push the door slowly open, and of course it makes the obligatory horror movie-esque squeal. Manon crashes into the back of me in her rush to get in, but I'm frozen to the spot.

'*Mon Dieu*,' is all I manage.

'It's a... secret library?' Manon asks, pushing my lower back so I have no choice but to trip into the suite. Every wall is lined with bookshelves that are double and triple stacked with books. 'I think your wish for a fully stocked library just came true,' Manon whispers, her voice full of awe.

'*Oui*. There are so many!'

Under the window is an ornate antique bed, the thick quilt lifted back as if someone just woke up and pushed it to one side. I inch closer. E. M. Foster's novel *A Passage to India* lies face-down on a bedside table – did whoever lived here not get to finish reading it? For some reason, that tugs at my heart. I suppose chances are that we'll all leave this mortal coil somewhere in the middle of an unfinished book, which makes me strangely sad. I lift it and check the publication date. It appears to be a first edition from 1924, so that means the guest came here sometime after that date...

In the middle of the room is a desk, cluttered and stacked with piles of paper. Novels. Dictionaries in various languages and a few gold-bound encyclopaedias.

The bookshelves are bowed with the weight of so many tomes, and the parquetry below them has stacks of books, as if they've spilled off the shelves over the years.

We're all silent as we take in the spectacle before us. It's like a time capsule going back to another era. I move to the shelves and run a finger along the spines of the leatherbound books. What would these be worth? While they're in disorderly dusty piles, they're in immaculate condition. I breathe them in, the scent of bygone times. Do I really want to share these special tomes with others? Part of me can't imagine disturbing one single thing in this room. It feels special, somehow. Like the occupant just stepped out for a moment...

Noah goes to the old-fashioned rolltop desk that's been left open and says, 'Do you mind if I—' He points to a drawer.

I don't want to miss a thing, so I step around spilled piles of books and join him. 'Go for it.'

The drawer is full of notebooks. He takes one and flips it open to find neat cursive writing, so curly that it's hard to decipher. 'Any idea who wrote it?' I ask, reading over his shoulder. I can't tell if it's a journal or a manuscript.

'*Non*, I'm not sure.' We each take a notebook and read, looking for some clue as to who stayed in this suite. The only sound is the rustling of paper as we turn the pages.

'Found something,' Noah says. 'She writes that she's escaped her husband and is relieved she won't ever need to write under the pseudonym any more. She doesn't go into much more detail, only that she hopes that he doesn't find her.'

I gasp. 'So the rumour is true? A mysterious writer from the twenties lived here, at L'Hotel du Parc!'

'It could be. She was clearly a "woman of letters", as they were so dubbed back then.'

I remember that day back in La Closerie des Lilas when Noah told us what he knew about the writer. 'Didn't you say she assumed another name when she moved to the hotel?'

'*Oui*, that's what the previous hotelier told me. But does that mean she took another pseudonym, or a whole new identity?'

'And why? To escape her husband, as she mentions?'

'Must be.'

'The plot thickens.'

Noah gently flicks the pages, looking for more details.

I take stock of the novels on the desk, wondering if our mystery guest penned any of them. I find an edition of *Gigi* by Colette, and under a stack of typed papers, there's a copy of *Chérie* by the same mononymously known author. My heart stops for a moment. 'It couldn't be Colette, could it? A French icon famous for writing about love and sensuality who was well ahead of her time and lived what was considered a scandalous life back then...'

'Let me check.' Manon takes her phone and types. '*Non*. It says Colette was living at number 9 Rue de Beaujolais in an apartment at the Palais Royal at the time of her death in 1954.' She pockets her phone.

'What a place to live.' Very rarely apartments at the Palais Royal are offered for sale, but when they are there's a hefty price tag attached for such a prestigious address.

Noah nods. 'Colette's life was well documented. She wrote semi-autobiographical books, and didn't shy away from society. Plus, she didn't write under a pseudonym.'

'*Oui.*' I'm surprised at Noah's knowledge about our infamous French author. 'Have you read Colette's work?'

'Most of them.' He shrugs. 'I'm a fan of literature of that era.'

Manon sidles up to him. 'So you wouldn't read an Anais De la Croix novel then? Too modern for your tastes?'

'Never say never. I'll read anything.'

I bristle at his use of the word 'anything', as if in desperate times a book written by me would suffice. 'How sweet,' I say with a wooden smile. 'As much as I'd love to explore every inch of this time capsule, I think it's best we press on with our hotel work, so if you can find your way out—?'

Noah's face falls. 'Of course. Thank you for sharing this room with me.' He puts a hand on his heart and gazes around once more as if taking it all in to consider later. 'I'd really like to help you investigate further.'

'*Merci*, but that won't be necessary. However, if you don't mind keeping your knowledge of this private, I'd be grateful. I'm not sure I'm ready to share this with the world yet.' This room is special, not only because of the beautiful disorderly books but because there's a real sense of a secret being kept inside these walls. A secret that I also feel is not mine to tell.

'My lips are sealed.'

After he goes, Manon confronts me, eyes ablaze, arms akimbo. 'Anais! That was rude. Why are you so prim and proper around him? You remind me of my *maman*, the way you're acting. Pursed lips, huffy faced.'

'Why did you bully him to come over here?'

Her eyebrows pull together. 'Without Noah, we wouldn't have the key for this suite, and he's a word nerd, it's practically tattooed across his forehead. Why wouldn't you two literature lovers want to share in this musty, dusty find? While this space is intriguing, it's also a little drab and boring for my tastes, so I figured he'd be the man for you. The person you could run to when you want to obsess over every little detail. Details, I might admit, that I would personally find excruciatingly boring to hear on repeat for the next lot of forever.'

I blow a lock of hair from my face. 'You didn't know what we'd find here, Manon, so how can any of that be true?'

'I had an inkling. And my heart, my soft squishy heart, hoped for the best for you. And my suspicions were correct, were they not? You've unlocked a secret library, an office hidden for however long, and now you can share it with the ink drinker next door, and leave your poor overburdened cousin out of exclaiming about every word you unearth here. While you're doing that, I'll get back to doing menial labour.'

'I see what you're doing, Manon, and it isn't going to work. Don't forget, I'm a romance writer' – suffering from crippling writer's block, but still – 'I can see a forced proximity ploy a mile away. This suite is a delightful, delicious literary mystery. Or it might well turn out to contain the mutterings of a reclusive woman who despised people and preferred to live out her days holed up in L'Hotel du Parc and, honestly, I can relate. But you putting Noah in my way isn't going unnoticed. And can't you see it's having the opposite effect? Did you hear the way he said he would read anything? As if a book written by me would be... tedious but doable, because he's so book smart and well read or something. Urgh, the man is pretentious.'

Manon takes a seat at the desk. 'How is that pretentious? I took it to mean he'll give any genre a go.'

'You're clearly not familiar with anti-romance bias. I am, and I can detect it a mile away. Men like Noah hate the fact that women write empowering stories where heroines take the lead and win against the ways in which they're often oppressed.'

'Not this oppression talk again.' She groans and makes a

show of dropping her head on the desk when there's a clunk. '*Aie!* That hurt.' Manon rubs her forehead while I move the stacks of papers to see what left a bump the size of a grape on her brow.

'*Ooh la la* it's a typewriter!' I practically hip and shoulder Manon from the chair so I can inspect it up close. It has a gold MAP logo and is an exquisite piece of history. 'There's a sheet of paper in the reel!'

'What does it say?'

Keep my soul in peace. Keep my last manuscript safe.

A shiver runs through the length of me and, for some strange and possibly stupid reason, I wish Noah was here to see this.

Manon's eyes sparkle with sudden interest. 'Her last words?'

'It certainly sounds like it. And someone, maybe the affluent family who owned the hotel through the generations, preserved the two suites, just as they were. Actively went to great lengths to hide them. Why? Do you think they were honouring her wishes? The way she wrote she was relieved to be finished with the pseudonym *and* had escaped her husband, as if both things were mutually exclusive, is odd to me. I'd like to find out more about that.'

'*Oui*, it does have an air of finality about it. Like she ran from an evil man, maybe?' Manon leans against one of the bookshelves and spins a sepia-tinted world globe.

'If the rumours Noah heard are correct, she lived here in the twenties, until... when? Her death? And for all that time, this secret library has been left alone? It can't be. Let's see if we can find anything online about L'Hotel du Parc's history. There might be old photographs archived somewhere. We might even be able to find photos of what these suites looked like originally.'

'Ooh, good idea. Let's look on the laptop.' I take a few of the notebooks from the desk to read later and hope to find clues on who our mystery guest was. We lock the door as we go.

In my suite, we sit together and look for any history about the hotel online but find nothing that fits with our mystery.

How has this secret been kept all this time? 'I wonder if we can find out the name of the family who owned the hotel before the previous hotelier?'

'Sure we can. We can even get on the dark web if you want?'

'What! *Non*.' My cousin has many a talent; if only she'd use them for good. Manon is a tech wizard, a gift that could essentially set her up for life, but, like with everything, she only uses this talent when it suits her.

With a few keystrokes, Manon has the sales history of the hotel, which is rather sparse; there's the Toussaint family, the previous owner, and then me.

'Toussaint?' she says. 'Why does that name ring a bell?'

I gasp when it comes to me. 'The paintings in suite twenty! L. L. Toussaint!'

'So do we think that our writer is L. L. Toussaint?'

I contemplate it. 'Could be. So she wrote and painted? But wait... If she left her husband and came here under an assumed name, wouldn't her family here think that strange? And if she *was* hiding from her husband, wouldn't he look here first, at her family's hotel?'

'*Oui*, it doesn't fit, does it?'

'*Non*. Even if she did in fact "escape" her husband for whatever reason, surely her family here would have protected her from him. They were obviously wealthy by the standard of items in suite twenty, so it's not as if they couldn't support emotionally as well as financially.'

Manon fidgets with the hem of her jumper. 'Not all of the items in room twenty were of the same quality though. There were some very plain dresses, made from coarse material. And there is a bed in each suite, leading me to believe there are two different people in this story.'

'But we didn't find any clothing in suite nineteen. It's a library, an office. Writers take naps, it's part of the process, so maybe that's why there's a bed in there.'

'Hmm. Maybe. Do you think Francois-Xavier heard the rumours and that's why he was so hellbent on buying this place? Hoping to find a pot of gold at the end of the rainbow?'

'No way. If he had half a suspicion there was a secret library, or the potential of a forgotten manuscript, possibly writing that is valuable, he'd have kept this in the divorce. He would have ripped this place apart to find it and sold whatever he could to the highest bidder.'

Manon's eyes open wide. '*You* could do that, Anais. What if we found her last manuscript like they did with Harper Lee's *Go Set a Watchman*?'

'It wouldn't be mine to sell, it would be her family's, or her estate, or whatever. Plus, she has expressly asked for the last manuscript to be kept safe. As a writer, I couldn't go against those wishes, and as a human it wouldn't be right.'

Manon slaps her forehead. 'You and your morals.'

I laugh. 'That doesn't mean I won't read the manuscript if we find it.'

'There's hope for you yet.'

I laugh. 'One issue has been solved.'

Manon's brows pull together. 'What's that?'

'The name of our hotel will be L'Hôtel Bibliothèque Secrèt.'

'The Secret Library Hotel! *Magnifique!*'

* * *

The next evening, I sit at my desk, laptop open, and wait for inspiration to strike. I wait and wait. And I wait. I tell myself just to write one tiny little sentence. Just one. How hard can it be? There are twenty-six letters in the alphabet; I just need to arrange those letters to form a word, and soon a sentence will appear, then a paragraph. Then a page. Simple.

I remind myself that, if I don't meet my deadline extension, Margaret will drop me, and my readers will be disappointed there's no Christmas book next year.

When Hilary locked eyes with the brooding man in the café on Boulevard Saint Germain, she felt a frisson of something. Was it love, lust or... murderous rage?

I cup my head. Why can't I write? I delete the sentence and sigh. Perhaps I'll find a little inspiration reading the notebooks of our mysterious author. I take one from my desk, inhaling the scent of the parchment. It smells like ink, like vanilla. Who was she? Why did she leave her pseudonym *and* husband behind?

As I read the flowery cursive words, an unhappy picture forms. It seems even the passage of time hasn't changed human nature. Our anonymous writer found her husband in flagrante delicto with a member of their household staff. I can relate.

This husband of hers also kept every penny she'd made writing, and threatened that, if she left him, he would tell everyone she was mad; the household staff would back him up, and he'd ruin her reputation. He was easily enraged and she feared for her life.

I must leave for my own sanity. While he may do his best to besmirch me, he cannot take away the words I am yet to pen. Those words, they are all that matter. I'll never publish another novel as long as I shall live, thus he cannot profit from me. That will be the best revenge. The man is dangerous. I must tread ever so carefully.

My pulse races at the entry. I have to show Noah! Manon's right. She will care not one jot about this, but I know he will. And maybe he can help me solve the identity of who this mysterious author is. But can I trust him with a secret as big as this? Perhaps I can give him some breadcrumbs, not the whole loaf, and see what he makes of it.

I swipe on some lipstick and head next door, only to see Noah through the window, in his element behind the bar, throwing cocktail shakers and joking with the small crowd who are dressed in reindeer ears and Christmas jumpers.

Perhaps he's hosting a work Christmas do? It's a Saturday night, probably his busiest time, so I don't bother interrupting. When he notices I'm hovering outside, he waves me in. I wave back and leave it at that. I suddenly feel protective of the mysterious writer, so maybe it's best I delve into this alone to ensure her last wishes of not only her manuscript being kept safe if I ever find it, but also her secrets.

20

24 NOVEMBER

By Sunday evening, the lobby hall is painted – begone, sunshine-yellow walls! – and we've spruced up the reception desk by hiding it behind a few plant pots with leafy ferns we picked up at the market for a song.

Manon's looped red tinsel around the plants even though all this area will most likely get dusty as work continues in the hotel and we'll need to clean it all time and again. 'That's it, I quit.' I put my hands on my hips and arch my back. I'm toy-soldier stiff. It radiates from my neck down every muscle, some I'm sure I've never used before. 'Maybe the words will spill now, because any excuse would do to not have to hold another paint-brush. The crick in my neck feels permanent, like I'll fall over backwards when I try to go forwards.'

'We've done a great job.'

I don't remind her how many other rooms we've got to do.

While I'm physically drained, I feel inspired by our accomplishments. My fingers tingle to write, which is a positive sign. 'Who knew backbreaking labour would be a potential cure for writer's block?'

Manon gives me the side eye. 'Cure or avoidance of said backbreaking labour?'

I let out a laugh. 'Both, probably.'

'I need dinner. It's well past my designated mealtime.'

In the laundry, we clean our paintbrushes and trays before going to the kitchen area. I take cheese and charcuterie from the fridge while Manon slices a baguette. We've been living on simple slap-together meals, and I do look forward to shopping and stocking up the larder so we can cook some proper dishes, but, at the end of a long day painting or rushing around, neither of us can be bothered cooking.

'I checked with the supplier about the delivery for our mattresses. There was an issue with the ones we ordered but it's sorted now and they're being delivered tomorrow.'

'And the linen too?'

'*Oui*.' I eat quickly, eager to get writing in the hope that the block is a thing of the past. 'I'm off to write.' I put my plate in the sink and leave Manon to it.

In my suite, I open up my laptop and begin to type.

Snow fell as Hilary made her way down the cobblestoned street near the Louvre. Her Parisian adventure had only just begun when she'd met a dashing Frenchman who...

Who what? Made her heart sing. Pulse race?

I'm internally cheering. One full sentence. Progress! I knit my fingers and stretch them out, readying myself for a long writing session, when there's a thump of bass. No matter. Paris is a noisy city and I am a professional. In my desk drawer I find my noise-cancelling headphones and slip them on. The pumping of the bass increases. Where is it coming from?

I take a steadying breath. It does not matter. It does not exist in this fictional world. Where was I? Hilary. How she feels about the dashing Frenchman. Does she feel rapture? Lust? Excitement? I picture my heroine with her straight blonde bob and China blue eyes. She's no nonsense. Has a take-charge persona. Doesn't suffer fools. She—

'*Bonsoir, Bonsoir!* Welcome to The Lost Generation Wine Bar! Tonight we have local death metal band, Pandemic, playing a set for you.'

How loud does the man have to be for his patrons to hear him in his tiny little bar? Is he using a megaphone? And a death metal band? It doesn't sound very Roaring Twenties to me.

I vow not to let him disrupt the flow of my writing. I stretch once more and try to get back into the headspace of my heroine. Hilary, black hair. Or was it blonde? Gah, it's no use. The thumping starts in earnest, so loud I'm sure the walls are shaking. Is this some kind of retaliation for the renovations?

I pull my headphones off and stomp downstairs and bump straight into Manon, who is dancing around the lobby in time to the music. 'Who knew Noah had such good taste?' she screams to be heard.

'Good taste? How can this even be called music? It's horrific. I'm going to go over there and give him a piece—'

'Yeah! Me too!'

'What?' She clearly can't hear me. How do the other neighbours let this sort of thing fly? As predicated, Noah is a hypocrite of the finest order. Whatever noise we make renovating makes his teeth grind, yet he hosts a death metal band that's so loud I'm sure the Eiffel Tower is shaking on its foundations.

My rage builds as I head to the exit. Manon grabs my arm. 'Where are you going?'

'NEXT DOOR!'

'*C'est bon!* Let me get my coat and I'll join you.'

I frown, confused. 'I'm not going for the... music! I'm going to talk to Noah about the noise pollution. It's a disgrace!'

Disappointment dashes over her features. 'Noise pollution? It's not that loud.'

'I can't hear you!'

With hands over my ears, I make my way to The Lost Generation Wine Bar. Noah stands by the front door in the crisp evening air, smiling and joking with patrons who are queuing to get in.

I tap him on the shoulder. When he turns to me, the smile slips straight off his face. Typical. I'm so riled up I don't speak; I rely on an extreme eyebrow raise and the cords twanging in my elongated exposed neck to get my point across.

'Do you need medical help?' he asks, his face pinched with worry. 'Did you... ingest—'

'What?'

His expression changes to relief. 'Ah, sorry. You had your neck stuck out like a giraffe, and that surprised look on your face. I thought you needed medical attention, but I see my error. Were you just...? In pain, or—?'

The hide of this man! '*Oui*, I'm in a lot of pain. Because I CAN'T HEAR MYSELF THINK.'

'Is this about the writer's block? Manon told me all about it.'

I'm going to kill her. But first I'll ask where to hide a dead body. And then I'll kill her.

'*Non*, it's not about that.'

'Well,' he says jovially, throwing an arm around my shoulders as if we're long-lost friends. 'Whatever it is, you've come to the right place. I'll even let you skip the queue, since you so clearly need to get out of your own head.'

'*Excusez moi?*' Is he joking or does he really think I'm here to unwind?

'No need to thank me.' He motions to a guy standing just inside. 'This is Anais, drinks are gratis for her. She's going through... some things.'

Before I can argue, Manon shows up. 'Ooh, can I skip the queue with Anais? I'm going through some things too.'

Noah throws her a bright smile. 'I bet.' He gives me a long look as if to imply that I'm the issue. I'm roiling, my head is going to explode, but it's so damn loud I can't form words fast enough to cut this fool to the quick.

Before I know it, we're being led inside the bar, Christmas lights are pulsing in time with the horrific bump of the base, it's so loud I'm sure this must be what hell sounds like, and we're deposited in a booth.

'If you had to dispose of a body, Manon,' I say through gritted teeth, 'where would you suggest?'

'Drink?' She mimes the action.

I give in to it. A drink would certainly help matters. It can't make it any worse, surely.

21
25 NOVEMBER

I wake to intense banging. Then it dawns on me it's coming from inside my own head. Gah. I piece the previous evening back together and groan, pulling the pillow over my head so I can hide from my bad choices. But it doesn't help. Mini jackhammers are drilling into my grey matter, while outside, actual hammers are hammering away in the hotel.

I glance at my watch and groan. It's well past ten. What must JP and his crew think of me, a no show? This is all Manon's doing.

One thing is certain: I need paracetamol and coffee, in that order. I throw myself in the shower and get dressed, going a little slower than normal due to my fragile state. Flashes of the evening before appear when I least expect them. Did I engage in a round of shots? Urgh. And... sing with the death metal band?

In the kitchen, I find painkillers and wash them down with some orange juice.

'*Bonjour, soleil.*' Manon saunters in looking bright and energetic. Life is not fair.

'It's not good morning, sunshine. Not even close.'

She takes a stool opposite the stainless-steel island bench. 'Suffering a little?'

'A lot.'

'You *really* let your hair down. That dance you did with Noah' – she pulls her collar out as if she's hot – 'certainly got everyone's attention.'

Mon Dieu. 'Ah – which dance was that?'

She shrugs as she pours coffee for the two of us. 'I *think* it was meant to be a kind of... tango?'

I want to curl up in a ball and die. 'But – but I don't know how to tango.'

'You gave it your best shot.'

'With Noah?'

'Uh-huh. He was just as surprised. You don't remember any of this?'

It's all coming back to me, in mortifying flashes. 'Manon, this is all your fault! I went over there to berate him, not... to tango with the guy. Then you ordered those blue-flamed cocktails that tasted like petrol and on it went, bad choice after bad choice and still no further along in my manuscript.'

'That's a lie. You told everyone last night you had written a sentence and then Noah was on about how Hemingway said something along the lines of only needing to write one true sentence and the others would follow, and then you got into a debate about toxic masculinity...'

'*Merci*, Manon. That's quite enough of a recap for me.'

Her cheeks are pinked as if she's just done a workout or had a brisk walk in the cold. 'I haven't had a fun night out like that in ages. I can't wait for this evening's festivities to start. We'll drink *vin chaud*, eat Brie de Meaux, jambon de Bayonne and partake in a Christmas movie quiz. A little more subdued so maybe it's not your thing?'

'This evening? Next door?'

'*Oui.*'

I narrow my eyes. Subdued. She's teasing me. 'Count me out. How are you so bright and bubbly today?' By the looks of her peachy complexion and clear eyes, Manon is suffering not one after-effect.

'One alcoholic beverage, one water. Those are my set-in-stone drinking rules. And I didn't partake in any shots. Honestly, I don't think I've ever seen that side of you before. I was a little blown away. Uninhibited Anais is a whole different person.'

I groan and lie my head on the kitchen bench. The cool of the stainless steel is a godsend for my thumping headache. 'How am I ever going to face Noah again?'

'What do you mean? He had a great time with you.'

'That's not the real me and you know it.'

Manon lifts a lock of my hair. 'Ah, she's under there somewhere.'

'We're supposed to be painting the guest lounge today, but I don't think I have the energy.'

'Why don't you write?'

With a hangover as ghastly as this, I'm not sure I can do much except suffer and wait for it to pass. '*Oui*, perhaps I'll focus on my book today. One thing I'm still confused about is, why the death metal band? It doesn't gel with what I know of our neighbour so far. It seems an odd choice.'

'Ah.' Manon leans her elbows on the bench. 'Every now and then he opens the bar for struggling Parisian musicians, so they get some exposure. He also gives them a percentage of the beverage profits to help them out. Due to his generosity, the bar has quite the cult following, as locals want to support artists, and I suppose Noah too, who is the brains behind it all. Not such a bad guy, eh?'

I don't want to give Manon the satisfaction of seeing my surprise, but I am a little taken aback by Noah's actions. It's a great opportunity for musicians to share their gift, and for him to share part of the spoils with them shows a sweet side to his character.

'It's good of him,' I eventually manage, and am rewarded with an eye roll. 'I better get to work so the entire day is not wasted.'

Manon yawns. Maybe she's not so bright-eyed and bushy tailed as I once thought. 'The new mattresses for the four guest suites are due to arrive today along with the new linen. How about I get everything washed and folded away, if we're not painting the guest lounge today?'

We have a small laundry at the back of the hotel. While the machines are antiquated, they're all in working order. 'Great idea.'

'Leave it to me.'

In my suite, I sit at the desk and wait for inspiration to strike. While I'm waiting, I open a new Word document and start typing up my Christmas card list. I even include Noah's name because it's the neighbourly thing to do. Once that's done, I go back to my manuscript and start over.

Rain lashed at the window while Hilary sat at her desk, waiting for inspiration to strike. She had a lot on her mind, what with the surly neighbour next door intent on ruining her life. Wild and robust in nature, the man was a walking cliché, but nobody but her could see it. Yeah, sure, he might have had a soft side to him, with his generosity helping local musicians, but that didn't give him the right to boss her about. Now she'd made things a hundred times worse, by drinking too much in his bar and attempting to tango with the damn man, and who knows what else. He was exactly her type, and that's why she had to avoid him. Short of vanishing, she didn't quite know how she was going to manage that. Unless he had himself a little accident...

A little accident? What is wrong with me? I go back and edit. ~~Unless, he had himself a little accident...~~ My keyboard keys are clattering in time with the pounding in my head and in the end I abort mission and decide a nap is the best option.

22

30 NOVEMBER

The following Saturday we're up early after a long night painting the guest lounge, which has taken far longer than we expected. The hotel is deathly quiet; JP and his crew have downed tools for the weekend and the backpackers are out. It feels suddenly strange that the place is bereft of so many bodies scuttling around, their radios blaring, the jokes they tell to make the day go faster. A scream every now and then when Manon pranks them.

'What are your plans today?' I ask Manon who is tucking into a buttery croissant, showering the island bench with crumbs. Around the corner we have the most beautiful boulangerie, Le Petit Lux, where we buy fresh croissants, pastries or a baguette that we heap with lashings of salty butter.

'I'm going out with, uh... Kiki tonight, but aside from that not much. Unless you've got more painting that needs doing and, in that case, I'm busy all day.'

I laugh. 'I was thinking we should start compiling books for the library room. We could use some of the collection from suite nineteen, but they seem too special, don't you think?'

'*Oui,* until we know more, we should leave that room as it is.'

'I agree.'

'We need to figure out what we're going to call the hotel library. I was thinking of Library Anaïs. What do you think?'

'After yourself? I love it!'

'Not myself! Anaïs Nin. One of the first and finest female writers of erotica, she was also a committed diarist who lived a more, shall we say... wanton lifestyle, and wrote titillating diary entries about it all. I've been reading a biography about her and she's wild enough to be endlessly fascinating. There are so many wonderful quotes attributed to her, but one of my favourites is...' I find my phone and pull up my notes app where I've been jotting quotes from the author herself and I read: '"I'm restless. Things are calling me away. My hair is being pulled by the stars again." Isn't that perfect for the library room?'

Manon nods. 'I must read this erotica... to make sure it's appropriate for our guests.' She winks, garnering a shake of the head from me. Trust Manon to get stuck on that part.

'Actually, you make a good point. It's not exactly child friendly. Perhaps we need a separate book area for children? We can set up some shelves and toys in a corner of the guest suite.'

'Ah – *oui*! When I cleaned out the cupboards in the laundry I found a box of toys. Not that old by the looks of it. An abacus, a xylophone, a train set, some board games. I'll take a closer look at them and see if they're in good enough condition for the children's area.'

'*Parfait*. And we can buy some picture books. Why don't we trawl round some bookshops today to find stock for the library? I want it to be an eclectic mix so there's a curated selection to suit every taste. We can buy second-hand books, which won't hurt the budget too much.'

Manon returns to her phone. '*Delta of Venus*, by Anaïs Nin. I'll start with that.'

'*Oui*, and we can hunt for not only her novels but biographies about her, with all the juicy details. Have you got that list of suite names?' Manon gives me a nod. 'Great. We can look for the books we named the suites after. Whatever we can't find we'll order online, but won't the fun part be searching for books to make the library grand?'

'I'll get ready now while you think about where you're taking me for lunch. I'll need stamina for all this book shopping.'

* * *

The cold wind whips my hair back as we wander along the streets of Paris, book shopping. Is there anything more fun? We've been to Shakespeare and Co., where Manon got remonstrated for taking a selfie beside the sign announcing that photos are prohibited. Then it was off to The Red Wheelbarrow Bookshop, before continuing to the flea markets where we found untold treasures at a fraction of the cost of new.

Now we're strolling along Les Bouquinistes, the booksellers along the bank of the Seine, looking for French language novels.

The tiny green book boxes run up and down the length of the river Seine and sell a variety of vintage novels, postcards and prints. We rummage through and find a copy of *Delta of Venus* by Anaïs Nin, and *The Hunchback of Notre Dame* by Victor Hugo. We make our purchases and head back in the direction of the hotel, arms laden with over-full carry bags and books.

'Let's go to the Rue Mouffetard Market,' Manon says. 'For *fromage*.'

'My hands are full of books, there's no way I can fit cheese in.'

'I'll find a way. *Fromage* is life.'

The bustling street market in a picturesque location is famous for selling the best and freshest produce and has been around for the longest time. Hemingway wrote about it in *A Moveable Feast*. He lived close by with his wife Hadley for a while at 74 Rue du Cardinal-Lemoine. And George Orwell stayed for a spell at 6 Rue du Pot de Fer. There's a lot of literary history surrounding the area that leads out from the market. I always get a little thrill at the thought of walking where they once did. Of picking up a ripe, juicy plum and inhaling the perfume, did they stop and take it all in too, a memory, a snapshot for their own writing about Paris?

The market is busy. Vendors display fat, juicy, plump olives, deep purple artichokes; the spoils are rich. Roasted chestnuts scent the air. There's a stand with oozy gooey raclette, melted cheese piled onto a plate ready to be eaten with a chunk of baguette.

Christmas bunting shivers in the wind. Children clutching hot chocolate shriek and laugh, dodging in and out of the crowds.

'*Fromage*?' Manon asks. 'Or *saucisson*?'

'Why not both?'

Manon orders thinly sliced *saucisson* with fennel and garlic and a thick wedge of aged Comte.

While Manon flirts with the vendor in the hopes of free samples, I move along to a flower stall. There's no excess funds for such frivolous purchases but the fragrant blooms are beautiful. Ideally, I'd like to start staging some areas for photographs for the website. I pick up a bouquet of soft pink peonies, whose petals fold in like a secret. As I'm debating with myself over spending ten euros for flowers, there's a tap on my shoulder. I turn to find Noah standing there, holding a large zucchini. It's rather phallic and laughter bursts out of me.

His eyebrows pull together but a smile tugs at his lips. 'I'm happy to see you, Anais.'

I flick my gaze to his long, thick zucchini and say, 'I can see that.'

I bite my lip but when he computes, laughter burbles from us both. 'It's for balls.'

My mouth falls open.

'Ah – deep-fried zucchini balls.'

'I, uh – see.'

There's an awkwardness between us, and I'm not sure if it's because of the pendulous zucchini or my drunken behaviour at the death metal evening. Probably both.

'So...?' I say, scrambling to think of something, anything, to say.

'*Delta of Venus*,' he says, pointing to the books in my arms. 'I wouldn't have figured you for a fan of erotica.'

Just when we get on solid ground, he says something jarring. 'Oh, why's that? Do I come across as a prude to you?'

He double blinks as if shocked by my question. '*Non, non*, not at all. In fact, after the other night I understand you've got two very different sides to you.'

I feel a blush go from my head to my very toes and only hope it isn't obvious to Noah.

'The other night I was clearly out of my mind after those petrol-flavoured cocktails. I mean, why would you sell a cocktail like that?'

'You said you loved them.'

'Drunk me is an idiot.'

He laughs again. 'Right. So you *do* like erotica then? I'm so confused.'

'Why does it matter to you?'

'It doesn't. It's just Anaïs Nin originally wrote that book for an anonymous client of hers who asked her to write only pure sex, without any poetic flourishes. I've always been fascinated by her, but her life' – he shakes his head, his eyes widening – 'was rather scandalous.'

'I'm aware of her life and the things she did.'

'I'm not saying you're not, but a lot of people don't know the... *scope* of it. It's a little eyebrow raising, wouldn't you say?'

'*Oui*, there's a lot of debauchery.'

He scoffs as if he knows better. 'And then some. And I see you've got a George Orwell novel too. Well, he...'

I hold up a hand to stop him nattering on any further. '*Merci*, Noah, but that's enough educating for one day, don't you think?'

Confusion dashes across his face. 'Oh, sorry. I tend to ramble... at times.'

'Is that what you call it?' I shoot him a pointed look.

'Sorry, I've done it again, haven't I? Acted superior.'

'You have.'

'I get carried away when I talk literature. Speaking of, did you find out anything more about the writer from suite nineteen?'

'A little.'

He waits.

I sigh and begrudgingly share in case Noah can shed any light on the matter. 'We found out the Toussaint family owned the hotel at the time. In suite twenty are Impressionist-style paintings signed by an L. L. Toussaint. Does that name mean anything to you?'

'Toussaint? *Non.* You think the painter is the writer?'

'I'm not sure. There are beds in each suite, so Manon thinks that implies two separate people stayed in suite nineteen and twenty. But there are no personal belongings like clothing, shoes or anything in suite nineteen. It's her library, her office; it's where she wrote in all those notebooks.'

'And suite twenty has clothing, shoes, things that belonged to a woman?'

'*Oui.*'

'It makes sense she used one as an office and one to sleep in.'

'I think so too.'

Manon finds us heads bent together, deep in conversation, going over possible theories.

'How can you expect Noah to speculate when he hasn't seen inside suite twenty? Why don't you stop past and take a look?'

The busybody meddler. Noah waits for me to agree, so I give him a small nod. Maybe two heads are better than one in this situation?

23

2 DECEMBER

JP and I stand outside gazing at the front façade of the hotel while he delivers what equates to bad news. *Very* bad news. 'The windows in the guest lounge will need resealing, an expense we didn't budget for. And the windows on the other side, near the laundry.'

As I survey the windows in the drizzly rain, my heart drops. Another surprise expense. Sure, natural light is a wonderful thing, but not when it comes time to pay for maintenance.

'Is there any other way we can get around it?' Short of scrunching up newspapers to fill the pockets of air whistling through, I'm sure there's no other option but to do it properly for the sake of our guests, but JP might be able to pull a rabbit out of a hat and come up with a solution that's... Oh, who am I kidding? Warmth, especially in winter, is crucial. They'll need to be fixed, no two ways about it. We only discovered this problem after noticing the fresh paint in the guest lounge wasn't quite drying and was dripping around the window frames, as the cold air came in. We'll have to sand and repaint that area, but it'll do for now. Drips are better than sunshine-yellow walls.

'*Non*. It's important, especially as winter is approaching.'

'*Oui*.' Rain falls on this grey day, matching my mood. 'Is there any way to cut costs elsewhere?'

He lets out a long sigh. 'We could but it would slow down the opening of the hotel. I know this isn't ideal, but it's necessary.'

'What's the estimate for the resealing?' I ask and brace myself for the answer.

JP rattles off a figure that makes my eyes water. 'Sorry.'

'*D'accord*. It must be done.'

'It'll put us behind too, but we'll do our best to catch up.'

'I understand.' JP gives me a nod and runs in out of the cold.

I think of the secret library and finding the hidden manuscript. Would it be mine to sell? The paperwork for the hotel said I own the hotel and all its chattels. But could I go against the wishes of a long-dead writer? She said, *Keep my soul in peace, keep my last manuscript safe*, but what does that actually mean? Really, I don't even know if such a manuscript exists. I don't know who she is. What if her writing is abysmal? Although, from reading her journals, I know it isn't. It's brave, bold and fierce, and deeply poignant at times. She writes with an eloquence of the time, but also strangely modern too, as if she was born of the wrong era, or else knew that traditional roles for women had to change.

There's been no time to search through the room properly as the hotel work has been interminable with deliveries and painting, not to mention my writing, which seems to have turned into some kind of ode to Noah, of all people. I'm not sure what my muse is playing at.

Then there's the financial concerns that pop up and are

always at the forefront of my mind. These have the ability to keep me awake so I feel like I'm always running on empty.

I pull my coat tighter and glance down Rue de Vaugirard, smiling when I see so many businesses have decorated for Christmas now that's it's officially clicked over to December. Père Noël's donkey stands tall out the front of Cépages et Fromages. In France, the donkey named Gui is the beast responsible for guiding Santa's sleigh, and the name translated means Mistletoe, which is hung for good luck here, not a device for kissing, although the romantic in me prefers the idea of a surprise smooch.

Each lantern along the street is adorned with red-beaded garlands. All of Paris is illuminated to celebrate Christmas.

Noah exits from his bar, carrying various colours of tinsel.

'*Bonjour!*' he says cheerily and walks over with his hands up in surrender, as if I'm going to take a shotgun from my pocket and blow him away, although he does look rather farcical doing it with tinsel wrapped around his arms.

'Erm, *bonjour*, Noah. I'm very busy so I'll leave you—'

Like the overbearing man he is, he cuts me off, not listening to a word I've uttered and says, 'Give me a hand, would you? I want to string this up along the windows.' More decorations? The man is Christmas mad. Secretly, I'm jealous. We haven't done much in the way of decorating because everything continually gets covered in a film of dust with the renovations.

I hold in a sigh and take the end of a length of golden tinsel. 'Wouldn't it be better taping this up inside the window?'

'*Non*, I've got Christmas string lights for that. I suppose you won't be decorating? No need just yet, is there? Not while it's still such a frightful mess.'

I reel back. Noah has the ability to get me on the back foot each and every time. 'What do you mean a frightful mess?'

The lobby still holds a range of detritus to be removed, but that's because things are constantly being moved there from other parts of the hotel. 'We've cleaned the windows to a streak-free shine numerous times and hung posters that announce "*Demande-moi pardon!* I'm having a makeover". So it's fairly easy for passersby to compute that we're not hoarding old bric-a-brac and the corpses of flatpack furniture just for fun.'

He gives me a loose disinterested shrug that is so offhand it makes me want to...

Hilary loved everything about Christmas, especially tinsel. It came in handy when you wanted to decorate or... decapitate. She wasn't surprised to find her neighbour had purchased top-of-the-line tinsel. She thanked him for investing in its sturdiness as she wrapped it around his neck, smiling when his ruddy cheeks went from red to white...

I shake the madness away and hope my face doesn't show my inner serial killer. What is happening to me? When I glance up at Noah, his mouth is a perfect O and his eyes are full of fear.

'Ah – everything OK?'

He gazes at me suspiciously. 'Did you say "decapitate"? You mumbled so I only caught—'

'You misheard. The word is "decorate". Story ideas hit me at the most inconvenient times. Anyway, back to your *incorrect* assumptions about the hotel. Our plan is to open a week before Christmas or so.' I hold the end of the tinsel by the arched window while he fixes it in place.

'What? That's crazy. You'll never get it all done in time. Not to a proper standard, anyway.'

I reel. '*Excusez moi*, how do you know that?'

'I renovated the bar; it took a solid two years. You're rushing ahead with no thought for the design process.'

He's always so contrary. If I dragged renovations out for two years, he'd be apoplectic. 'Is that so? Did you have a team the same size as JP has?'

With a jerk of his head, he gestures for me to move along to the next section of window. '*Non*, I did most of it by myself. I wanted to make sure of the workmanship.'

Does he not realise how egotistical he comes across when he speaks like this? 'So you're a licensed builder, as well as bar owner and book lover? Is there no end to your talents?'

He grins. 'I'm not licensed, but you're being sarcastic. As for literature, I've studied it. And I'm good with my hands, always have been.'

My eyebrows shoot up. 'I see.'

'Go to the end of that window.' He orders me about like I'm an employee. The man is just too much. I duly comply but I go slow, so he knows he does not do my bidding.

'Well, I have an entire team of licensed renovators working to a schedule to achieve our goal of opening before Christmas.'

'That's a great goal but it won't happen.'

Why is he always obsessed with having the last word and being so negative in the process? Why can't he be encouraging? Enthusiastic, even?

'We'll be open by Christmas.' If it's the last thing I do!

'We'll see.' He gives me an affable smile.

He just can't let it be.

'We will.'

'If you say so.'

'I do say so.'

'OK.'

'Noah!'

'*Oui?*'

'You're insufferable.'

'I've been called worse. Now can you lift your side a little higher. It's uneven.'

There's no escaping him!

'Now,' he says, dusting his hands together. 'Have you got time to properly show me suite twenty?'

24

2 DECEMBER

'This is incredible,' he says. 'May I go in?' I'll admit, he has good manners at times, always asking permission when it comes to suites nineteen and twenty.

'You may.'

He flicks through the clothes in the wardrobe. Lifts each painting and inspects it. He mumbles to himself as he goes. He kneels in front of the travelling trunk and lifts the lid. I sit on the bed and open the bedside table. The first drawer has a bible and a comb. In the second drawer is an envelope.

I open it and find a letter, and I settle back on the bed to read.

My dearest,

I write to you with an ache deep in my heart. I wish I was with you. I wish to be free of him, the constraints of writing his way, and to follow my heart. Do you wish for the same?

You are the keeper of my secrets. Our secret. While our love affair must remain private and I must burn every letter you send to me, I pray that one day we will be in each other's arms again. I hope that day comes soon. After your last visit, he became suspicious. Aggressive. Perhaps it was the happiness radiating from me. The smile I could not swallow. Should we make plans, audacious plans, for my escape to join you in Paris at the hotel? I warn you, I will come with nothing except my heart and soul and an abundance of love. Your parents, are they still supportive?

I cannot wait one more day.

Please say yes. This life is impossible without you.

Je t'aime.

'Noah.'

He turns to me.

'A love letter! She found love after being so cruelly treated by her husband, who'd already slept with the help, I might add.'

'With who?'

'It doesn't say. They were obviously being careful as there are no names on it at all.'

I pass him the letter and he reads it. Once he's finished, he hands it back to me and I return it to the envelope.

'What does she mean, she'll come with nothing?'

'I suppose her husband would keep everything, as would have been the case back then. Especially if she wasn't planning on telling him. In one of her notebooks, an entry said she had to leave for her sanity and that he'd do his best to besmirch her name. And something along the lines of he couldn't take away the words she'd yet to write but she vowed never to write another novel so he couldn't profit from her.'

'Ah. So he had control of her career.'

'*Oui*. She mentions "the constraints of writing his way" as though she had no power, even in her writing,' I say. 'And no control of her life.'

'So she came here. To stay with L. L. Toussaint. Who is L. L., that's the next question. The son of the owner of L'Hotel du Parc?'

'There is no men's clothing in this suite. Nothing here at all that points to a masculine presence.' I gaze around the room full of women's belongings and it all clicks into place. 'The daughter! L. L. was a woman. They lived in *this* room together. That's why the women's clothing is different sizes, different styles. Did our writer wear plain clothing in an effort to disappear, blend in, in case her husband came looking and made enquiries? And it's why she asks in the love letter if L. L.'s parents were still supportive. She means supportive of their relationship, their romance. The women probably felt the need to hide their love from strangers, or society at least. Our writer clearly hoped to find sanctuary here with L. L. and her family, a family who, by the sounds of it, were understanding, which is rather refreshing for the time.'

Noah gives me a slow, warm smile. '*Oui!* It makes perfect sense. Paris back then was more progressive than a lot of places but love between two women would probably have still been very much hidden for the most part, disguised, except when they were among trusted friends. We need to find out more about L. L., confirm she is the daughter of the owners, and hopefully that will lead to finding out the identity of our writer.'

My heart expands sensing that these two women made their way back to each other, despite all the obstacles they must have faced at the time. There's a part of me that already feels protective of them and their story, I only wish we had confirmation we're on the right track.

'Anais! Where are you?' Manon calls, her voice shrill. What now?

'I better go see what that's about.' Have Noah and I called a truce? It certainly feels that way, and we make our way downstairs together. When we're wrapped up in the suite nineteen mystery, he's less bossy, less big-headed.

25

---

3 DECEMBER

Manon and I drive to Galeries Lafayette in the 9th arrondissement near Opera Garnier to find the perfect star for our tree. While I much prefer shopping at all the Christmas markets across Paris, Manon convinced me we'd find what we need here.

Every window in the department store is extravagantly decorated with Christmas scenes. The shopping centre is famous for its floating Christmas tree that sits under the glass Neo Byzantine dome. We visit all the displays while humming Christmas carols. It's impossible not to be swept away in the magic and the need to recreate it at The Secret Library Hotel.

We choose a few small ornaments for the tree and find the perfect glittery star. Manon exclaims over two life-sized Nutcrackers, and I do my best to keep her moving. 'But we need them!' She's like a child on Christmas morning, surrounded by all these luxury ornate decorations. 'They'll guard both sides of the entry, standing like Christmas sentries to welcome our future guests!'

'They're frightfully expensive.'

'I'm buying them, not you.'

'Manon, it's a waste of money.'

She won't be told and hoists them under her arms, knocking into shoppers as she goes.

'Oooh, I need that cute-as-a-button Père Noël!' Manon nods to a jovial chubby Santa Claus with ruddy cheeks, holding a beer stein.

'Do you think that's the right message? A drunk Santa?'

'*Oui!* It's Christmas, time to drink, laugh and be merry! My hands are full. Can you pick it up for me?'

'I will not.' Note to self: don't bring Manon here ever again. 'We have those gorgeous Christmas decorations from suite twenty.'

'But he's holding a beer stein!'

I've never had children, but I assume this is what they're like when they've had too much sugar and are overexcited by the magic of Christmas.

I do splurge on some Christmas lights for the windows, and I hide a smug smile when I note they're bigger and better than Noah's rather lacklustre strings.

'We'll get a real tree, *non*?' she asks.

'*Oui*, of course.'

'*Parfait*,' Manon says. 'I can't wait for the *vin chaud*.' My cousin and I have a lot of Christmas traditions, and one of them is making an evening out of decorating the tree. We feast on Christmas snacks and listen to carols on repeat while drinking far too much mulled wine. Without fail, we usually end up on the sofa watching Christmas flicks. My all-time go-to is *Les Bronzés font du ski – French Fried Vacation 2* – an oldie but a goodie that most French families watch around this time of year. It's the same kind of wacky comedy as *National Lampoon's Christmas Vacation*. Manon always chooses *La Bûche – Season's*

Beatings – as she does love a good drama in her life and on screen. They never get old and I love those cosy evenings with her each and every year.

We load our haul in the car, and sputter slowly back. There's no parking to be found so I'm forced to do a circuit before a space finally opens up out the front of Noah's bar. It's a tight spot, so I reverse park, holding my breath as I navigate backwards, trying hard to focus as Manon natters on about making and decorating a gingerbread house, which fills me with dread. Manon is many things, but baker she is not. She's more likely to burn down the hotel, so I do my best to temper her plans.

'Let me order a gingerbread house from Ladurée instead.' I run up the kerb but successfully fit the car into the small space, only just kissing the bumper of the car behind me. *Succès!*

Before I can even open my door, Noah strides from the bar, index finger at the ready. 'Here comes the king of Rue de Vaugirard,' I mutter as I unplug my seatbelt and exit. So much for the idea of a truce.

'Can you not *see* my car there, Anais?' He gesticulates wildly as if I've side-swiped his oversized SUV. No one drives such a huge vehicle in Paris, they're just not practical, so part of me wonders if Noah is making up for a lack. Big SUV, small man, if you get my drift.

'I can see your SUV. It blocks out the sunlight, so how could I not? What's the problem?'

'You reversed right into it!' He goes on to berate me about Parisian parking etiquette as if I'm new to the city and haven't lived here all my adult life.

I hold up a hand to stop his tirade. 'That's enough mansplaining for one day, Noah. Parking in Paris is an art form, and if you knew any better, you'd know that a light graze like that is totally normal. It's expected.'

He folds his arms across his chest. 'Is that so? And just how am I supposed to get my car out? You're "grazing" the back and the other car is "grazing" the front.'

'Perhaps you should invest in a smaller vehicle if you have trouble manoeuvring such a beast as the one you drive.' I give a loose shrug, just like he always does, that implies I don't care one bit. 'Pro tip: usually if you find a good car space such as this, you don't move, as they're hard to come by.' I can't help but grin. It's a stupid silly rule of thumb that has us leaving our cars for days while we walk or catch the metro. I only have a car because Francois-Xavier insisted on it, claiming we'd need wheels to get around when the hotel was up and running for errands and whatnot. So far, it's been a blessing and I'm glad I got to keep it in the divorce, though that's mostly due to the fact we got a loan for it. But, for now, it will stay parked because of the handy location, and also because I don't think I'll be able to get out easily either. It's just the way street parking is here. Chaos.

'That's the most ridiculous thing I've heard you say, Anais, and you've said some real doozies before.'

Hilary eyed the arrogant mansplainer coolly while he once again tried to belittle her. If only he knew about her past with men just like him. Men who were now not of this world.

'*Moi?* That's rich coming from *you*. He who puts the P into patronising.' At that he frowns. Did I cut him down to size? I'm internally bubbling with anger and my mind is a muddle.

Manon watches us bicker back and forth before she finally bursts out, 'I could cut the sexual tension with a knife!'

If only I had a knife at hand; I'd slice that smarmy look straight off his smarmy face!

My very witty comeback to Noah dries right there on my
lips. '*Manon!*' I admonish. 'Can't you see we're two adults
engaging in warfare? The only tension I feel is the expanding
of my head when Noah tells me the rules about parking in
Paris as if I'm a complete novice, when the opposite is true.
And does he stop there? *Non*, he will school me in the best
way to clean a window so it's streak-free, or give me a lesson
on how much noise my builder can make. I could go on
and on...'

'Please don't.' He shoots a glare my way. 'I'm trying to be a
good neighbour and, if you can't see that, that's on you. I'm only
trying to help as I've been in your position before and learned a
thing or two.'

'Except when you're being a massive hypocrite.'

'Like when?' He cocks his cocksure head.

'Like when you suggested our industrial skip go right down
the back and around the corner when you did no such thing.'

'I got permission from the previous hotelier to put mine out
the front; that's the difference.'

'Oh? So if I'd asked your permission you'd have agreed it
could stay just like yours did?'

He mumbles under his breath.

I put a hand to my ear. 'Sorry, I can't hear you.'

Manon's head looks like it's on a swivel going back and forth
from me to Noah. She's got a triumphant grin in place like she's
enjoying every quip being flung back and forth.

Noah blushes. 'Truthfully?'

'No, why don't you *lie*, Noah? Like all men do!' I fight the
urge to stamp my foot. This guy frustrates the hell out of me.

'Not all men lie.' He pushes his hands into his jeans pockets
while I shoot him a galactic-force glare that is so fierce I'm sure
it's going to melt the skin off his bones. 'Fine, *truthfully*, I'd still

have suggested the location out the back for the benefit of all interested parties.'

Point, Anais! 'And yet, it was different for you.'

'We've covered this.'

'And still you stubbornly refuse to play fair. It says a lot about your character, Noah.'

'Hardly.'

'*Oui*, it does. Rules for everyone except you!' And with that, I spin on my heel and dash inside, determined for once to have the last word. My heart thunders and I can't help feeling a little thrill that I won that battle!

Just as I'm feeling on top of the world, taking down one arrogant man at a time, Manon reappears. 'Are you going to help bring the Christmas shopping inside? There's a Nutcracker with your name on it.'

'Has *he* gone?'

'Where do you want them?' Noah asks, hoisting the two Nutcrackers under each arm.

Mon Dieu. I shoot Manon a glare, which she grins at. 'Oh, anywhere.'

Noah deposits them by the entrance and turns to me. 'One more thing, Anais...'

'*Non, merci.* I don't need any more of your advice, Noah.'

He holds up his hands. 'OK, then I won't tell you that you left your car running.' I slap my forehead as he takes the keys from his pocket and hands them over. 'I hope I'm not being *too* presumptuous by turning it off and locking it for you. Don't want to overstep.'

I roll my eyes and get ready for Round Two when Manon says, 'Knock it off for the sake of *les enfants*.'

'Who are *les enfants*?'

'I am! I'm your younger cousin who didn't come here to

referee each and every argument. Don't get me wrong, I love drama as much as the next person, but not at the rate you two are going. Just kiss already.'

Kiss! That will never happen! Duly chastised, I hang my head like a recalcitrant child. 'Drink?' I ask Noah. That's as far as I'll go with any conciliatory efforts to make peace.

'Sure.'

Manon takes the car keys from me. 'Allow me to get the rest of the Christmas decorations while you pour the *lait de poule*.'

'Chicken milk?' Noah queries the translation in English. 'I've never tried that before…' He wrinkles his nose as if dubious why anyone would drink chicken milk.

'It's eggnog; there's no chickens involved.' Even though he's proficient in French, I suppose there are always strange phrases that when translated literally make no sense.

Relief sweeps across his face. 'Ah, *oui*.' He pretends to wipe sweat off his brow. 'I was lost to wondering how on earth one would milk a chicken, and then *why*, and how such a thing would be palatable.'

The earlier tension evaporates and we fall into easy laughter. I wonder why it's called chicken milk; it's never occurred to me before because I've always known it's the French version of eggnog.

'There's a jug in the fridge,' Manon says. 'I made it this morning. I'm going to unload the car.'

We leave the lobby area and wander into the kitchen.

Manon's not only bad at baking, but she also can't mix drinks. She gets carried away and doesn't measure anything, is always heavy-handed on the alcohol. It's likely to blow our heads off and Noah's already seen me not at my best after the death metal evening. The more I think about it, the more I wonder if Manon set me up with those drinks on purpose, and how do I know she's not trying that again now? I'm suddenly tongue-tied around Noah and, by his silence, I guess he is too. If we're not arguing, what else is there to do?

I find the eggnog and pour two glasses and we sit around the kitchen bench.

Noah holds his glass up to mine.

'*Santé*. Fair warning, this might be the best drink you've ever had, or it could be the worst, and potentially lethal at that.'

He gives me a lopsided smile. 'I'm a gambling man.'

We grin at one another and take a sip at the same time. It doesn't taste lethal, so maybe Manon followed a recipe this time.

'Not bad. Now, far be it for me to make assumptions, but I get the feeling that you despise me. Or is it all men in general?'

Says he, who then makes a huge assumption like that! Have I been a little hard on him? Hasn't he deserved it? My first reaction is to tell him off again, but am I being unfair? I decide to lead with the truth and he can make of it what he will. 'Manon already blurted to you that my husband, ex-husband, had an affair. Well, it was not once, not twice, but multiple times with multiple women. That betrayal has made me see the world through a slightly jaded lens when it comes to men.'

'Where is he now, your ex? Still kicking or did you give him one of Manon's concoctions?'

I laugh. 'I wish I'd thought of that. No, the poor man went to Thailand and was crushed by an elephant in a freak accident. Very sad. For the elephant.'

Noah smiles. 'I better be on my best behaviour around you. It's strange, though, my wife also died under mysterious circumstances. She was struck in the left temple with a golf ball and died right there on the 9th hole.'

'Wow, did you live near a golf course?'

'*Non*, I wish. The man she was having an affair with did.' We share a laugh over the joke about the fictional demise of our significant others, but Noah's confession about his wife cheating gives me pause. I'm a little surprised he was once married, as I'd pegged him for the non-committal type. Not a settled-into-wedded-bliss sort. Well, until he wasn't.

But I'm way off the mark with my assumptions about Noah. He knows what it's like to be betrayed, and it does make me slightly soften towards him. If my heart wasn't bruised, I'd probably admit that the man sitting opposite me is rather attractive and makes my heart beat double time, but I can't trust my own judgement. Not after Francois-Xavier.

'Should we move into Library Anaïs?' I ask. 'I can light the fire. The chairs aren't great. We'll be replacing the cushion inserts eventually but they're OK for now.'

'Library Anaïs?'

'I knew you'd latch on to that.'

'I'm not saying a word.'

'Go on,' I say, gathering up our glasses and the jug of eggnog. 'Tell me everything you know about her, like you wanted to the other day. It might spark more ideas with what to do for the room itself.'

26
5 DECEMBER

A couple of days later, I take notebooks back to suite nineteen to exchange for others. One thing is certain: the writer who resided in this room spent many hours a day in here, writing her thoughts in beautiful calligraphy. She also explored the many parks and gardens in Paris, so she wasn't entirely reclusive. So far, I've learned that her marriage was not a happy one, even before she caught her husband philandering. According to her journals, he was a cold, cruel man who sailed through life on the back of her success as a writer – sounds familiar. But, back then, things were so much harder for women, and she suffered in silence for a long time, claiming she only survived because she had the outlet of her writing. She could escape inside her own mind and create fictional worlds where men like her husband didn't have control. There are also many passages written in ode to being newly in love and being welcomed into a supportive environment. This love helped her slowly lower her guard and each day she wrote how she felt safer, more in control of her destiny.

Now, I sit at her desk and go through the papers that lay in messy piles. Where would her manuscript be? I feel such an affinity with her, and the thought of a secret manuscript is intriguing.

A knock at the door interrupts me. Noah sticks his head around. 'I thought I'd find you here.'

'I'm obsessed,' I say truthfully. While my own novel is coming along, the pull of this room is too much and I often find myself here, late at night, like now. 'Is the bar closed?'

'*Oui*. From tomorrow I have a Christmas function almost every day.'

'Do you ever get tired of it?'

'Sometimes.'

'Take a seat,' I say, and I motion to the bed and then blush. It's the only place in the room that's not covered with books or papers. Since our chat over eggnog the other evening, I've softened towards Noah; some of the ice around my heart has melted. While he can still be insufferable at times, I'm coming to learn it's mostly when he's passionate about the topic, like the jazz era and classic writers.

'Did you ever want to write?' I ask. Noah seems to enjoy learning about the minutiae of writers' lives, like Hemingway, F. Scott Fitzgerald, Orwell. Not only does he understand the volume of their work, but he also knows all about how they lived, and who they loved.

He shakes his head. 'Never. I don't have that talent, I'm afraid. I enjoy reading too much to worry about the mechanics of such a thing.' I raise a brow at this admission. 'OK.' He dips his head. 'You've caught me out there. I might like dissecting and discussing literature, which probably comes across pompous at times, but I know for a fact I don't possess the skills to write.'

'You, pompous?'

'It's been mentioned once or twice.'

'*Oui.*' I smother a grin. There's been a slight shift between us, but can I trust Noah when it comes to this room and its secrets? Trust him in my life?

'I'd like to help you in here. You might be surprised to know in my past life I was a literary scholar and critic.'

I search his face in case he's joking. His expression is earnest, and I suppose it fits: his literary bar, his swagger, the whole Noah persona.

'Why does that not surprise me, especially the critic part? So you *do* know about the mechanics of such things?'

'A little.' He's kept this close to his chest.

'*Quelle* surprise.' Noah is more of an enigma than I first thought. No wonder his bar is an ode to Hemingway if he studied literature. 'Why did you leave that world behind and open a bar?'

He glances out the window. From here, the gates of Jardin du Luxembourg are visible, the copse of trees swaying in the windy weather.

'My ex-wife and I worked together at a college in the States. When I found out about her and her golfing buddy... I lost the heart for my work. Lost my heart for everything, as a matter of fact. I couldn't sit in my office every day, across from hers, and pretend nothing had happened. Work with her as normal, as if she hadn't detonated a grenade in our marriage.'

We lapse into silence with just the beat of heartbreak between us. What can you say in this instance that actually helps? 'And so you came to France?'

When he turns back to me, the sadness in his eyes has dissipated. I suppose that hurt, that betrayal, never goes fully away, but it seems at least Noah has control of it. 'I'd always wanted to live in Paris. How could I not, having studied The Lost Generation? But my wife wouldn't entertain the idea. Wouldn't even consider holidaying here. Aside from our work, I see now that we didn't have much in common. When things ended, and they ended badly, I packed a bag and left. I applied for a long-term visa, and the French Consular Authority granted it based on my extensive studies in literature and the fact I planned to incorporate it into a business. The Hemingway effect. They love him here.'

We exchange a grin. 'How long ago did you move here?'

'Six years ago. The first thing I did was pick up French language lessons. I'd studied a bit in high school but was very rusty.'

'And then you found the bar?'

'*Oui*, a damp, little rundown bar that I knew on sight would be the perfect spot to make my own.'

'Are you still in contact with your ex-wife?' I don't know why I ask but I wonder if Noah forgave her, or if he holds that hate in his heart still. I suppose I want to know if this feeling of betrayal, of humiliation, ever fully eases.

'Not directly. We communicated through lawyers and settled our divorce in record time because she wanted to get remarried, and I wanted to buy the bar. It gave me no pleasure when I heard her second marriage also ended recently. I wish her well, but I don't think she'll ever find what she's looking for.'

'What's that?'

'The next best thing.'

'Ah. And what about you? Would you marry again? Do you want to have a family?'

'*Oui*, I'd like that very much, but I don't know if that will happen for me. I'm forty this year, and while that's not old in the scheme of things, it does seem rather difficult to imagine a wife and family when you're single. What about you? Do you see marriage and children in the equation?'

I consider it. 'I've been too heartsore to imagine anything except hurt and possible bankruptcy. I'm thirty-eight and I wonder too if that ship has sailed since there's no man on the horizon.' I do want to find my happy ever after, but how do I allow myself to trust again? What if I make the same mistake? 'Right now, my sole focus is this place and my writing. If I don't make this work, I'll lose everything I've got left.' Before I can overthink it, I say, 'I wonder if we put our heads together we can figure out who she was?' Could this writer be the key to making the hotel successful? Solving a one-hundred-year-old mystery in the process? Or do I keep it all quiet? Keep her secrets safe from the world?

'I'd love to be involved. I hate to say it, but I know a thing or two about 1920s literature, so perhaps I can be of some assistance.'

'Well, I will gladly accept that assistance, but I'd like to keep the room and its contents on the quiet for now.'

'*Oui*, you can trust me, Anais.' I feel the truth in his words. There's a sincerity about Noah and I only hope my intuition about him is correct. If I take him at face value, he's sensitive, wise and often soulful, but then so was Francois-Xavier. Is Noah the real deal? I wish I knew for certain because I feel a flutter in my heart when we share time together as nice as this.

'*Merci*. There's one other thing. We found a typewriter on the desk under a stack of papers. There was a piece of paper in the reel that said: *Keep my soul in peace. Keep my last manuscript safe.*'

At that, his eyebrows shoot up. 'There's a hidden manuscript from a writer of the twenties that hasn't seen the light of day?'

I nod. 'And I believe she was someone of note, due to other notebook entries she made.'

I catch Noah up about what I've read so far in the personal journals and offer them to him to read in his own time.

'Did she date the journal entries?'

'The ones I've read so far were all written in the year 1924.'

He rubs his chin, thinking. 'And she alludes to being traditionally published before that date?'

I nod. '*Oui*, she talks about varying publishing success with a range of books and then there's excitement about a "runaway" novel that superseded expectations, but there's never mention of the title of the book; she just refers to them as "the summer novel" or "the novel set on the coast", so there's not much to go on.'

'Getting published back then was difficult. Rare. Especially for women, who often used a pseudonym, which we know she did. Still, there's enough here for us to start making notes of points to research later. And her husband, no ideas who he was?'

'A "brutish bull of a man with an intolerable countenance" if I remember correctly.'

We share a smile.

'The sad thing is,' I say, 'from what I can gather, once she escaped her marriage, her royalties were still going directly to him, hence her desire to cease publishing. Why would that be? Why couldn't she retain her own royalties?'

We lapse into silence, reflecting on it all. '*Oui*, why?' he muses, eyes sparkling from the mystery of suite nineteen.

'She escaped to L'Hotel du Parc and promised herself she would never write another word that her controlling husband would benefit from. She lived here and wrote in these notebooks for her own enjoyment. L. L.'s family must have protected her privacy here, but how did she afford to live? Surely their generosity didn't equate to paying her living expenses as well as her private suite.'

Noah rubs the back of his neck. 'We can investigate who L. L. was. Surely there's a record if they were a prominent family. We'll learn more as we sift through all these papers. The other notebooks in the desk. Even the novels that lie scattered about might offer up a clue.'

I pick up a book from the desk. Inside is a notecard filled with reflections of what she enjoyed about the novel, and what she didn't.

'Yes, perhaps we'll find more here. It's strange; I want to unearth her secrets, but it feels like sacrilege, delving through her dusty papers, rifling through her private journals. Suite nineteen has been kept locked up for all this time, and it feels like we're intruding.'

Noah surveys the room. 'The big question is, why was the room hidden away?'

'*Oui.*'

'While I understand your reservations about rifling through her suite, don't you get an overwhelming sense that *you're* the exact right person to uncover her secrets? A writer yourself, who inherently understands why she wants to keep her last manuscript safe. You could quite possibly solve a literary mystery, the fate of this escaped author and share her last works.'

There's a hush, a sense that the room itself is holding its breath. How can that be? Is she here, somehow, stuck until we right the wrongs done to her? There's that one gnawing concern...

'That would mean going against her wishes to keep it safe.' I blush when I recall I had considered selling the manuscript when JP told me the budget would blow out because of the need to reseal the windows. It had simply been panic taking over. I'd never really do it – would I? Not for my own financial gain, at any rate. 'But what does she mean by that?'

'I take it to mean she didn't want her husband to get his hands on it or profit from the royalties from it.'

There's a faint echo, as if the words inside this room have a pulse. Is she showing us the way or is this mystery making me a whimsical mess?

Noah runs a hand over the lace quilt cover. 'Do you think they left the hotel, the author and L. L., but planned to come back, and that's why they had the wall made?'

'Why not just lock the rooms?'

'It's a mystery.'

We spend the next little while going through papers and diaries, jotting down points of interest to delve into further.

* * *

Juliette and I walk along Rue de Seine holding umbrellas aloft. 'Timothee and Zac got the Père Noël job. Kiki found work in a bistro as a dish hand. I'm still doing the walking tours, but they're not generating much income with the weather like it is and Christmas approaching.'

'So what will you do?'

The apples of her cheeks colour. 'I know you're renovating with a strict budget, but would you consider me for any work around the hotel? Any amount of money would help so I don't deplete my savings before we go to the Netherlands. Maybe I could help paint?'

We're so behind with the painting, I'm sure Manon would

jump for joy having extra to help. There are still some funds left from the windfall of the items we sold from the storage room.

'*Oui*,' I say, giving her a bright smile. 'We'd love your help to paint, Juliette. We'll work out a figure that's fair for both of us.'

'*Merci!* I really appreciate this, Anais.'

'So do I. Another pair of hands means I can escape earlier to get back to my book…'

'Speaking of books, this is the park I wanted to show you. Another location for your literary map of Paris. This is Square Gabriel Pierne.'

It's a small cobblestoned park with statues and a fountain, but what draws the eyes is the benches shaped like open books. 'This is gorgeous.'

'It's beautiful when the cherry blossom tree blooms with pink flowers. It's usually quiet; not many people know this park exists. It looks so inconsequential on the map of Paris.'

'It's the perfect place to read. Thank you for showing me. Guests will love knowing this place exists and visiting with a book to enjoy the solitude.'

'You're welcome.'

'This is close to Bibliothèque Mazarine on the Quai de Conti, so guests could visit both places easily.'

'While not literary, there's also a stunning *parfumerie* nearby, Officine Universelle Buly 1803. They make *parfums* and lotions with natural products and are very popular with tourists. The shop looks like an old apothecary.'

'Let's go take a look.'

27

6 DECEMBER

Christmas lights twinkle festively up and down Rue de
Vaugirard. Manon and I shuffle from foot to foot in the blis-
tering rain awaiting delivery of our Christmas tree that was
supposed to be here an hour ago. 'Should we wait inside?'
Manon asks, her breath coming out like fog.

I check my phone again. 'His text says he's a few minutes
away.'

Manon groans. 'He probably can't find parking.'

'Here he is!' I point to a truck laden with fresh fir trees. The
man pulls up over the kerb and jumps from the cab. '*Bonsoir*,
sorry I'm late. Traffic.'

He unties the tree and hefts it over his shoulder as if it
weighs nothing. 'Where do you want it?'

I direct him into Library Anaïs, by the window where we've
placed a mat to protect the wooden flooring. JP's crew finished
the library room yesterday, the parquetry is polished to a shine
and the space is almost empty, bar the fresh tree, ready for us to
paint the walls tomorrow.

The man gives us instructions on how to care for the tree and is off before we can even offer him some *vin chaud*.

'Now the fun part!' I say. 'Decorating the tree. I suppose you're going to fight me to be the one to put the star on the top.'

'Ah – *oui*.'

'Shall we make a Christmas platter before we start decorating? Earlier today I bought a wedge of double crème brie and gingerbread macarons and...'

She lets out a string of sighs. Usually, Manon and I spend a whole evening decorating the tree. We space it out with glasses of eggnog and eat our bodyweight in aged *fromage* and spicy saucisson before indulging in sweets. Now, she's looking everywhere but at me, as if she doesn't want to be here.

I narrow my eyes as she steals a glance at her watch. 'Got somewhere to be?' I ask.

She averts her gaze.

'*Manon*.'

She toys with a Gui donkey ornament. 'Fine, *fine*. I've got a date, but I didn't want you to make a big deal about my cancelling on you for it, especially on our traditional decorating-the-Christmas-tree day.'

I take the Gui donkey from her hand because she's about to decapitate it with all her handwringing. 'We can decorate another day, that's no problem. Honestly, I'm happy to write instead because I've got such a long way to go with the first draft. Why didn't you tell me you had a date?'

'Because you're going to fuss and ask me questions relentlessly until I give you every last detail.'

'*Oui*! Isn't that my job as older cousin? Who is he?'

'Never you mind!'

This is always the way it is with Manon and men. She is not

the commitment type, so I will always quiz her relentlessly, fascinated by the fact she doesn't want long-term relationships, doesn't subscribe to committing to only one man, and is very open and honest about it. It's not like her to try and keep it from me.

'OK, I won't ask about him. Where are you going?'

She looks under her lashes at me. Coy Manon is not a Manon I'm familiar with. 'Jardin des Plantes, the winter festival of lights.'

The botanical gardens are in the Latin Quarter in the 5th arrondissement. Every winter, the gardens are illuminated in a grandiose fashion, and each year there's a different theme, usually relating to conservation. It's quite the spectacular immersive experience and is popular among locals and tourists alike.

'*Bonne journée.*'

She gives me a hard stare. 'That's it?'

'What?'

'Come on, Anais. You never give up so easily. Aren't you curious?'

'But you said...'

'When do you ever listen to me? You normally browbeat me into submission.'

'I'm getting whiplash here, Manon. All these twists and turns.'

'Fine, if you're not going to let this go. I'm going on a date with JP and I don't want to hear a word about why it's a bad idea.'

I gulp. 'JP, our building supervisor JP?'

'The very same.'

I hold up a palm. 'I trust you to make good choices that won't affect the working relationship we have with JP.'

'No, you don't. You don't trust me one little bit.'

I frown. 'What's going on, Manon? You're speaking in riddles.'

The wringing of her hands continues. She's fidgety and distracted; it's so unlike her.

As she struggles to respond, I say, 'Ah. This isn't your first date, is it?' I recall all those times recently where I've been holed up in the secret library and she's stepped out to meet 'friends'. I never thought much of it, because Manon does have a lot of Parisian friends.

'*Non*, it's our third. And' – Manon's face is pinched – 'he's very sweet. A real gentleman. I, uh, I haven't quite felt this way before, and I don't really like it.'

'What do you mean you haven't felt like this? Why don't you like it?' I consider the fall out if Manon breaks JP's heart. It won't be ideal, but we can deal with any awkwardness if we have to.

'I like... love him?' She covers her face with her hands. 'It's insane. He's cast some spell over me, and I absolutely despise it.'

My jaw drops. Manon in love? My wayward cousin who claims love is a concept for romance novels? Who says she'd never commit to one person because the world is full of too many options? 'You *love* him? After three dates?'

'*Oui*, and I hate him in equal measure for making me feel this way.' She cups her face and wails. I'm so shocked I don't quite know how to react, or what to say. This has never happened before. Manon always casts men away as soon as they get love hearts for eyes. She's ruthless and I've been on the end of many a call when her significant other has reached out and asked why she's disappeared and if there's any hope.

Too many times I've had to be the bearer of bad news and

enlighten the poor men that if they've received the obligatory break-up text *I'm not into this*, then there is no hope. I've never faced a lovelorn Manon before, so I grapple with how to navigate this.

'But... but... how do you fall in love with a guy after three dates?'

She shrugs and pulls at the sleeve of her jumper. 'It just happened. I felt all gooey and dazed and sort of struck by him. How do I turn it off?'

'You cannot! You're love drunk. *Mon Dieu!* This is serious.' She nods sadly. 'And how does JP feel?'

Her face is a picture of angst. Only Manon could fall in love and hate it. 'I'm not sure. Probably the opposite, because *suddenly* I can't form cohesive sentences in his presence. I blush and stumble when I try to arrange my thoughts. It's the worst!'

I can't help but laugh and pull her in for a hug, even though she has issues with anyone encroaching on her personal space. Breaking the rules in this instance is warranted. She collapses into my arms like a ragdoll. 'How long until this feeling goes away? I can't sleep, I can't eat. I'm going to waste away and die. He's on my mind when I wake up, when I eventually fall into an exhausted sleep. I wish I'd never played all those practical jokes on him! Men love that stuff, and now look what I've done.'

'Not that you're dramatic or anything, Manon. Most people enjoy the sensation of falling in love.'

'That's the biggest issue: I feel simultaneously like I'm literally falling and floating, like I'm unmoored, unanchored, unsafe! Why him, why now?'

'You poor thing.' I bite down on laughter.

'I know,' she mumbles against my shoulder. 'And now he's coming to take me out to some spectacular light show where I'll spend another evening *unable* to make cutting sarcastic remarks or to keep him at arm's length. I'll probably kiss him again and feel like I can't breathe for how good it makes me feel.'

'Have you found the hero in your own love story, Manon?' She wiggles out of my grasp and steps back, smoothing down her hair.

'I don't believe in all that romance novel gibberish. I only said that to hype you up after your divorce, and because you *do* believe in all that schmaltzy heart-on-sleeve, soulmates, love at first sight nonsense.'

'Ah – *merci?*'

With a grimace she says, 'I better get this over with.'

I laugh and give her arm a supportive tap. 'That's the spirit. Go and have fun and we can decorate another time.'

Manon leaves, her shoulders slumped as if she's walking to her death. I shake my head, as always perplexed by her, and put the donkey ornament safely back in the box.

Time to write. Back in my suite, as I review my earlier attempts, it occurs to me the reason I'm struggling to have my heroes remain alive is because I doubt their motivations, even though they're fictional and my own creation. How wild is that? My own trust has been broken so completely that it's seeped into the very men I conjure in my imagination!

So why don't I create men who *aren't* like my previous heroes? Men who've also had their hearts broken, men like the surly, gruff guy next door who wears that bluster as a shield but deep down has faced the very same betrayal as my heroine has? Thus can relate and also *be* trustworthy.

Snow fell thick and fast as Hilary snuggled under a blanket in front of a roaring fire, wondering not for the first time what her neighbour, the plain-speaking, literature-loving Joel, was doing this evening. Not that he mattered in her world. Not at

all, in fact. She was simply curious as their paths kept cross-
ing, and what else was there to ponder about on a cold
wintry evening such as this? Since her divorce, she found
the evenings the hardest to cope with. The stretch of night
when couples usually dined together, snuggled in front of a
movie or shared a bottle of wine. Alone, it felt like a great big
void of time, a hole, where loneliness crept into her heart.
She should call a girlfriend, go out, but it felt like too much
effort. They'd question her about the end of her marriage,
that same shameful story of her ex-husband's cheating, and
who could be bothered retelling all of that and seeing pity
reflected back at her?

No, instead she'd watch a Christmas romantic comedy
and dream of her neighbour, Noah.

I read it back, remembering Margaret's advice about getting
the word count up. And then I spot the great whopping big typo
and correct it:

No, instead she'd watch a Christmas romantic comedy and
dream of her neighbour, ~~Noah~~ Joel.

Why is he on my mind, when really it's not so much that I'm
taken with him, not at all! It's more that we share a common
bond, in that both our marriages imploded due to our spouses'
infidelity, so there's an affinity between us now. Or is that a lie
I'm telling myself to protect my fragile heart? On paper, Noah is
perfect, despite his obvious flaws, but all heroes have flaws and
his are surface level, petty grievances, like getting the last word
in, or being bossy. Not great big character flaws like cheating, or
being duplicitous. Still, I don't have time for love. I have to get

this manuscript done, save the hotel and solve a hundred-year-old mystery!

I get back to work, typing whatever comes to mind, trying not to edit as I go. Every word matters as the clock ticks, loud and clear.

Make it messy but make it happen.

28

7 DECEMBER

After a semi-successful night writing, I wake early, keen to get the library painted so we can later decorate not only the tree but also the entire room, which is visible from the street. Juliette's going to focus on the second guest suite that JP has finished, while Manon and I focus on the library, including painting the cheap plywood shelves black so the colourful spines will stand out, and to help disguise the fact the shelves have seen better days.

JP still has to install a simple bar area, which we plan to dress up with colourful bottles and glassware. It won't be anything as fancy as Bar Hemingway in The Ritz, but it will be a nice addition for our guests, who can help themselves to a complimentary drink or two with Anaïs Nin looking down coquettishly, from the many pictures I've framed of her and will hang around the room. None of that can happen though until we slap the paint on the walls.

Where *is* Manon?

I spread plastic matting along the far wall and tape up around the light switches and windows. I check my watch; it's close to my cousin's regimented breakfast time and there's still no sign of her. In fact, I haven't seen JP either, but he's usually dashing up and down the stairs supervising his staff and dealing with issues as they arise.

Before I open the tin of paint, I go to Manon's suite to check on her. I knock and receive no response, so open the door to find her and JP asleep curled in each other's arms. It's so unlike Manon to invite a date to stay over so part of me wonders if this could be the real thing for her. I creep backwards and let the lovebirds snooze. JP's worked hard and I'm not going to begrudge him a lie in. Just as I'm sliding the door closed my mobile rings; I dash away so I don't disturb them.

'*Allo?*'

'How's the word count? What numbers are we talking?' Why didn't I check caller ID! At least to have given myself a moment to brighten my voice, to make myself sound upbeat, like everything is just *fine*.

'*Bonjour* to you too, Margaret. I take it you're well.' I can't help but tease her for her curt question and the usual lack of a greeting.

'Cut the crap, Anais.'

I grin. 'Now that we've got the pleasantries over with, I'm happy to report I have written three chapters and, while this is not ideal, or enough, at least it's something. I can build from here, but it will be... messy.'

'Three chapters? That's it?' Her voice is so loud I have to pull the phone from my ear. 'What have you been doing since we last spoke to have only written three measly chapters? And don't tell me it's the renovations, when I know you've got a builder doing the heavy lifting. I've seen the social media posts.'

'Well, we found...' I am about to tell her about the secret library and think better of it. Margaret might just get on the next flight over if there was a hint of a hidden manuscript that might be of value. I can picture her, vape clamped between her lips, eyes narrowed in concentration as she tears room nineteen apart, looking for treasure.

'Found what?'

'Found that renovations are – ah – time consuming. Yes, JP is doing the "heavy lifting", but we're still sourcing items for the hotel and building the website and social media pages. Painting, cleaning, sorting fire extinguishers, safety protocols, all the fun stuff. There's a lot of behind-the-scenes work that goes into such a project.'

'And that affects me how? Come on, Anais. I need this done, OK?'

I sigh. 'I'll get there, I promise.'

'Good.'

Less than a month to go for the deadline. I can write a messy first draft fairly quickly, but that was before I took it upon myself to maim and dismember all my heroes. Still, I feel like I'm finally past that now. I confess to my agent what I've discovered about the longest writer's block of my career. 'I figured it out! The block was caused by writing unrelatable heroes, heroes just like my former husband, all suave and showy with very little else going for them. Sure, those kinds of men are attractive but only on the surface. This new hero I'm conjuring, well, he's got the soul of a poet, but he's also good with his hands. He's robust and wild and takes charge. Though he says stupid manly man things, but that's because he's hiding his own hurt.'

'You've just described Noah!' I jump out of my skin as Manon appears out of nowhere and yells over my shoulder. She's got the stealth skills of a ninja when she wants to.

'Noah, eh?' Margaret says. 'The guy next door? Maybe it's

time I paid you a visit, eh? Just to talk shop. Actually, it's not a bad idea. It'll get me out of a publicity tour with that two-bit celebrity creep Wells,' she says, almost as if she's musing to herself.

I push Manon away, who is intent on listening in on my phone call. 'A visit won't be necessary, Margaret. Not yet. Wait until the hotel is open and I can offer you a refurbished suite so you're comfortable.'

'OK, OK, all I'm suggesting is perhaps you *do* need a little inspiration of the romantic kind. Would it be so bad to have a quick fling with this Noah guy? Restart the clock, so to speak. Get your ex-husband out of your mind for good and get those words on the page.'

'And you don't think a quick fling would complicate matters and steal away what little writing time I have?' Only I could have a job where my boss, or at least the person in control of my earnings, advises having a romp with a man to increase my workflow.

'Of course not! It would inspire you! Call it research if you must.'

Now I've heard everything. 'Ah, I'll definitely keep that in mind.'

'You will not. But you should. Call me in a few days and let me know what you're up to.'

'Will do. *À bientôt.*'

Margaret ends the call without a goodbye, on to terrorise her next author. While she's sharp and short and can be brutal, she's a force to be reckoned with and I've learned how to deal with her over the years. Under that acerbic demeanour, she's a softy at heart. Well, sort of. If I don't meet my deadline, I'll certainly hear about it. Right now, I'm distracted by Manon, who's leaning against the wall, eyes glazed, lost in a daydream.

'Earth to Manon.'

'Huh?'

'That's not exactly painting attire.' I point to her black flannelette PJs that feature skulls, of all things.

'Oh, *oui*. It's just that I'm a little tired today, I'm coming down with a bug.'

'Ah, *punaise d'amour*?'

She screws up her face. 'A love bug? That is disgusting, Anais!'

I laugh. 'It's meant to be romantic. Bitten by the love bug; have you never heard of such a thing?'

'This is why I steer clear of romance mumbo jumbo. It's nonsensical.'

'You know what else is nonsensical?'

'Let me guess: me trying to avoid painting because I had a late night with JP?'

I make a show of feigning surprise. 'You can read minds too!'

'Urgh, why are you so spritely this morning? I much prefer it when you're grumpy and monosyllabic.'

'Because...' I make jazz hands purely to annoy her further. 'I wrote three chapters last night. And not once did I butcher the hero. I'm at the start of Chapter Four and he's still alive and well with all his appendages intact.'

She heaves a sigh. 'How depressing. I hoped you really were going to pivot into writing crime novels. You might try and hide it, but underneath that sweet romance writer persona lies a black heart, just like your favourite cousin.'

'Who, Eloise?'

Manon gasps. 'See, you *are* evil!' Our cousin Eloise is rather elitist and doesn't often have a kind word to say about anyone. Eloise is the child my uncle talked about in the group chat who demands a new wardrobe of designer label clothing every summer. Even though we're adults now, our parents still expect us to attend gatherings at their family chateau on the outskirts of Lyon whenever we're invited. Which is far too often for Manon's liking.

'Oh I don't know, maybe we judged Eloise too harshly in the past. Shouldn't we let bygones be bygones? Why don't I invite her here for Christmas?'

With that, Manon takes it upon herself to tackle me like the lady she is not. When I finally disengage from her octopus-like hold, we're on the floor, legs akimbo, hair a mess, breathing hard and laughing uncontrollably, when I glance up to see Noah standing there, hands in pockets, a look on his face that implies he's been there for some time and still doesn't know what to make of the scene before him.

'A writer in her natural habitat, eh? I've always hoped to see one in the wild.'

I bite down on my lip in embarrassment. What must he think! Manon crash-tackling me to the floor, like she's some kind of wrestler putting me in an arm bar. I wish I could say this didn't happen often, but Manon often practises her jujitsu submissions on me. She's shockingly strong, especially when she boa-constrictors herself around my poor body in her efforts to bend my limbs in unnatural ways until I'm forced to tap out.

'Not so haughty now, is she?' Manon teases, holding a hand to help me up. She keeps insisting I'm acting stiff and modulated around Noah, like a well-mannered robot; well, that just went out the window.

'Can I help you, Noah?' Best to pretend he hasn't just witnessed two adult women fighting to the death, me to survive, Manon to win. I give him a wide smile that feels a little forced, but still.

Manon frowns and steps close, whispering, 'What's with the lockjaw?'

'It's my "nothing to see here" smile.'

'Please don't. Rethink that for everyone's sake.'

Noah coughs and clears this throat. He probably heard what Manon said, but at this point can it really get any worse? 'I wondered if I could steal a moment of your time? I did some research into our mystery. If we could chat in' – he darts a glance around the room – 'the secret library?'

'Sure, sure.'

Manon yawns. 'So I guess I'm painting alone?'

'Unless you can get JP to help, but last I saw of him he was still sleeping.' Two can play at that game!

'You little spy!'

29

7 DECEMBER

I open the door to the secret library and am once again assailed by the scent of the past, the vanilla smell of thick parchment and the earthiness of leatherbound books. Dappled wintry sun shines through the lace drapes, bathing the room in a sepia tone.

'What have you found?' I ask as Noah takes his position on the bed, and I sit at the leather chair.

'I did some digging into published female French writers in the twenties and compiled a list of names for us to research. There's a few we can rule out immediately like Colette, Anaïs Nin, Gertrude Stein...' He rattles off a number of well-known female authors. 'Because they were married or in relationships and published up until their deaths. However, there are a few that fell off the radar and who I haven't been able to find many details for. It's like they vanished. Of course, there could be various reasons for this: they settled into more maternal roles, gave up writing, moved away, or any number of legitimate reasons, and so the history books go blank at that point.'

'Ooh, exciting to have a shortlist already though. Let me see.'

Noah hands me a moleskin notebook. 'More interesting is that these three authors used pseudonyms. Their real names were kept quiet, whatever they were, but interestingly enough they chose to stick with feminine pen names.'

'Right.' Back then it was routine to use masculine names, or initials, to disguise the fact the author was female, which is awful and sexist, but that's how it was for a lot of female writers. The names Noah has compiled are:

Thérèse Fournier
Adeleine Deschamps
Clothilde Labelle

'These authors were all published?' He nods. 'Do you know the titles of their books?'

'Turn the page. I made a list of their works.'

I turn the page and try to recall how our mystery author described her published works, something along the lines of 'the summer novel' and 'the novel set on the coast'. These titles don't mention either of those, but that doesn't mean they're not set in summer or by the sea.

'We have to find these novels and see if they match up with what we know so far. Actually, our best bet is to look on the shelves here first. You'd think she'd have copies of her own novels, wouldn't you?'

'Great idea.'

We search high and low, gently moving the double and often tripled-stacked books, including all the novels that spill out onto the floor and those plonked on the desk and tucked away in drawers.

I yelp when I find *The Year Time Slowed* by Adeleine Deschamps and hold it up for Noah to view. 'Shouldn't I feel a thrum, a pulse, a sign that this is *her* book?' I asked, giddiness taking over that we might be one step ahead in figuring out who she was.

'*Oui*, a hundred years is sufficient time for her to work out how to message from the afterlife.'

I fall back on the chair and run a hand over the cover. It's green, featuring only the title of the book and her name. I open it to see if there's any inscriptions, any clues, but find nothing.

'No other Adeleine Deschamps where you found this?' Noah queries.

'*Non*, and isn't that weird? I have triples of every edition of my own work waiting to be shelved when the library is renovated.'

'That's what I'm thinking too. Unless... when she escaped her controlling husband, she didn't want to be reminded of them and what she'd lost: her royalties, her voice.'

It makes sense. 'If she was running for her life, then the books wouldn't have mattered; all she'd have been thinking about was her safety and getting out of his clutches. You're the literary scholar, Noah – would you like to read this first? You might be able to tell if the writing style is similar to what's written in the notebooks.'

He grins. 'Sure. I'd love that.'

I hand him the novel, which he holds tight to his chest as if to protect the words within. I lean back on my chair, excited to share the spoils of my own investigations. 'I did a little digging too, back through old archives on the internet about the Toussaint family. They were renowned for their patronage for supporting aspiring writers. This literary philanthropy continued with their daughter... Lily-Louise, who would often pay house calls on writers she admired.'

'Lily-Louise must be L. L.! Great work, Anais.'

'Oui! Merci.' It's thrilling to see the same level of enthusiasm from Noah as I felt when I discovered what her initials stood for.

'She paid house calls, you said? So, she could have visited our writer and that's how they met? By chance...'

'I sense Lily-Louise saw an unhappy woman in a controlling marriage and vowed to help...'

Noah nods. 'And our author found true love with Lily-Louise? We know from the love letter you found in the bedside drawer in suite twenty they were plotting her escape from the controlling husband, and she asked whether she could come here. And that she'd come with nothing but her heart and soul and an abundance of love... which was my favourite part of that letter.' So, Noah *is* a romantic? I loved that part of the letter too and it strikes me as sweet he's memorised that part of it, just like I have.

'Oui. I sense they made plans to be together quickly after that letter. You could *feel* the urgency in her words about the need to escape, not only him, but because she yearned to be with the woman she fell in love with.'

'I agree. The writer arrived here, we think sometime after 1924 under an assumed name with support from the Toussaint family, who kept her real identity a secret, we presume so her husband couldn't find her?'

'Looks like it.' From what I've read in the notebooks, the Toussaint family had welcomed her with open arms.

'What happened to the Toussaint family?' Noah asks.

'There wasn't much on the parents themselves, but they had a son, Jean, Lily-Louise's older brother, who took ownership of the hotel around 1931. Then *his* son Jean Paul sold the hotel to the previous hotelier, the one you met.'

'So, if the son Jean took over in 1931, what happened to the parents and Lily-Louise? We need to find out whether our author wrote any journals after that date to find out their fate.'

'*Oui*. But I have the strangest feeling about it. Why would their rooms have been sealed up? If the two women left for whatever reason – travel, escape, family issues – wouldn't they take their special things? The author's precious notebooks, her manuscript? Lily-Louise's artwork?'

'Yes,' Noah says, gazing around the suite full of disorderly piles of books. 'It doesn't make sense. How old were Lily-Louise and our author, do you think?'

I search the drawer for one of the notebooks I replaced last night. 'In this one she talks about being married for a long time, almost two decades of mistreatment, so I suppose around forty or so given marriage happened at an earlier age back then? As for Lily-Louise, I'm not sure. I can't find anything about Lily-Louise's parents either. Not even a death notice.'

'The mystery deepens.'

'*Oui*. I hope we've found her.' I shake the novel by Adeleine Deschamps.

'It's not enough to go on, is it? One fictional work. Why don't I look further into the Toussaint family? See if I can find out where they went, when they died. We might be able to track backwards from Jean Paul, to Jean, Lily-Louise's brother.'

'That would be great. As much as I want to solve this riddle, we have so much to do before opening in a couple of weeks.'

I wait for him to tell me it's not possible, but he remains silent. Progress? I check my watch and swear under my breath. 'Sorry, Noah. I've got to go. I'm interviewing a chef today.

Manon has found a candidate who has experience in French kitchens. I'm not used to interviewing staff so wish me luck.'

'*Bonne chance.*'

'*Merci.* After I've met my self-enforced word count this evening, I'll compile dates from the notebooks and see where they end? Meet here again in a few days?' We lock eyes and for a moment time stops. I put it down to being swept away by a love affair from a century ago. I step to the doorway, breaking the spell.

'*Oui,* I'd love that.' Noah takes the Adeleine Deschamps novel with him, and I lock up and dash to the kitchen to find our potential new chef opening and closing drawers and familiarising herself with the layout.

'*Désolée,*' she says with a laugh. 'I wanted to see what I'd be working with. I'm Camille.' We shake hands as I introduce myself and give her a run down on what we've achieved so far and what we hope to achieve with the hotel restaurant.

Camille asks a lot of questions and offers suggestions that make no sense to me, like doing American breakfast waffles at dinner, but I gently steer her back to our culinary vision of serving French bistro food and decide to reserve judgement.

'I'm not experienced in a kitchen, but simple French dishes will appeal to our guests and locals alike.'

She holds up a hand. 'Say no more. Why don't I make you one of my signature dishes and you can let your palate decide? If you enjoy it, we can talk about the ideas I have for this kitchen and whether it aligns with yours.'

'*Parfait.*'

'Would you mind giving me some money and I'll go and buy some supplies?' I find my purse and hand over some euros.

Manon appears, wearing her overalls, which are now paint

splatted. Somehow they suit her. 'Did I hear talk about a signature dish?'

'*Oui*, this is Camille. My cousin Manon.'

'*Enchante,*' Camille says. 'Give me a few hours and I'll serve you both lunch.'

Manon calls out to her but she's already out the front door.

'What is it?' I ask.

'Is Camille American?'

'*Oui.*'

'Huh. I'm sure she said she was French on her application.'

'Does it matter as long as she can cook?'

'*Non*, it's just I was sure she said she was from Paris. And her references, I haven't called them yet. I'm sure it'll be fine.'

30

7 DECEMBER

Camille returns with fresh produce and gets to work in the kitchen while Manon and I get back to painting Library Anaïs. The cutting in has been done, so all we have left to do is roll the middle.

'You achieved a lot this morning, Manon,' I say, marvelling at the amount she got done while I was chatting to Noah.

'Uh-huh. Work horse, that's me.'

I hold my roller still over the plastic mat and narrow my eyes at my wily cousin. 'You roped JP into it, didn't you?'

She grins. 'Well, he did start late; it was the least he could do to make up for that. I might be in love with the guy but that doesn't mean he can take advantage.'

'You're the one who made him late, and now you're taking advantage of him!'

Her mouth falls open. 'How did *I* make him late? Isn't he a grown man with a brain in his head?'

'Because I know you, Manon! You would have bullied the poor guy to do whatever you wanted, and point proven: look at this room.'

'I can't be everything for everyone all the time. He can't expect me to paint all day and then have the energy to wander the streets of Paris on his arm all night like some love-struck teenager.'

'You evil minx. I thought you were having trouble communicating basic sentences with the guy?'

'*Oui* but I can text. I sent him a message saying how I lacked energy after our evening out and one thing led to another, *et voilà*, the high bits and low bits are done.'

I shake my head. She is the limit and gets away with it, the lucky devil. 'Noah and I are having fun trying to solve the mystery of room nineteen.'

'Is that all you're doing?' She waggles her brow.

'Unlike *some* people, I can control myself.'

'*Touché.*'

'So shall we decorate the tree tonight?'

'*Non, non.* How about tomorrow? That way JP can help. He's got dinner with his *maman* this evening.'

'Are you going too?'

She blushes. '*Oui*, he is insisting on it.'

'*Ooh la la.* Meeting the parents already!'

She pinches the bridge of her nose, smearing paint across her freckled skin. 'Parents are never thrilled when they meet me. I'm not sure why. Do you think it's all the black clothing? The big boots? The dramatic winged eyeliner?'

I consider it. Manon is edgy, but that's her style and it suits her. 'Does it matter? Those things are all cosmetic and they're what make you, you. You're not thinking of changing your look, are you?'

'I don't know, maybe it's time for a change? For the first time ever, I *care* what the parents think of me, you know?' She massages her temples, spreading yet more paint. At this rate she's going to have black and white hair like a dalmatian.

'It's lovely that you care what they think of you, Manon, but what you wear doesn't define who you are as a person. If they judge you because of your style, that's a bit of a red flag.'

She's only half listening and gives me a distracted nod.

A few hours later, Camille finds us packing up the plastic mats in Library Anaïs and asks us to wash up and head into the dining room. Our feast awaits. Manual labour really does increase a person's appetite, so I'm excited to try her signature dish.

After we've scrubbed paint from our hands, we take a seat in the dining room. 'Is that smoke?' I sniff, looking towards the kitchen.

'The oven probably needs a good clean,' Manon says distractedly as she swipes her phone open.

'Manon,' I say more urgently. 'The kitchen looks like it's—'

Camille comes out bearing two plates. 'This is *cote de bouef* with *café de Paris* butter and duck fat roast potatoes. I've also made a side salad of fresh leafy greens. *Bon appetit*.'

Manon and I exchange a glance. The thick cut of steak is burnt; not charred, but blackened to a husk. The roasted duck fat potatoes have suffered a similar fate. I'm frozen, unsure what to do or say because Camille's expression is so hopeful. Maybe she had an issue learning her way around a new kitchen, yet she's happily served us charcoal with a smile on her face.

'I've also made an apple tarte tatin, so I hope you're hungry.'

'Uh, I – um...' How can I be the person who steals her dreams away? She is clearly not the chef for us. There's a very big chance she's not a chef at all.

Just as I'm about to drop a bomb on her culinary hopes and dreams, something catches my eye, or more accurately something catches fire. 'FIRE!' I yell in case the flames licking the rangehood aren't as obvious to Camille and Manon. There's an ear-piercing chirp as the smoke detector bleats a warning. At least we know for sure they do in fact work.

I run to the kitchen and see Camille's left a pot of oil on the stove – did she deep fry the steaks?! – and it's caught alight. I switch off the gas and put a lid on the pot, trying hard not to burn my arm in the process. The flames soon dissipate, and I suck in a lungful of oxygen. The rangehood is sooty but doesn't appear to have sustained long-term damage; I can't say the same for myself. I'm sure I've sprouted a hundred grey hairs at the thought of the hotel burning down before I found the manuscript in suite nineteen. *And* I suppose because my money is tied up in the place.

I take a deep centring breath and face Camille.

'I didn't get the position, did I?' Her eyes are glassy with tears.

I give her an apologetic head shake. '*Non,* Camille. You did not. Are you really a chef?' She nods her head vigorously. 'A *properly trained* chef?'

'Oh, no, I don't have a formal education or anything. Self-taught. I learned a lot from—'

Please don't say YouTube.

'—TikTok.'

I bite down hard on my lip to stop any sound from escaping as I teeter between anger and fear at what might have happened with a TikTok-trained 'chef'.

Manon reads my mood and says quickly, '*Merci*, Camille. Perhaps stick to TikTok for the safety of others?'

When Camille leaves with her head hung low, I fold my arms and stare down Manon. 'Let's make a hard-and-fast rule that we check all references from now on, *oui*?'

Manon does her best to look contrite but fails. Manon doesn't do contrite. Soon her eyes pool as laughter finally bursts forth and I can't help but join in. Once we get a handle on ourselves, I say, 'TikTok?' And the laughter starts again. We have one of those ridiculous uncontrolled moments, almost like a release of all the good, the bad and the ugly, that, by the time I'm finished giggling, my stomach muscles hurt. It takes an age but we eventually compose ourselves.

'What if we don't hire a chef? What if instead we offer *formule petite-dejéuner*?' The kind of typical breakfast you see at most Parisian cafés. Coffee, juice, croissants, baguettes and pastries. 'We can get morning deliveries from the boulangerie, L'epi du Prince, around the bend of the *jardin*. Keep it simple.'

Manon considers it before asking, 'And just who will be serving the handful of guests their orange juice at seven a.m.?'

I pull a face. I'm not a morning person and never will be. '*Toi?*' I ask hopefully.

'*Moi?*'

'*Oui?*'

She harrumphs to get her point across. Neither of us are morning people, although my writing block has changed me somewhat and I've found myself getting up earlier, wanting to get stuck into work around the hotel. I'm sure that will soon pass when I'm back in the zone and bashing away at my laptop into the early hours. 'Let's do alternate breakfast days, then? Will that work?'

'*Oui*, breakfast isn't so bad. We can set up a table with everything and they can help themselves. We'll just replenish drinks and condiments as needed.'

'*Parfait*. And we won't have the added expense of a chef. Let's find a good fromagerie and charcuterie nearby too for our cheese platters.'

'And for the dessert boards? We need to find a patisserie.'

Kiki and Juliette appear, waving their hands through the residual smokiness. 'La Parisienne Madame is very close and is one of the best patisseries in Paris, although Juliette has her own favourite but that's in Montmartre. Dare I ask what happened in here?'

I take my phone and jot down the name of the patisserie for later.

'Oh,' Manon says. 'We did a safety check, to make sure all the smoke alarms were working, and you'll be happy to know they are.' We exchange a smile. No one need know we interviewed a TikTok hopeful.

* * *

That evening, just as I'm preparing to go to my suite to write, I meet Manon coming down the stairs. At least, I presume it's Manon. Gone is the black winged eyeliner; her dramatic makeup has been toned down and replaced with shades of subtle pink. She's wearing a long beige and white knit dress, *my* beige and white knit dress, paired with my white cashmere coat and white high-heeled boots.

'Ah – whoa, Manon. You look beautiful, of course, but do you think it's the best idea to hide who you really are?'

She gives me a decisive nod. '*Oui*. It's time for a change.'

I keep any further opinions to myself. 'OK, well, be safe. Have fun.'

31

---

8 DECEMBER

I spend the day buzzing around the hotel, completing one chore before moving on to the next. There are so many items on our to-do list but they're easily achieved if I just keep my energy levels up and eye on the prize – partially opening by 18 December, which is ten short days away. We still haven't decorated the tree, or the lobby. It's been all hands on deck trying to get the place painted. The words written. And the mystery of suite nineteen has been on my mind, but time slips away so fast here at the hotel.

JP meets me in the lobby for a walkaround. He points out a few jobs they've got left to complete. Really, it's just smaller finicky work, patching up scuffed skirting boards, removing the last of the clutter and junk from the suites and the shared spaces. 'We're slightly ahead of schedule,' he says. 'So most of our crew are going to move on to the next project. I'll stay here with just a few of my staff to get the last of it done.'

'Are you confident we can take bookings now? We have a guaranteed completion date?'

He nods. 'December eighteenth, but, like I said, I'll stick

around and fix the cornicing, the smaller detailed jobs, but I'll be quiet so I don't disturb guests. Then I can quote you for the remaining work, but nothing there is urgent, unless you choose to renovate more suites.'

I let out a whoop. While the hotel is coming along nicely, there's still scaffolding in hallways and tradespeople everywhere; there's plastic covering our coffee station trolleys, and there are boxes of books stacked in a corner of the guest lounge.

'*Merci*, JP.' I swipe at sudden tears. With only ten days to go, it brings this stark reality into focus. We are going to make it! Not only has JP and his team completed their work to a high degree of quality, but they've also done it fast and made me fall in love with what this place will become. A sanctuary for bibliophiles, a haven for Francophiles. A cosy, welcoming hotel for those who want to stay in one of the best locations in Paris.

We finish our walkaround, noting a few extra jobs that need to be completed, and JP goes off to have a team meeting with his crew.

I note the time and head to the guest lounge area and find Manon there already, wearing a black pant suit. I give her a slow up and down and she laughs. '*Oui*, back to the real me.'

'How did dinner with the parents go?'

Manon uses a screwdriver to tighten up a brass handle onto a navy-blue bedside table. 'Well, I dressed in your elegant but extremely dull ensemble.'

'Stop, I can't handle all these compliments.' Switching the silver handles out makes all the difference; the bedsides now have a regal air to them. Well, regal if you knew how bad they looked before paint and flea market-find brass handles.

'His *maman* is one of those tactile types. She grabbed hold of my hands as soon as I walked through the door, squeezed and hugged. It was… a lot, but I liked it. I suppose, as much as I can like all of that touching.'

'His *maman* sounds really lovely and welcoming.'

'And she blurted, "Why are you dressed so pretentiously like that?"'

I bristle. 'Wow, Manon. My clothing isn't that bad!'

'*Non,* she didn't mean it like that. She follows me on Instagram and wondered why I went from wearing all black to arriving in white cashmere. She told me I should never change who I am, especially for their sake.'

I lift a brow. 'I did say all that to you as well.'

'*Oui,* but you're not the one I'm trying to impress.'

As always, I'm slightly bamboozled by my cousin. 'OK.'

Manon's eyes shine with happiness. 'We had a great night. His *maman* is hilarious, cheeky and silly and not at all like I imagined she'd be. After dinner we went to the Fete de Noël and had so much fun playing the sideshow games. I'm going to fit in just fine in that family.'

'I knew you would. Everyone loves you, Manon, and if they don't then there's something wrong with them.'

'*Merci.*' She accepts the compliment as if it's fact, which draws a small smile from me. Oh, to have Manon's confidence in life. 'I'm sorry to say, there was a slight accident and your cashmere coat came off a little worse for wear.'

I groan. 'Red wine?'

She drops her head in mock shame. '*Oui.* This is why black is the safest option for me.'

'Gah. Did you soak it?'

'Uh-huh.' She surveys her nails.

'You did not. Where is it?'

'I'll get it later. Look, here they are.'

We're holding a job interview for maintenance staff today.

We're hoping to find a team of two superstars who'll handle making up the suites and doing the laundry in-house. I placed an ad online last night and a husband-and-wife duo contacted me for more information. They've got great references and have worked in and around Paris at various hotels. And this time I took it upon myself to call those references and make sure they were legitimate.

'*Bonjour,*' I say and welcome them in. They're in their sixties and are lively and energetic. After we've shown them around the hotel, we sit down in the guest lounge to chat.

'We've worked in prestigious hotels all our lives,' the wife, Lina, says. 'While that's been great, we'd like to slow down a little now. Eighteen rooms, including the owners' suites, is an achievable number for us.' We didn't include suites nineteen or twenty on our tour and they didn't question it. 'We're a great team and we work well together. If you take a chance with us, we can offer you long, loyal service and a wealth of experience.'

Manon and I exchange a glance. It's an obvious choice. 'We'd love you to join the team. We're learning as we go so we are really lucky to have experts such as yourself willing to help. One thing you should know is, once the hotel is up and running, I'll be looking to sell. I'm not sure if that will sway your decision, but if so I understand.'

They confer in whispers before saying, 'We'd love to accept the position. However, our daughter is about to have a baby and we're going to stay with her for a couple of months.'

'Oh.' I deflate. A couple of months! 'So when would you be ready to start?'

'We're planning to return to Paris early February. Do you think you could hold the position for us until then? We know it's a big ask, but it's important we're there for our daughter and our grandchild.'

I weigh it up. Manon and I would have to handle all the cleaning and washing on top of our other work around the hotel. It's probably doable as we're only soft launching, and hopefully by the time the couple are back from visiting their daughter we'll have a few more suites renovated, funds depending. Manon gives me a surreptitious nod. '*Oui*, we can wait for the right staff, that's not a problem.'

Once they leave, Manon turns to me. 'Do you really think you'll still sell this place?'

I frown. '*Oui*, of course. All my money is tied up here and I don't have the time or inclination to be a hotelier. The sooner I can extricate myself, the better.'

Manon's face drops. 'It's just... hasn't it been fun? Even all those marathon painting sessions and washing so many white sheets I saw snowy spots for a few hours. Pranking the tradespeople, meeting Camille who is going to set TikTok on fire, and hopefully not an actual kitchen. It feels like we're on the brink of something special. I don't know – maybe this is the stupid love-struck phase I'm battling, but this place has a heart and a soul and, for the first time in my entire life, I feel like I fit. Even though the salary is woeful. So woeful it's actually non-existent.'

'It really is woeful, but it will get better once we have paying guests. I'll make it up to you when we sell, I promise.'

'So you won't think about keeping the hotel, not even if it's wildly successful when we launch?'

I search her face. It's evident Manon has fallen under the spell of L'Hôtel Bibliothèque Secrèt, but my cousin is fickle at the best of times. How do I know a few months from here, her enthusiasm won't wane? And what am I even saying? There's the mortgage to consider, the loan from my parents. It's too much. 'I don't think so, Manon. How can I? This place needs an owner who is hands on, there for any dilemma twenty-four-seven. That's not going to be me, is it? While I might have been going through a tough patch with my writing, that's where my passion lies. Not in running this place, as much as I have come to love it, like you have.' It does grow on you, this little boutique hotel across from the *jardin*, the history, the story we are slowing unfurling...

'What about the secret library?' she asks. 'You'd give that up?'

The secret library. That does give me pause. How can I entrust that space, and the history it holds, to just anyone?

I purse my lips together and I envision the sale, and the next owner. It's a worrying thought. 'I don't know, I guess I'll have to.' My brain is telling me to be practical, but now my heart has other ideas. How can I abandon the mystery writer and her secrets?

What makes it worse is I've had the most amazing idea to honour suite nineteen. I wonder if we can pull it off? And what will that mean when it comes time to sell...?

* * *

I'm winding my scarf around my neck when Manon finds me in my suite. 'Where are you off to?' she asks.

'We. You and me.'

'OK, where are *we* off too?'

'La tour Eiffel.'

She tilts her head. 'You've got a burning desire to visit the Eiffel Tower?'

'*Oui*. Hurry, we've got tickets so we can't be late.'

Thirty minutes later, we're herded into the glass elevator that hangs on to the *outside* of the tower and are making our way slowly up to the summit. The view is incredible from this vantage point. We exit at the very top onto the open-air balcony located just below the spire. 'What are we doing here?' Manon asks. 'While I joked about you being afraid of heights, this is a little... high.' Wind whips her hair from her face and carries her words with it too.

'*Oui*, but you're lucky we didn't have to take all of the 1,665 stairs to get here.'

'*Non!* Are there really that many?'

I nod. 'But visitors are only allowed to climb 674 steps. The rest are not open to the public, so the elevator is necessary after that stage.'

'That's still about six hundred steps too many.'

'Look,' I say, indicating to a small queue of people, shuffling to keep warm.

'What are they waiting for?'

'You'll see.'

When it's our turn, we move to the portal-like window and peer in.

'Ah! I see!' says Manon.

'This is known as the secret apartment. Gustave Eiffel used the space as an office. It's been restored back to its original layout. Back then he'd invite notable guests here, or would conduct science experiments.' Now there's a tableau of wax sculptures featuring Gustave Eiffel, his daughter Claire, and guest Thomas Edison, who gifted the engineer the first sound recording device ever made. The display features a piano, desks and sofas. The secret apartment is one hundred square metres, but some of the space is obstructed by the elevator chute and stairwell.

'This has to be the best apartment in Paris. I can't believe I had no idea this existed.'

The queue grows behind us, so it's time to move on. 'We can do this too, Manon. With the secret library.'

'*Ooh la la!* Giving our guests a sneak peek into what effectively is a room where time stopped a hundred years ago. You're a genius, Anais.'

'Perhaps not only our guests but the public too?'

We hold off discussing it as we make our way down in the elevator, but, once we're deposited on the ground floor, we resume our excited chatter.

'Would you make it like Gustave Eiffel's secret apartment? With a portal window? Or...?'

'Why not remove the door and put a three-quarter partition up? That would prevent guests from walking into the suite itself, but not obstruct their view. And...' My words come out thick and fast as I picture how we could best honour our mysterious writer, not just for our guests but for literary fans alike.

'There's also suite twenty to contend with...' Could we make it a museum exhibit of sorts? Displaying her clothing, her trinkets? There are so many options, but most important is to preserve the legacy of our mysterious writer and Lily-Louise and celebrate them in a way that is respectful.

* * *

JP pours us each a glass of *vin chaud* and plays Christmas carols from his phone, the tinny sound reverberating around Library Anaïs. 'We'll need a proper sound system in here, won't we? Background music for the guests.'

'I'll make a note to do that tomorrow,' Manon says, reaching for her phone. The more I consider Manon wanting to stay working at the hotel, the more I'm tempted. My cousin never sticks with anything. There's always a new hobby, new career;

dare I say it, new man around every corner. She's fully aware of her fickle nature and makes no efforts to curtail or change it, so for her to share those feelings of finally fitting in somewhere, having a place like the hotel that feels right – it does make me consider it from her perspective. What if this is meant to be – for Manon?

I've never seen her focused and in control like she is here. I'm suddenly the nutty distracted one making mistakes, hoping to god it all comes together, but the truth is that it's only going to because Manon has upped her game and picked up the slack.

'Why don't we invite Noah to help decorate the tree?' Manon asks, putting her phone on the table, and picking up her mulled wine to take a sip.

'Sure,' I say.

'I'll invite him over.'

A few minutes later, she returns with Noah, whose hair is mussed like he's just woken up.

'Did we interrupt a nap?' I ask and hand him a glass of mulled wine, the scent of the orange and star anise perfuming the air between us.

'I prefer to call it a power nap. It's been hectic with one Christmas function after another. *Merci*,' he says, holding the glass aloft.

Manon opens a box of ornaments. 'Anais has decreed the tree should be decorated ombre-style, which means we go from colour to colour cascading down the tree. She's quite pedantic about placement so make sure they're equidistant or we'll never hear the end of it.'

I laugh. I am a stickler for symmetry. 'Go wild; who cares what distance they are?'

Her forehead wrinkles. 'And you won't sneak down at midnight and redo them?'

'Of course I will, but have your fun now.'

Noah and JP laugh. We gather around the tree, each holding an ornament.

'OK, so you're both lucky to be included in our annual Christmas tree tradition, and with that responsibility comes question time. I'll start with you, JP. Tell me, what makes the perfect Christmas gift? Novelty socks that say *All the Jingle Ladies*, or a more heartfelt gift like homemade gingerbread and a handwritten card?'

JP loops a Santa ornament at the top of the tree. 'Why not both?'

'Good answer! OK, your turn.'

He rubs the back of his neck while conjuring a question. 'What's the best night for Christmas feasting?' Traditionally in France the Christmas feast is called *Le Réveillon* and is held after returning from Mass on Christmas Eve; however, there are plenty who prefer celebrating on Christmas Day itself so there's more time to prepare and enjoy the food and festivities.

'Why not both?' Noah says, grinning as he hangs a candy cane on the tree.

'*Oui!*' Manon laughs. 'All that effort should last a few days at least.'

I take a step back and survey the trio of happy, smiling faces. How did we get here? We feel like a little found family. It wasn't what I expected to find when I stood out the front of the desolate grimy hotel all that time ago when my interfering neighbour waltzed over to complain about the mess. Now Noah is part of our everyday lives and that brings its own little thrill, but I keep that secret close to my chest. It's too soon to contemplate another relationship... but it's nice to know that my heart hasn't shrivelled and withered away completely. There's hope for me yet.

Like Manon, have I found the place I'm meant to be? Perhaps my life needed a shake up too. While I had success with my writing, what else did I have? A marriage based on nothing but hot air, a sterile apartment that didn't bring any joy and a sort of emptiness that I'd put down to worry over money, fatigue from writing so much. But was it more than that? Was it that my life had become so bland and insular that I didn't even recognise how bad it was until Francois-Xavier exploded our marriage? All the hurt and pain I've held fast to evaporates as I suddenly understand he did me a favour. Without him, my life is so much better. I'm surrounded by people who irk me, make me laugh, give me hope and at times make me want to throttle them – the whole gamut of emotions; the very antithesis of bland.

It's a revelation, as if I've been sleepwalking the last couple of years and have woken up to this explosion of colour. If I sell the hotel, if I take this away from Manon, will I go back to that humdrum life?

32

10 DECEMBER

Noah and I are meeting at Bibliothèque Mazarine, the oldest public library in Paris, on the left bank of the Seine. Somewhere in the cavernous library there is a vault that holds a thirteenth-century Gutenberg Bible, a treasured artefact that will never see the light of day – although the library does have a replica of it on display. That's part of the magic of libraries – what secrets do they house? There are so many historical documents and scrolls, and this library is known for being the keeper of a range of rare medieval manuscripts that were seized from noble families after the French revolution.

I quicken my pace and enter the library, to be greeted by the regular sour-faced librarian. 'What's the purpose of your visit today?' she asks in a shrill tone. I've written here for years, but she asks me every single visit. I suspect it's because my British-accented French makes her suspicious of me, as if I'm here to discover the vault and steal the Gutenberg Bible itself. There are several librarians working here but this one, who I privately call 'The Gatekeeper', always leaves her place at the reception desk to follow me around as if waiting for me to commit a

cardinal library sin like talking above a whisper or taking too
many books to my table. I could easily write in any of the other
beautiful libraries around Paris, but that would mean she's won
and I don't want to give her the satisfaction. I can be petty.

'I'm here to work, Madame,' I say with a bright smile, just
like always.

With a distrustful frown, she waves me inside.

Does Noah get the third degree when he visits? I make my
way around the library and find him sitting at a table in the
back.

'*Bonjour.*' We kiss cheeks in the French custom and I get a
little zap from the smell of his cologne. Huh. I push it from my
mind. We've got serious business to attend to and I need to
focus. Why does he smell so good? A spicy evocative scent that
distracts me from my purpose here today.

I take a seat opposite him and shake the fog from my mind.
'*Bonjour.* Did the librarian ask you what the purpose of your
visit is?' I ask as I unwind my scarf and sit opposite.

'*Non?*'

'That's grossly unfair!'

'Isn't she a darling little thing?'

I cock my head. Is he toying with me? 'Are you joking?'

A grin splits his face. 'She told me I reminded her of
Hemingway, and that if only I was him, despite her advanced
age, she'd court me, no two ways about it.'

Muted laughter spills from me and I turn to find her behind
me, finger to her lips to shush. I do the adult thing and point to
Noah, blaming him. Her harsh expression softens when she
locks eyes with him, and she gives him a fluttery little wave
before she flounces off to berate another library member who
has the audacity to take a selfie. There are no photos allowed in
these hallowed halls!

'I have no words. OK, *oui*, I do! The woman is a tyrant. She's sweet on you because you remind her of Hemingway and I face her wrath if I happen to breathe too loud? It's a disgrace!'

He shrugs. 'Hemingway survived two plane crashes. She mentions it every time I visit, as if she thinks I might be him reincarnated or something. If he can survive that maybe he can survive death – who knows?'

'*Oui*. That would explain it.' Hemingway really is alive and well in the hearts of Parisians, even after all this time. It makes me think of our secret author, and whether she is too. Could she still be celebrated here and we just don't know because we don't know her identity?

Noah must read my mind because he says, 'Sorry to say though that Adeleine Deschamps is *not* our author. After reading her novel, I did some research and found that she died a few years after publication. I found an article from her publisher who shared the news.'

I am instantly deflated. 'She died?' I'd also done some investigating and hadn't found much on Adeleine Deschamps at all. Obviously we're going back a hundred years, but the history books made little mention of her.

He shakes his head. '*Oui*. From smallpox. She was only thirty.'

'It's always sad when a literary light goes out so young.'

'I looked into the other two women from our list, Thérèse Fournier and Clothilde Labelle, and they're accounted for too. Thérèse gave up writing when she married into a wealthy family, and Clothilde swapped writing for nursing and later published a memoir under her real name, her married name, about her time nursing on the battlefield.'

'Well, I guess we knew they were a longshot. I had a thought, and I could be totally off base, but could our mystery

author have published under her husband's name? We know
that happened a lot back then, women writing under a man's
name, or a nom de plume, because of gender bias, but could
that be why the royalties still went to him even after she left the
marriage?' It would explain why she so vehemently wanted to
drop her pseudonym, which wasn't really a pen name; it was *his*
name when she escaped from her husband.'

Noah slaps his forehead and yells, '*Oui!*' He draws the attention of the librarian, who smiles. 'That would explain it. It fits
with why she never wanted to publish a book ever again, if she
indeed wrote under his name and maybe he took all the credit
for her hard work?'

'Shall we look through the archives here? Make a list of
names of men who were prolific and then suddenly stopped
publishing around 1924?'

He gives me a quick nod. 'I'm sure we're on the right track.'

We split up and spend the next few hours going through the
archives and make a solid list of potential writers. It saddens me
that so many more men were published back then than women.
And perhaps in order to get their words in print, they had to
make sacrifices, like allow their husband to take the credit.

When we meet back at the table, we make a plan to investigate our long list of names further and meet up again later as
soon as we happen on anything that feels like it might be him.

As we're packing our papers away, Noah says, 'Would you
like to go to the Christmas market with me tomorrow afternoon
before the bar opens?'

'Sure, I'd love to.' I'm not sure if Noah's just being a friendly
neighbour or there's more to it on his part, but I decide in the
interest of not reverting to a bland and boring life to say yes, to
whatever comes my way. We've bonded over our shared heartbreak and now we're bonding over the mysterious writer from

suite nineteen. Whatever is in store for the future will only happen if I open myself up to possibilities. Even just the thought of a 'one day' romance is enough to send tingles down my body. The more I get to know Noah, the more I like him, even though he's a mansplainer of the finest order.

33

---

11 DECEMBER

I'm meeting Noah at the Tuileries Marché de Noël, across from the Louvre. Every year at Christmas, the garden is transformed into a Christmas market with pop-up wooden chalets, serving festive fare and warm drinks. There's an ice-skating rink and a Ferris wheel, as well as stalls selling gifts and plenty of places to sit and take in the ambiance.

The nutty smell of roasted chestnuts is enough to make my mouth water, so I hope eating is part of the plan when Noah finally arrives.

I catch sight of him at a kiosk, chattering away. I take a moment to survey him. He really is the whole package, a man who drinks words like they're life-affirming; and let's be honest, to us bookworms, they are. He also has that *je ne sais quoi,* a certain appeal that can't be explained. If I were writing a hero like him, the heroine would be at a crossroads right now. Facing the dilemma of the whole *will they, won't they* thing, but this is not a romantic comedy. This is not fiction. Am I actually falling for the guy? Am I the heroine here?

Noah turns away from the kiosk and catches me daydreaming, gazing adoringly at him like he's the delicious crème pâtissière in the centre of a profiterole. I squint and pretend to look straight through him, acting oh so surprised when he gets to me. 'Noah! Sorry, I was a million miles away.'

His lips twitch as if he doesn't believe me, so I press on. 'There's *such* a glare off the white of the rink. Makes it hard to see, doesn't it?' Why don't I stop talking?

'These are for you. If the size is wrong you can exchange them.' Maybe the glare really is harsh because Noah is holding two pairs of ice skates, which can only mean...?

'Ah...'

'Let's skate!'

I scrunch my nose. 'But the markets, the roasted chest—'

'We'll work up a good appetite burning off some energy.'

'I don't know how to skate.' OK, it's more like I can't skate and stand upright at the same time.

Noah's busy unlacing his boots so I reluctantly follow suit. This is going to be a disaster. I despise exercise at the best of times but add in some public humiliation and possibly a broken ankle when I fall, and I think we might have the trifecta of embarrassment.

'Why don't I watch? I can get us some *vin chaud*?'

'Let me help.' Noah drops to his knees and unlaces my boots, as if we're the best of friends and this is totally natural, which it is not. It feels wildly intimate as he wiggles off my boots and replaces them with skates, looking up at me every now and then as if to check he's being gentle enough. My heart bongoes against my ribs and I remind myself to remain at least outwardly calm. I give him a toothy smile to express my absolute feelings of ease and he frowns. Perhaps that smile needs some work.

'Ah – are you OK?'

'*Oui*, just a little cold.'

'I can help with that. May I?' He gestures to my jean-clad legs.

I nod.

He runs his hands up and down my calves, trying to warm them. 'You'll be OK when you're on the ice, you'll warm up then.'

Not if I faceplant.

'Ready?' He stands and holds out a hand to me. I clasp it like my very life depends on it and, if you'd seen my previous attempts at ice skating, you'd know that to be true. I send up a prayer to the ice-skating gods: *Please don't let me fall in a bloody messy heap. If I must fall, please let it be one of those delicate swan-like kisses with the ice.*

We crunch our way to the rink, my breath coming out in foggy gasps. As soon as the metal spike from my skate hits the ice, my legs slip out from under me and I let out a very unlady-like scream.

Noah jumps out of his skin at the sound but grabs me around my waist and rights me.

'Breathe,' he says, holding me tight. I'm sure he can feel the thundering of my heart, which isn't helped by us being pressed against one another. 'Breathe. You can do this.'

'I'll need a few more minutes.' I rest my head on his shoulder so I don't have to look into the intensity of his gaze.

He wraps his arms tighter around me. 'I've got you.'

'*Merci.*' In his arms, I feel warm and safe. 'If I accidentally take you down with me and we end up losing consciousness in a bloody heap, I want you to know I've really enjoyed today.'

'It's been all of twelve minutes.'

'And I've loved every single one of them.'

'Me too, Anais. But do you actually want to skate or shall we follow your suggestion and drink some *vin chaud* and keep warm that way?' He must now realise there is a high probability that we will both be injured with the lack of my skating abilities.

'*Vin chaud* seems the safer option.'

I don't want to leave the comfort of his warm embrace. If this were a romcom, the heroine would strategically slip over as she exits the rink, thus the dashing hero would have to wrap his arms around her and support her as they wandered the Christmas markets and chatted about everything and nothing.

'Let me help you out of the rink,' Noah says. 'I don't want you falling and hurting yourself.'

'I'm fine. I can take it from here,' I say, giving him a bold brave smile as I step out of his arms and slide to the exit gate.

'If you're su—'

'ARGH!' And down I go in a messy heap.

'Anais! Let me help you.'

He scoops me up, into his arms. Who knew romantic comedy moves would come in so handy in real life?

34

12 DECEMBER

Manon and I are at Saint Ouen Flea Market shopping for furniture for Library Anaïs when we happen upon an antique shop called Palais. We peek through the window at the gorgeous ornate gold furniture, the exact style I want for the hotel.

'Can you see any price tags?' I whisper. From the quality of the range, I have doubts it's in our budget but part of me hopes for the best.

'*Non,* and you know what they say: if you have to ask the price, you can't afford it,' Manon says. Inside, there's a woman of indeterminate age, dressed in a flamboyant fluffy coat and matching fluffy beret. She clocks us peeking and waves us in.

'*Bienvenue*, I'm Geneviève. Mimosa?'

'*Oui,*' Manon says as if she shares mimosas with Geneviève all the time, despite us never having met her before. 'Anais would love one too.'

I paste on a smile and grip Manon's arm. What if this is some sales ploy? The antiques in Palais are breathtakingly beautiful, but we'd come in search of more overlooked beauty with a flea market price tag.

Geneviève returns with three mimosas. I take the proffered glass and a sip to be polite. There's more champagne than orange juice and already I feel the alcohol warm me from the inside out.

'What brings you to Saint Ouen?'

Manon takes more of a guzzle than a sip and says, 'We're renovating a boutique hotel in the 6th and were looking for some furniture for what will become the library. While we're in a bourgeois location, sadly we have a tiny little budget. Unfortunately, I'm not sure it would stretch to these magnificent pieces.'

'Ooh, let me be the judge of that. While most of the range here are genuine antiques from chateaux all over France and *castellos* from Italy, I do stock some replica pieces for those who have an eye for luxury. I've also got some pieces in need of refurb; they might suit?'

'*Fantastique!* What about this beauty?' Manon points to a ruby-red chaise longue.

'Replica, and not excessively priced. I have matching Louis XVI bergère chairs that will suit a library. I've got a range of occasional tables with marble tops; some need legs tightening, others the marble is marked or slightly chipped. I can do them for a discount.'

I'm still not convinced we can afford replica or even the in-need-of-refurb antiques, but I hold my breath and hope.

'What about this?' I've never seen a world globe as big as this. It could be a feature in the middle of the library. Library guests can sit with a book in their lap, a glass of wine in their hand, and spin the globe, a finger landing on the next city they'll visit. We have a globe in suite nineteen but I'm still not sure about sharing those treasures.

'This,' Geneviève says, her eyes twinkling, 'is more than just a globe and utterly perfect for your needs. Let me show you.' She removes the surround and opens the globe to reveal a bar. There is room for bottles of spirits, and it has six highball glasses sitting in brown velvet lining.

'*Ooh la la!*' I say. 'I've never seen anything like it.'

'Do you have two of these?' Manon jokes.

'You don't need one for your suite,' I say with a laugh, admonishing her. Truthfully, I'd love one for my personal space too. What could be better than curling up in front of the fire after a long evening writing, pouring myself a cognac and spinning the globe, wondering what people on the other side of the world are doing right that second?

'You're making this very hard for us, Geneviève. I knew we'd fall in love with everything in here.'

'No pressure but I can tally these up and see where we're at. I offer deposit down, interest free payment plans to local Parisian businesses, so that might work too.'

'*Merci.*'

'That sounds good, right?' Manon says, tugging on my arm. 'You want the library to be the showstopper, and with those ruby-red chaises, it will be. You've got to spend money to make money.'

We've been so frugal with funds and have made do with what we've got and could repurpose, but the library room will look spectacular with furniture like this. Do I splurge, just this once? The payment plan is very tempting.

When Geneviève comes back, she slips me a sheet of paper with a figure written on it. It's utterly French not to talk so openly about things as gauche as money. The price is more than I'd bargained on spending today, but the replicas are worth it and will add such elegance to the library.

Manon surreptitiously peers over my shoulder. 'Do it, Anais.'

'You've been very kind, Geneviève. We'd love to feature these antiques in Library Anaïs. If we could arrange the payment plan and delivery, that would be wonderful.'

We sort payment and logistics when a woman with a pixie haircut wanders in and greets us with a wave. She's strangely familiar but I can't think why.

'Sorry,' I say. 'Won't be long; we're just finishing up.'

She sits on the ruby-red chaise we've just purchased. 'Ooh, it's OK, no rush. I'm Lilou; I work next door at Ephemera.'

Geneviève smiles as she hands me a receipt. 'You might also know her as Paris Cupid.'

'*Geneviève*,' Lilou says with a sigh. 'She just can't help herself.'

'Ah! That's why I recognised your face!' A few months ago, the name Paris Cupid was on everyone's lips as no one knew the identity of the anonymous matchmaker who set up so many Parisians, including movie star Emmanuel Roux, AKA the Playboy of Paris.

'Have you ever thought about writing love letters?' Lilou asks.

'Well, I sort of write ninety-thousand-word love letters in the shape of romance novels.'

'Ooh, what's your name?'

'Anais De la Croix.'

With that, Lilou jumps from the chaise and comes over to me, pulling me in for a hug that is strong despite her petite frame. 'I've read every single one of your books and I cannot wait for your new book next Christmas. Can you give me a hint of what it's about?'

'At this stage it's under wraps I'm afraid, but I can tell you it's set in Paris.'

'You absolute tease! I can't wait.'

We leave the market and go for afternoon tea. Lilou from Ephemera has given me a much-needed confidence boost about my writing, by reminding me that my books are special to readers, even when I've lost my mojo and am suffering a block, or imposter syndrome or whatever the case may be. I've been in a rut, thinking only of myself, not my faithful readers, some who've been with me since book one. That's the kind of magic that usually has me plugged into my characters, hyper-focused on their lives as if they're real, so I can take readers on a journey. While I escape my own life writing, readers escape theirs by reading if I do my job well enough.

Lilou doesn't know it, but her words have zapped that part of me that needed rebooting. I've got a Christmas book to finish and I'm going to make it my best one yet, because that's what Lilou and everyone who has supported me deserves. My fingers itch to write, and there's not one thought of bludgeoning. Well, not much. When we get back to the hotel I go to my manuscript and jump straight in.

Hilary was certain no other city was as pretty as Paris at Christmastime. The four hundred chestnut trees along the Place de la Concorde were strung with glittering fairy lights, as if showing the way to the magnificent Arc de Triomphe. Even with the sparkling display of joie de vivre around her, she felt that something was missing from her life. Love, actually...

And it was time to act on her feelings.

The words pour out of me like a dam that's burst its banks.

Time is forgotten as I type like my life depends on it and, for the first time since my divorce, I enjoy writing about love. Complicated, messy, beautiful love. Soon the characters become three dimensional and real to me, as if I'm writing about people whose every secret I know, and I can sense just what they need, even if they can't. But... that doesn't mean I'm going to give it to them. Not yet anyway, because one thing I know for sure is that love might be a long journey, but it's always worth it when the timing is right...

35

14 DECEMBER

I'm up early ready to furnish and decorate Library Anaïs. JP has installed a beautiful walnut bar shelf as an early Christmas present for us, which is so touching I promptly burst into messy tears, which Manon gives me the side eye for.

'Will you stop with all the crying? What's gotten into you?' she admonishes.

'These are happy tears. Look at the hotel! We achieved the dream, in such a short amount of time. Sure, it's not perfect, but we worked with the budget we had, and it'll do for now. It's a million times better than it was. And better yet, it feels warm and welcoming. Like it's always looked just this way.'

'It really does have a good feel. I've had so many enquiries after we posted those updated photographs on the website and across social media yesterday. Once we get the library done, I'll take some snaps and post those too.'

'No bookings yet though? Isn't that a concern if we plan to open by December eighteenth? I'd hoped by now we'd have at least one or two confirmations.'

'Not yet. But we will. Don't worry. I've been fielding calls and replying to lots of emails.'

'OK. Let's finish Library Anaïs.' I give the newly painted shelves a dust while Manon carts boxes of books in and deposits them by my feet.

I shelve the books in alphabetical order while Manon makes a start on the Books of the Month table.

We've chosen to highlight the jazz era and all those Lost Generation authors who made Paris their home. Seems fitting when we have a selection of those novels in a few languages.

We've got a string of tinsel hung along the stand that features our 'Blind date with a book'. Novels that we've wrapped in butchers' paper, with a few clues about each novel and what genre they are. In the corner close to the fire is our Annotation Station. We've supplied pens and annotating paper sets that guests can use to make notes as they read.

'Coming through,' JP grunts as he carries in a ruby-red velvet chaise longue.

'Ooh, the furniture from Palais has arrived!' Manon and I go the lobby and I help carry in bergère chairs and the occasional tables while JP rolls in the globe that's conveniently on wheels.

He places it in the middle of the room. 'That's the biggest globe I've ever seen.'

'Wait,' Manon says, and she dusts her hands on her black jeans. '*Voilà!*' She opens it to reveal the bar. 'Anais is no fun and said I can't have it for my suite.'

'Shall we toast this room?' I say, feeling a well of emotion sweep through me that we're almost at the finish line. While the library is still a mess of disorderly piles of unstacked books, it already has a warm comforting feel to it with the plush ruby-red chaise longues and gold accented marble-top tables. Also the chandelier, which we polished to a shine after replacing a few crystals that were the wrong size. But isn't that beauty in itself – loving and carefully mending the damaged thing; hearts, chandeliers – so they can thrive in the next reincarnation proudly wearing those marks of character? In the corner, lights on our Christmas tree flash and sparkle, drawing the eye of pedestrians, who peek in the window.

When all the books are shelved and the fire is crackling in the hearth, it's going to be an oasis for bibliophiles. There are baskets of throw rugs, and library-card stamped cushions. I can't wait to add more to it as we go and as funds allow so our guests never forget their stay in L'Hôtel Bibliothèque Secrèt.

Manon comes back with a bottle of champagne and pops the cork. 'To new chapters!' I say as we clink our glasses.

A few hours later, the room is complete. Books line the shelves patiently awaiting to be read. On the mantle are black and white pictures of Anaïs Nin from over the course of her life. There's a stack of her books on a coffee table and a range of memoirs written about the woman, who was once called a provocateur. We hang Christmas stockings under the framed photos, and decorate the rest of the room, including moving the Nutcrackers to the doorway, as if they're standing guard over the many novels on display. For now, the room is finished, but we could always use more books...

* * *

That evening, I dress warmly for the wintry weather. Mid-December brings heavier rain and high winds. Still, that's what *vin chaud* is for – to warm up those cold bones.

I find Manon in Library Anaïs, writing up notecards. 'What's that?' I ask.

'Index cards. I just bought the most beautiful old library

cabinet catalogue. We can squeeze it to the right of the fire-place. Let me show you a picture.' She brings it up on her phone. It's gorgeous, like the catalogue drawers in Bibliothèque Mazarine, only smaller. The wood is marred with thick gouges, and a couple of the drawers are bowed and twisted.

'Wow, where on earth did you find it?'

'Geneviève from Palais found it at another flea market and called me and asked if we wanted it.'

'Of course, it's gorgeous.'

'*Oui,* it cost very little because of the condition it's in. She's asked a friend to deliver it to us.'

'What a find. There's cash in my top drawer, just use whatever you need.'

'I know where your cash is, and your diary.'

I tut. 'And I presume you've read it?'

'*Oui,* I tried but it's so boring! You and all your talk of feelings. It really is a bit much, all that lamenting.' At least my secrets are safe. 'So I'm making an index for the library. Although, I didn't factor in how time consuming it would be. Won't it be fun for guests to rifle through the catalogue drawers and search for books the old-fashioned way?'

'It's a book nerd's dream. I can help later.'

'Where are you off to?'

I wave my hand in the vague direction of outside.

Manon waits me out with a look that implies she can wait all day.

'To the Marché de Noël Notre Dame.'

Manon claps her hands in delight. 'Ooh, the Christmas fair! This can wait. Let me get my gloves and coat.'

'Ah, *non, non,* we can go together another time.'

'But we always... oh. You're going out with Noah!'

I try and tamp down her excitement about me going out

with a man who isn't my ex-husband by acting completely disinterested as I rummage in my handbag for my beanie. 'It's not like that. It's to discuss our findings about the author from the secret library.'

She holds up her hands in surrender. 'OK, OK, don't let me stop you. Go find Noah and talk about dead people.'

I roll my eyes, wave goodbye.

* * *

I tap on the window of The Lost Generation Wine Bar and Noah jogs over to open the door. 'Come in, come in. I'll just be a minute. I'm setting a few things up for tonight. Drink?'

'Sure.'

He pours me a robust red wine as I take a seat at the bar before excusing himself to change into warmer clothes. I take my glass of wine and walk around the bar while it's closed to customers, enjoying the freedom of having the place to myself to take it all in. After all, I don't exactly remember much from my last visit, except maybe the drunken tango, and that I avoided the Christmas movie quiz Noah held the following evening because I was suffering from a bout of pure embarrassment and a hangover from hell.

There are booths along one side and bookshelves at the back that I didn't see the night of the infamous death metal band. Like any good bookworm, the first thing I check is what's on the shelves.

There's an entire collection of Hemingway, F. Scott Fitzgerald, Don Passos. And Oscar Wilde, whose *A Picture of Dorian Gray* is one of my favourite novels. Gertrude Stein, Colette, Henry Miller, Proust; all the usual suspects. I run my finger along them before crouching down by a lower shelf that has a range of more colourful spines. I gasp when I see a collection of my own novels that stand out in their absolute pinkness among the more subdued covers. I take one from the shelf. Did he just purchase these? I thumb through *The Billionaire's Runaway Wife* to find it's well loved; some pages are dog eared, others are bent as if it travelled in someone's knapsack.

'Sorry, I had to...'

I stand with the novel in one hand and glass of wine in the other. 'What's this?'

Colour creeps up his cheeks. 'It's your eleventh book, if I remember rightly, and it became your first global bestseller, but I could be wrong.'

'Ah – how?'

'I'm a fan, always have been.'

'But you said...'

'When you were on the phone to your agent, the day Manon had that horrific incident with the very heavy bookshelf' – now it's my turn to blush – 'you said you were a romance writer, but I didn't put two and two together and realise you were *that* romance writer.'

'Your face fell though, I saw it as soon as I said I write romantic comedies.'

'That was nothing to do with your writing.'

'What was it then?'

'I – I...' He drops his gaze to the floor. 'I felt instinctively I could very easily fall for someone like you. And then you asked if what you wrote wasn't literary enough and glared at me so forcefully, I felt it was best to keep my trap shut for my own safety.'

'Post-divorce me is a terrifying thing.' He could easily fall for someone *like* me? Still, while it's vague, I feel a small thrill at his confession. When I met him outside that very first day, I felt a pull to him until an alert went off in my mind, warning me to be on guard because I couldn't suffer another upset like the one before; and men, who could trust a word they said? It was heartbreak driving the engine. Noah isn't like that. Is he?

'After that encounter, I had to know what you wrote. I bumped into Manon the next day at Marché Biologique Raspail and she mentioned you were the romance writer Anais De la Croix. Truthfully, I was confused. How could you be so funny on the page and so irate in real life?'

'Here we go again.' I roll my eyes. 'Tell me more.'

'I don't dare.'

I laugh. Poor Noah. I did lash out and put him in the same category as Francois-Xavier, which was unfair and unwarranted. 'When I met you that first time and you berated me about the mess of the broken sign, I knew you were main-character material. I wrote you as my hero many times, but sadly you suffered tragic ends. Once you were even wrapped in Christmas lights and rolled into the Seine.' Main-character material? Why am I suddenly talking so openly with him? There's something about Noah that makes me want to share. To be truthful.

'Wow. I hope I was dead before I hit the water.'

I shake my head. '*Non*. You were not.'

'Brutal. And now... am I still suffering horrifying ends?'

'I'm up to Chapter Twelve and you've made it this far, but there's a big conflict coming and, between us, I'm concerned for you.'

'I hope I make it.'

'For your sake, me too.'

'Shall we go to another Christmas market? I feel like we need to check them all out,' he asks. 'I could use a *vin chaud*, and you can tell me what hero Noah is up against.'

* * *

The market is a hive of activity with stall owners serving long queues of people. Children tug on parents' sleeves and point to the puppet show. A live band plays jaunty music. The scent of garlic is heavy in the frigid air.

'Ooh, escargot,' I say, pointing to a pan of delicate little garlicky snails.

Noah screws up his nose.

'Oh, come on,' I say. 'Have you actually tried them?' Escargots are a delicacy in France and, if you can separate the fact they're snails, you'll enjoy a buttery garlicky taste explosion.

'*Non*, and I will not.' Serious-faced Noah is back, standing ramrod straight as if ready for flight, like I'm going to force-feed him snails or something.

'You're missing out, Noah. Really.'

He shudders. 'I'll take your word for it, but isn't Christmas at the Paris markets all about the potatoes?'

I laugh and lace an arm through his as we wander slowly around. '*Oui*, markets like these were originally a German tradition, which then spread to Paris. Now we get the best of both worlds, German and French food.'

At a stall with a smaller line, Noah orders a plate of *Tartiflette*, which is similar to a potato bake but elevated by the use of reblochon cheese and salty crispy lardons. From the stall next door I order *Choucroute*, an Alsatian dish, and am given a plate heaped with sausages, meat, sauerkraut and boiled potatoes.

We find a table. '*Vin chaud*?' Noah asks with a smile.

He soon returns with two aromatic glasses of mulled wine.

'Sit here,' I say and pat the bench seat next to me, 'so we can share our food.'

We eat in companionable silence, delighting in the rich dishes, as part of me wishes Christmas lasted all year.

'Try this,' Noah says, lifting a fork with cheesy potato goodness to my mouth. 'Good, isn't it?'

He's a whisper away from me, and it's all I can do to *think* as the man feeds me and takes great care doing it, as though his only concern is my enjoyment. What is this? I'm not used to a man who is so kind and considerate. Eventually, I manage, '*Oui*, it's delicious. Try mine.' I don't go so far as to feed the man from my fork because my pulse is racing, and it feels so intimate. My thoughts turn to mush as his leg brushes against mine. I'd forgotten what this felt like, being fuzzy with the hopes of what might be.

I close my eyes, willing myself to get back on track. Make a joke about snails again; something, anything. Noah surveys me as if the mild panic I feel is evident on my face.

'We should, uh, go,' I say. 'Have you tried *Galette des Rois*? The king's cake?' I don't give him time to answer. I'm out of my seat and edging away. 'It's *feuilleté* pastry layers filled with frangipane and citron. It's a tradition to serve it January sixth to celebrate the Feast of the Epiphany...' I'm rambling, and worse, I'm rambling about a cake, for crying out loud. A very nice traditional Christmastime cake, but still.

'Anaïs.'

'Usually there's a *fève* hidden in the layers and whoever finds it is celebrated as the king or queen for the day. And, one year, Manon swallowed it and she...'

Noah laughs. 'Is this how I am when I'm prattling about authors to you?'

My jitteriness soon evaporates as I make sense of what he means. Is Noah just as anxious and unsure as me, so he fills those awkward moments with inane chatter that I've put down to him being some sort of literary grandstander? An egotistical maniac? But, really, it's his nervousness around me?

I swipe a lock of hair back at the same time Noah steps forward, and manage to elbow him straight in the face. '*Mon Dieu!* Sorry, Noah.' My cheeks flame. How am I so bad at this?

He rubs a spot on his forehead. 'I'm fine. But, for safety's sake, would it be all right if I put my arm around you as we walk?'

I bite my lip before saying, 'You'd better. These elbows have got a mind of their own. But first—' I step forward and grab the collar of his jacket to pull him close. I gaze into his eyes and see the same desire reflected back. *Kiss him!* My body vibrates with longing. I close my eyes as I—

'Anais! *Bonsoir!*'

My eyes snap open and I jump back from Noah. 'Père Noël?' I try to shake the muddle from my mind.

'It's me, Timothee, under all this padding.' He slaps his oversized belly. What unfortunate timing!

I cough, clearing my throat as I'm sling-shotted back to reality. 'Ooh, of course, Timothee. How's the new job going?'

'It's hectic. Kids are the *worst*. Zac has it much harder being stuck in the photo booth where they rip his beard off or scream in his ear. But the stall owners give us plenty to eat, so it's not so bad.'

I laugh, thinking of these twentysomething backpackers who probably have no real experience with children and are having to play the part of Father Christmas for hours on end every day.

A spotty-faced teenager rushes by and yanks Timothee's red velvet cap off before letting out an evil cackle and making a run for it. '*Give that back!*' Timothee yells. 'Guess that's my cue to leave!' He chases after the teen, his white curly wig flapping in the wind behind him.

'I don't know,' Noah says, 'Something tells me he's not the real Santa.'

I laugh. 'I think you might be right.'

The earlier spell is broken, so I clasp his hand and lead him away from the chaos of the market, my lips tingling at the almost kiss.

36

15 DECEMBER

The next evening, I'm tossing and turning in bed, unable to sleep. My mind spins from Noah to the hotel soft launch and lack of bookings, to money and everything in between. Eventually, I give up and wrench the covers back. I pull on my robe and find the key for the secret library.

I go through the books once more, looking for titles by men this time. I'm hoping to stumble on a range of books by the same author, an entire collection. I take my time but find nothing that fits.

There must be one clue, something in this room that will point the way to who she was. I sit at the desk and pull open the drawers. At the back I find a small notebook, more like a jotter than a journal. There is a scribble of names; could be character names? Maybe guests from the hotel? Did she use her assumed name when she dined downstairs in the restaurant, make up a whole fiction for her past? Or were her meals ferried to her here?

I flick through the jotter.

Chateau Beauchêne in disrepair.

It stands out because the handwriting is different from all the other samples. It's as if someone left her a note on her jotter. I take my phone and google the name of the chateau to see if it's a real place. I get a hit and click the link.

Chateau Beauchêne in the region of Bergerac is now derelict, almost a ruin.

I speed read the article that mentions it was once owned by a prominent family at the turn of the twentieth century before the owner, Benjamin Marceaux, let it fall into disrepair after the disappearance of his wife, Chloe. It goes on to say Benjamin Marceaux was a famous novelist who couldn't bring himself to write ever again after his wife's mysterious disappearance.

Chloe! Is she our writer?

The lights in the room flicker.

The reason he couldn't write was because the wordsmith was her! I'm sure he garnered a lot of sympathy for that absolute lie about his writing too. I've read many a Benjamin Marceaux novel! They're on the syllabus at most high schools, having been translated and studied around the world, as famous as novels that came later, like *To Kill a Mockingbird*, or *Catcher in the Rye*. Did this Chloe actually write those books that have stood the test of time?

I check the shelves for books by Benjamin Marceaux, but don't find any. Do I go and find Noah? I check the time. It's just past midnight on Friday; his bar might still be open. I call his mobile, and he answers after the first ring.

'*Bonsoir*,' I say. 'Sorry to call so late. But I've found something. Can you come to the hotel now?' My words come out in a rushed jumble.

'*Oui*, of course. I'm about to lock up for the night.'

'Great. Meet you at the front door.' I dash downstairs to change out of my PJs. I check my reflection and swipe on some lip gloss, my heart thumping against my ribs. *Chloe! Have we found you?*

I unlock the front door and let Noah through. A gust of wind blows the door open and I fight to close it. Noah stands behind me and helps push it shut. I can feel the heat of his body against mine and my legs go weak. *Focus on Chloe!*

When we get the door closed, I lock up and explain what I found scribbled on the jotter as we make our way upstairs.

'So I googled the chateau and an article popped up. According to that, his wife "Chloe" disappeared one day and he never wrote again. The chateau eventually fell into disrepair.' My words tumble out fast as my body thrums with adrenaline. I don't know if that's because of Noah's proximity or the idea we might have found our mysterious writer – probably both!

'Chloe! You've found her?'

My eyes go bright with tears. 'I think so!'

'And what was his name?'

'Benjamin Marceaux!'

'*The* Benjamin Marceaux? *Mon Dieu!*'

'*Oui*, it's...'

'It's *huge*, Anais. If Chloe did pen the Benjamin Marceaux novels and never got attributed for them, this is one huge literary wrong.'

'That we're going to right!'

Back in the secret library, we sit together on the bed. I take my phone and google the name Benjamin Marceaux. I click the link to 'his' collection of works. 'This says he wrote books for children originally before pivoting into books for adults. According to this website, his children's books received a mediocre reception. It was when he turned his hand to a more mature style that literary critics took notice. Is that when he married his Chloe?'

Noah nods, his face bright with excitement. *'Oui*, it must be.'

I search for her name and find nothing. Not one mention. The lights flicker again.

I gaze up. 'It's her!'

'A sign from Chloe?' Noah, says. 'Stranger things have happened.'

I search once more for Benjamin Marceaux and find an article that celebrates his life and achievements. There's a timeline we can work off. 'This says he married Chloe in 1910. OK, so that's later than we imagined. And she disappeared in 1924. He told investigators she suffered from "female hysteria" because she'd been unable to bear children and it had left a mark on her. Oh, wasn't he just a prince! It goes on to say this was a common malady, so investigators closed the case, suspecting the woman had taken her own life. The husband never wrote again. He claimed this was due to losing the love of his life, but we know that it was because the real author was safe and warm and away from his clutches right here in the secret library. He moved another woman into the chateau in 1928 but later lost everything after some bad business decisions. He abandoned the chateau and died penniless in Bordeaux; even his royalty income couldn't pay the debts he'd racked up.'

'Ah, *oui*, I remember reading about that story! I believe he got caught up in some bad business, but I can't remember what it was. Gambling, maybe? Even though his life ended in such disarray, he was hailed a literary genius. A *haunted* literary genius who could have gone on to even greater things, had his wife not disappeared and ruined him. When, in reality, it was she who was the literary genius.'

'Well, we *presume*. How do we prove it for sure?'

'We go through this library with a fine-tooth comb.'

'Now?'

'Who needs sleep?'

I laugh, slightly hysterically, but I'm wired at the idea we might be able to right a literary wrong that has survived for a hundred years. If we're correct in our assumptions, Benjamin Marceaux has been hailed a genius when he was nothing of the sort. In fact, he robbed the world of Chloe's literary genius, and thus those history books need to be rewritten.

37

16 DECEMBER

Our main renovations come to end and, when we finish the
walkaround with JP, I'm once again fighting off tears so Manon
doesn't scold me. His team have worked wonders on the old
hotel and now it will have a new life with a fresh look until the
next owner comes along and decides to change it. I only hope
whoever owns it next appreciates the amount of love that went
into the design and the amount of hard work the tradespeople
put into it to achieve our dreams. JP will stay on in a casual role,
fitting us in between other jobs, and take more time to renovate
suites as funds allow.

'This is it,' JP says, holding out a hand. 'Thanks for trusting
us with the job.'

'Don't be so dramatic. You'll be back after work, right?'
Manon says, shoving him with her hip.

'Well, *oui*, if that's all right?'

'Of course, you're part of the fabric of this hotel now, and
part of the family.' Things have progressed fast for the lovebirds. I guess, when you know, *you know*. If I could have
dreamed up the right guy for Manon it would have been a man

like JP, but she would have laughed in my face so I'm glad she's been bitten by the love bug because there's no way she would have listened to me anyway.

'Don't get so maudlin,' Manon says as I swat at more tears. 'I've got news to cheer you up! Our first guests have booked, arriving in three days on December nineteenth! Six pax coming from Germany.'

'Pax?' I ask.

'Oh, it's a fancy hotel term that means "people". I've been studying up on hotel management, you know, just for fun.'

'You know a condition of sale could be that I insist you're kept on as manager.'

'*Merci*, Anais, but somehow I don't think an investor would choose an employee who learned hotel management from the internet. It's not as bad as learning from TikTok, but it's not far off.'

'You could study hotel management while you worked here part-time?' But, really, what am I saying? I can't make promises like that. The fate of the hotel is still undecided. Even with the place running as a going concern it would be tight, and I never envisaged myself as a hotelier even if I'd love to hold on to it for Manon's sake.

But... there is hope on the horizon. An idea I have that might just work out for all parties. I give JP and the wider team a hug and thank them for all their efforts. Manon walks JP to the door, before latching on to his back like she's a koala bear.

I go to my suite and call my literary agent.

'Margaret,' I say with a determined edge to my voice. 'My Christmas romcom is almost done. At this juncture I'd like to remind you, you said make it messy but make it happen. So prepare yourself for a very *rough* draft.'

'Did I say that? It doesn't sound like me at all.'

'*Margaret*.'

'Fine, fine. Get it over to me when it's finished and I'll see if I can make sense of it.'

I grin. 'Sure. There's something else I wanted to talk to you about. At the hotel, sealed behind a makeshift wall, we discovered a secret library, hidden away for almost one hundred years. And in that library we found a great wrong had been committed by a man called Benjamin Marceaux.'

'The *writer* Benjamin Marceaux?'

'Yes and... no. We think Benjamin did write the children's novels, but he didn't write the adult fiction he's credited for. His wife Chloe did.'

'*WHAT!*' She screams so loud I'm sure birds outside scatter from the trees. 'You have my full attention.'

'First we found what amounted to be her last words: *Keep my soul in peace. Keep my last manuscript safe.*' I explain the treasure trove of papers that we found. Notebooks, love letters. The fact she was a literary genius who never got any credit and escaped to the hotel to be with her true love, a painter and patron of literature, a woman named Lily-Louise Toussaint. There's so much more. 'We unearthed letters from friends; many people who supported her knew she was the real author but were sworn to secrecy to keep her safe from her husband, who she felt would surely kill her if he found her, not only because she had the hide to leave him for a woman, but because she could also share the secret he wanted kept from the world. She wrote all of his books and we've got proof. This hundred-year secret is now ready to be shared.'

'The manuscript? Did you find it? Please tell me you did!'

'*Oui*, we did.' A tingle runs through me. 'It was hidden behind one of the bookshelves in her library.' My gaze drops to a leatherbound notebook on my desk, and I smile. 'And there was a note.'

'What did the note say?'

'Well, that is rather special and I'd really rather prefer you read it yourself.'

'*Anais!* The suspense is killing me! The manuscript – is it like her others?'

I stifle a laugh. Margaret is not exaggerating – this will be killing her, the not knowing. '*Non*, it's a memoir. At its core it's a love story told with her usual candour. It's her life story, how her family forced her into marriage with a violent man. How he discovered her writing talent and used it for his own gain. And how, just when all hope was lost, Lily-Louise stepped into her life and gave her something to live for. With Lily's help, as a patron of literature, Chloe went on to earn a small income writing articles for journals and newspapers under a nom de plume to pay her expenses. But she saved her greatest work until the end. Her memoir. I haven't come across a novel that reads so well, Margaret. It's incredibly special. A great, lost, love story, about two women who found each other, against the odds. You haven't read a romance like this before, and it's even better because it's all true. It's one for the ages.'

'And I hope this means you're passing this manuscript on to your cheerleader, your voice, your fierce and loyal literary agent?'

I laugh. 'Would I choose anyone else? With Noah's help, I've vowed to prove who Chloe was and I want to get her novels re-released under her own name. She deserves that much. And that's just the start of my plans to honour Chloe and Lily-Louise.'

'I can help with that too. This is just... great timing for me. I better come and see this secret library myself.'

'We'd love to welcome you to The Secret Library Hotel.'

'Ah, clever. So one thing... Why did they seal those rooms up and where did they go?'

'That you will have to read for yourself...'

38

17 DECEMBER

Noah closes the cover on the manuscript and lets out a long sigh and puts his hand on his heart. 'What a book. It's heartbreaking yet hopeful, poetic yet fast paced. And still, I want to cup my head and cry.'

'I know. The way it ended for them.' For a book written so long ago, it's still so relevant, so raw and unflinching, with an overarching theme of finding love after betrayal. Of finding joy and hope in simple things. The story of two women who braved it all for love. And how that love grew despite every obstacle thrown in their path. Then the bittersweet end. I still can't think of it without bawling myself. 'Did you get the sense she was talking directly to you, or do I feel that because we've grown so close to her reading her private journals?' I ask.

'*Oui*, I did. She had such a gift. Do you think she really didn't publish ever again? And only wrote for newspapers and the like?'

'I'm not sure? Maybe that's another avenue we'll have to look into. Lily-Louise being a patron for the arts could have facilitated a deal for her under another name. But part of me feels like she truly did lose her love for writing for others and instead focused on her memoir, writing her side of the story. Her truth.' My emotions are all roiled up after reading her last manuscript together.

Noah places the notebook on the desk and turns to me. 'What they went through only cements in me that life is short, and the time to act is now.'

He motions to the space between us that grows smaller as I take a tentative step closer to him, staring into the blue of his eyes and getting lost there.

Quietly, I say, 'Chloe taught us to act when you have the chance or live with regret.'

He pulls me tight against him. 'It would be remiss of us to ignore that.'

In the secret library, it feels like there's magic in the air, so I take Noah's face and kiss him softly on the lips. He wraps his arms around my waist. It feels like the first chapter of a new book, like the beginning of a love story.

* * *

Later that day, I'm singing Christmas carols, feeling very festive indeed when I run into a pinch-faced Manon in the lobby. 'What's wrong?' I ask.

'He's here.'

'Who?'

'Francois-Xavier.'

I feel colour drain from my face. Why now? Why when I finally open my heart to another man does he reappear? 'What does he want?'

She shrugs. 'You, apparently. And he's not leaving until he sees you. I tried everything to get rid of the fool.'

I rub my temples. 'OK. Let me give him his marching orders.'

I find him sprawled like he owns the place on the sofa in the guest lounge. '*Amour*,' he says to me in a silky voice. He doesn't get up but widens his arms as if he thinks I'll fall into them.

'I'm not your love, Francois-Xavier. Has Ceecee figured you out already? Before that there was Helga, Renee, Sofia... I could go on.'

'You absolute pig!' Manon adds. I squeeze her hand to quieten her.

He sweeps their names away. 'They lie! I messaged them, but that's as far as it went.'

'Is that so? And the thing with Helga? Maybe my eyes deceived me because I swear I saw her naked in our marital bed. I had to burn those sheets, and they were organic bamboo, which I'm still not happy about. And that's really saying something, the fact I miss those breathable sheets more than I miss you, which is not at all for the record. I'd like you to leave.'

He baulks. 'Leave? But this place was *my* dream! *My* vision.'

I'm almost at a loss for words. 'You cannot be serious right now, Francois-Xavier.'

Manon stage-whispers, 'Do you want me to escort him out in a chokehold? Because I will.'

And she would too. He'd have no chance against my jujitsu-proficient cousin. 'It's OK, Manon. I'm sure he's not going to make us use brute force in an effort to get him to leave. But I'll keep it in mind.'

Francois-Xavier rolls his eyes and I'm sure I hear Manon growl. She's never liked the guy and is probably hoping she'll get to throw him down and cut off his air supply. Still, it wouldn't look good for business, even if we don't officially open until tomorrow, and don't have guests booked until the nineteenth. We'd wanted to host a party to celebrate the achievement, but there's still so many odd jobs that need doing so we've shelved that plan for now.

Manon bares her teeth, like she's a wild animal. It's all I can do not to laugh. I squeeze her hand once more, but her expression must intimidate Francois-Xavier because he says, 'Fine, I'll go but can I at least call you?'

I give him a winning smile. 'You can call my lawyer, would that help?'

'*Anais.*'

'*Au revoir.*'

He saunters out slowly, as if he doesn't have a care in the world. 'You should tell Ceecee what he's up to,' Manon says.

'If he's here, that means Ceecee dumped him.'

'*Oui*, that's probably true. What do you think his end game is?'

I shiver. 'He'll hope he can slot back into my life until a better offer comes along.'

Manon goes to the window. '*Merde*, he's gone into Noah's bar.'

My chest tightens. 'You don't think Noah will mention anything about suite nineteen, do you?'

Manon screws up her face. 'He wouldn't tell anyone; besides, he doesn't know that's your ex-husband, so I can't see how anything about you, or the hotel, would come up at all.'

I'll have to be careful. If he's sniffing around and hears anything about the secret suites I'll never get rid of him, and worse, he might try and get the hotel back. He's got a free legal team on his side and I don't have anything left to fight him with. 'True. Let's leave him to drown his sorrows. I'm sure he'll be sitting at the bar, phone in hand, trying to find the next woman to fleece.'

Worry shines in Manon's eyes. 'I hope he doesn't come back, but I've got a feeling he will. Look at this place. Most of the hard work has been done and he'll imagine he can slide right in as hotelier.'

'Over my dead body.'

'*Non*. Over his.'

I laugh. 'OK, I'm going to write. I'm on a roll and I don't want to let him steal my good mood away.'

Manon narrows her eyes. 'I noticed you were floating around, singing carols at the top of your lungs, flushed complexion. What's *that* about?'

'The joy of Christmas!'

'Or is it the possibility of ending your bout of celibacy?'

'*Manon!*'

'Well? The signs are all there. You're living in a daydream and your passion for writing about love has returned with a vengeance. What happened with Noah in suite nineteen today? You were gone for the longest time.' She makes a bawdy gesture, which I duly ignore.

'Not that it's any of your business, but we kissed.'

She lets out a screech.

'Shush! We don't want Francois-Xavier to hear that and come running!'

'Tell me everything or I'll scream again.'

It's my turn to narrow my eyes. The old Manon doesn't do boy talk. Doesn't do lengthy chats about anything so messy as feelings. 'You want the details? That's not *like* you.'

She grins. 'Isn't it the worst being in love and then hoping that everyone around feels the same ridiculous giddiness? I hope I settle down soon. These feelings are intense and *quite* the distraction.'

I smile. 'It's nice seeing you so happy.'

'*Oui,* I guess. But what about you, will you open your heart to Noah?'

'Now you sound like a true heroine from a romance novel, Manon.'

'*Kill me.*'

'I will not.'

'Stop avoiding the question.'

I let out a long sigh. 'I like Noah. I did from the very first moment we met and then he spoke and the rage-fuelled me took over. But I was hurt and now I'm not. Things are clearer. I can look at him and not mentally write a scene where I strangle him.'

'You mentally wrote that?'

'Many times. Not just him. Any man.'

'Heartbreak is intense, I'm guessing.'

'Heartbreak and humiliation. What a combination. Noah is a good man and I have strong feelings for him, but we'll have to see how it pans out. *Is* dating the neighbour such a good idea?'

Manon clutches her head as if she's frustrated. 'There you go, obsessing over things that are of no consequence.'

'How can I not think ahead like that? What if...'

'What if you stopped all the chatter in your overworked brain and listened to your heart? What does it say?'

'My heart would say that, looking out at the sea of people all over the world, how lucky am I to have found a man like Noah? A man of substance. A man who will keep me on my toes. Who won't agree with me just for the sake of it, but will still put my best interests first. Even when I tell him I don't want him cleaning my windows.'

She grins. 'He's got a real thing about windows, hasn't he?'

'The man likes order in a disorderly world.'

'*Mon Dieu,* there's two of you.'

'And then there's you, who expects me to clean up in your wake.'

'*Oui*, but I paint the high bits and the low bits, so that's only fair.'

'*Touché.*'

In my suite, I sit at my desk with the wobbly leg and stretch my fingers. I have fourteen more days until my manuscript is due and I vow to make it on time.

39

18 DECEMBER

The next day, I'm up late after a long evening writing. The words spilled out of me, almost as if the heroine was writing the story herself, and I was merely the conduit transcribing for her. That doesn't happen very often, so I'm counting it as a win, as if the romance gods are on my side and want me to succeed after suffering a block that I thought I'd never recover from.

I make myself a coffee, smiling when I see Manon's found some literary mugs. Half-asleep still, I follow a noise and find Manon behind the reception desk, hanging a string of fairy lights across the front that cascade down in pretty loops.

'What's this?' A pretty Christmas gift box wrapped in silver ribbon sits on the counter. 'Papillote Christmas chocolates. For you.'

My heart expands. There's a whole story about how Papillote chocolates came to be. As it goes, in the city of Lyon in the late eighteenth century, there was a shy apprentice who loved a girl but didn't have the courage to tell her. Instead, he pilfered some chocolate from the *confiseur* and wrapped it in a love note to gift to the girl he hoped to make his sweetheart. The love-struck thief was caught by his boss, Mr Papillote, who thought the idea was genius, and so the Papillote Christmas chocolates were born, and they're still popular today during the festive season.

'When did Noah drop them off? I should thank him.' It's such a fitting gift after we've been surrounded by secret letters from the past.

Manon finishes tacking the last loop of Christmas lights. 'I'm not sure if they're from Noah. They were out the front when I opened the doors for the tradespeople. There's a card under the box with your name on it.'

'*Merci.*'

I take the box and envelope along with my coffee back to the kitchen. I open the card and it reads:

Christmas chocolate and a love note, what could be sweeter? Would you like to go to a Christmas concert at Sainte-Chapelle this evening? Send me a love note back. Noah

I grin. It's a sweet and utterly romantic gift and he's put a lot of thought into it. I open one of the chocolates, a rich dark chocolate delight that melts on my tongue while I think of a reply.

I find a piece of notepaper in a drawer, not as fancy as Noah's card, but needs must, and write:

Merci beaucoup for the Christmas chocolates, they are my favourite. I'd love to go to Sainte-Chapelle this evening. Herewith is your chosen chocolate. I hope you like hazelnut. Anais.

I wrap the note around the chocolate.

'Manon!' I yell. 'Can you deliver this to Noah?'

'Now I'm UberEats?'

I laugh, picturing Manon on a vespa ferrying food all over Paris. 'You'd eat their chocolates if you were an Uber driver, wouldn't you?'

'I wouldn't be able to resist.'

'Take one of these for your trouble.' I hold up the box and she chooses an almond praline for herself.

'Just the one. Wow. So generous.'

We laugh as she cradles the note and chocolate as if it's sacred and goes to deliver Noah's.

* * *

We take a pew inside Sainte-Chapelle. It's one of the most beautiful churches in Paris, from the rayonnant period of Gothic architecture. But what makes it particularly stunning are the stained-glass windows, shooting prisms of colour around the church. It's breathtaking and, no matter how many times I visit, I'm still rendered speechless by its beauty.

The carollers start, the young choir who have the voice of angels. My eyes well up at the pure sound that's so haunting and sweet and I try surreptitiously to dab at my eyes, wishing I'd thought to bring a tissue, or at least not worn a white jumper.

I'm sniffling and snuffling when Noah exits the pew, before returning with a small sachet of tissues. 'The usher said it happens all the time.'

I send him a grateful smile. It's the magic of Christmas, their cherubic voices, being bathed in pools of light, like we're actually in the belly of a kaleidoscope, it's Noah, the warmth and strength of him right beside me. It's grace for myself and letting go of what came before. It's a new start. It's a new stronger me. Once bruised and battle scarred. Now healed.

I lean my head against Noah's shoulder and put my hand on his chest. The beat of his heart is in symphony with mine.

After the concert, we take a walk along the Seine, hand in hand. Stars sparkle overhead as dinner cruises decorated for Christmas chug along the river. There's a festive air as families walk in large groups, out late to attend markets. Revellers spill from bistros, smoking cigarettes. In a doorway, a couple embrace, laughing breathlessly before kissing. I catch Noah's eye and we exchange a smile. 'Love is in the air,' I say.

'*Oui*,' he says, and he turns to face me.

I don't hesitate; I stand on my tiptoes and kiss him. The world around me fades to black as I melt into his arms and our kiss deepens with an intensity that feels right.

40

19 DECEMBER

Loud banging wakes me up. Squinting, I check the time. It's not even six. Our first guests aren't due to arrive until later in the day. I throw a jumper over my PJs and slip on my boots and head to the lobby to see who is making so much noise so early in the morning.

Is that Margaret *and* Francois-Xavier?

Mon Dieu. Margaret's arms are flailing and Francois-Xavier has his crossed tight against his chest. Uh oh, my literary agent is giving him a mouthful and by his scrunched up features he doesn't like it one little bit.

I twist the lock and they spill inside.

'Now you listen to me, you snivelling, snide sex fiend...!'

Sex fiend? I press my lips together to stop laughter escaping.

'*Excusez moi!* You cannot talk to me in such a way. I demand you stop.'

I stand between the pair. 'Francois-Xavier, what are you doing here? And Margaret, I didn't realise you were arriving so soon.' Although, I should have expected it. She wants to read Chloe's manuscript.

'I'm here because this is my hotel, my dream, my...'

I sigh. 'Don't start all that again.'

'But I love you,' he says, in his best beseeching tone that used to sway me and now makes me cringe.

'Where's the manuscript? Point me in the direction of the secret library,' Margaret bellows. 'I'll take a café crème.'

I shoot Margaret a look. The very last person I want to know about any of this is Francois-Xavier.

'What do you mean, secret library?' he asks, calculation shining in his eyes. He's probably already counting euros in his head.

'It's nothing,' I say. 'It's, uh... the new name of the hotel.' Margaret gives me a tiny nod to acknowledge her mistake.

'And the manuscript?' He laser-focuses his gaze directly at me. How did I not see this shrewd side of him early on?

'*My* manuscript, obviously. Margaret is my literary agent, as you well know.' I keep my voice modulated so he doesn't pick up on my lies. If he knows there's the potential for a pay day, I'll never get rid of him. If all goes according to plan, he'll hear about it in the press, but that's a worry for another day, a less important day.

'Is that so?'

Margaret purses her lips as her complexion pinks. She's going to blow if I don't put a stop to this and get him on his way.

'Today is a very big day. We're welcoming our first guests, so if there was nothing else?'

Francois-Xavier leaps forward and pulls me into his arms. I let out a surprise bark of shock. 'What are you *doing*!'

'Please, give me another chance.' He nuzzles my neck, a move that used to drive me wild and now makes my skin crawl. Suddenly my family's warnings all make so much sense! Did he act as smarmy as this when I fell for him? It's so obviously a ploy.

'Get your slimy hands off her!' Manon yells. Oh, this day just keeps getting better and better. 'I warned you about the chokehold, did I not? Now you leave me no choice but to...'

'Everything OK here, Anais? I heard yelling?'

I want to cup my head and scream. 'All OK, Noah. This guy is just deciding whether he'll leave or suffer a chokehold.'

'Ooh, *this* is Noah,' Margaret says, winking at my neighbour. Kill me.

Manon grabs Francois-Xavier and has him on the floor in one quick sweep. She loops her arms around his neck in the next breath. Not long after, his eyes pop out of his head. Do I look that unattractive when Manon practises her submissions on me? It's not a good look, but I worry she's going to cut off the oxygen to his brain, and violence is never the answer, so I say, 'Tap out or she won't release you!'

Francois-Xavier reluctantly taps the parquetry floor and Manon pulls her arms from his neck.

'Who is he?' Noah asks with a curious frown.

'I. Am. Her husband,' Francois-Xavier sputters as he pulls himself up, trying to catch his breath.

What is he playing at? 'Ex-husband. The one who drained my bank accounts and slept with half the women of Paris, *that* ex-husband.'

'Ah.' Noah gives me an understanding nod. 'I'd offer to escort him out for you, but Manon has this covered, more's the pity.' He gives me a cheeky smile.

'Would you like an arm bar next, Francois-Xavier? Or a foot lock?'

'Manon!' I'm all for getting rid of him but she's enjoying this far too much.

'I'm leaving,' Francois-Xavier says, 'I'm leaving.'

Manon can't help herself and has one more parting shot. 'Anais has already replaced you so there's no point trying to win her back.'

His eyebrows pull together. 'Replaced me with who?'

Manon jerks a thumb at Noah.

'That guy?' Francois-Xavier explodes. 'He's a misogynist of the finest order.'

What? 'You don't even know him,' I say, hoping I'm right.

'*Oui,* I do. After my last visit I went into his bar. You know to take the edge off, because you... you broke my heart, Anais.' His voice cracks with emotion that I presume is all fake. 'And I got into everything with him. He agreed that women are not worth it. That the world would run more smoothly if women kept quiet and did as they were told.'

'*Noah?*' I ask, my heart dropping. If this was a romance novel, this would be the misunderstanding that drives the couple apart while the reader rolls their eyes at their stupidity. This is real life and Noah isn't that type of guy. No one who cares about Chloe the way he does, about a love story as special as hers, would say such a thing. 'Actually, don't answer that.'

Noah gives me a reassuring smile, like we're already a team, a team of two. I get a flutter deep in my belly at the thought. 'No, let me explain. He did come into my bar, but I didn't know who he was, and I didn't recognise him today either until he spoke about the misogynistic stuff, which I hate to say happens every now and then. There's a certain type who prop themselves up at the bar and drink to forget their mistakes. They get sad and sloppy or mean and nasty. I learned early on to let them talk, to be agreeable for the sake of other patrons in the bar. They're mostly itching for a fight and I'm not there for that, and so the best way to handle it is to nod and water their Scotch down with soda water.'

'You watered my Scotch down? That's criminal.'

'So sue me.' Noah gives a lofty shrug.

'You can't fight stupid,' Manon says with a laugh. 'But you can take their money. Very clever, Noah.'

We're interrupted by a woman wheeling a suitcase towards us. 'Hello, erm, everyone. Is this The Secret Library Hotel?'

'*Oui.*'

'I'm Renee. Checking in for the next few weeks.'

Our first guest! 'Welcome!' I motion for her to walk with me towards the reception desk, but she's rooted to the spot, gaze going from face to face. 'You're staying in the suite called *Meet me in Paris*. On the bookshelf in your room, you'll find the book by Juliette Sobanet.' It's such a sweet touch, I hope the guests get as much enjoyment out of the themed suites as we've had searching for the perfect Paris memoir to highlight their stay.

'Great. I hope I do meet someone in Paris. Maybe a hot French guy.' With that, she gives Francois-Xavier a wink.

* * *

The smoke alarm goes off in the middle of the night and I wrench the covers from my bed and race downstairs, tumbling into our guest, Renee, who wears a sheepish look.

'Sorry, I lit a cigarette in the dining room, figuring everyone was asleep, and doesn't everyone smoke indoors in Paris?'

'Ah.' I grimace. 'Not any more. And we do have other guests staying here. The dining room is a smoke-free zone.'

'Right. Can I have one of those cheese platters brought to my room? I am allowed to smoke on the balcony, am I not?' Her voice is suddenly clipped.

I check the time; it's almost three in the morning. Why does everything weird in the hotel happen then? 'Erm – sure, cheese platter coming right up. And *oui*, you can smoke on the balcony if you want, but not in the suite.'

'Yeah, yeah. And a bottle of wine.'

'A bottle of wine what?'

'To my room.'

'Oh, right, OK.'

Merde! I make a note on the computer system Manon has set up so the cheese platter and wine are charged to Renee's room and start preparing it. The life of a hotelier is really a twenty-four-seven gig. I only hope the noise of the alarm didn't wake the family of six who are staying on the third floor.

41

---

20 DECEMBER

Renee comes downstairs, her lips pursed in a tight pout. 'Last night, there was so much noise from the bar next door, I couldn't sleep.'

I find it slightly jarring switching back to speaking English for our British guest after speaking French for so long, even though it's my native language.

'Is it like that all the time?' She folds her arms across her chest.

Day one and I'm on breakfast duty for our very first guest, who has woken up on the wrong side of the bed. Although her noise complaint is fair, she was up at 3 a.m. smoking in the dining room and never mentioned the pumping of the bass at that point. Still, we'll have to warn guests that this does happen every now and then when Noah hosts his up-and-coming bands. At least it wasn't death metal this time!

'Sorry, it's not usually that loud. Every now and then our neighbour holds an evening like that with live music to help aspiring musicians in Paris.' I'm exhausted myself. I knew I wasn't cut out for life as a hotelier. My exhaustion is soon replaced by shock when Francois-Xavier pads downstairs.

'How did you get in here?' I hiss.

He gives me an oily smile and joins Renee at the table. 'I'm with my girlfriend.'

Of all the... 'Girlfriend?'

'*Oui*, perhaps my future wife.' He gives her shoulder a squeeze. This is farcical. Absurd. But it's so very much in fitting with Francois-Xavier and the way he responds when he's got his eye on the prize. The prize being the hotel and whatever information he can gather.

'Renee has paid for a suite for one person, not two.'

'You can amend the booking,' she says, leaning over to give him a long, loud kiss.

How can this be happening? 'Seriously, Francois-Xavier? Why are you doing this? I'm finally back on my feet after what you did.'

'What *I* did?' He faces Renee. 'I made mistakes, I admitted that. Anais wouldn't even try couples' therapy.'

I scoff. 'Couples' therapy? That's the first I've heard of that.'

He shakes his head sadly as if I'm the one who let him down and not the other way around. 'I'll admit it's a strange coincidence that I found my next great love at the Trocadero Christmas Market. There I was, taking a photograph of our beautiful La tour Eiffel, as she sparkled under the moonlight in her special Christmas colours. No matter how long I've lived in this wondrous city, it never gets old. The Trocadero is the best spot for photographs, and then, *voilà*, Renee appeared, and it was *le coup de foudre!*'

Love at first sight? Didn't they meet right out the front of the hotel though? He will spin it any which way he can to fit his narrative and subsequent plotting...

'Ooh, I love it when you speak French,' Renee says. 'Say something else.'

'*Je t´ aime infiniment.*'

Her face lights up. 'What does it mean?'

'I love you endlessly.'

It's too early for this farce and there's not enough coffee in the world to be able to make sense of the tableaux in front of me.

'Help yourselves to breakfast, and I'll be adding another guest to your account, Renee. If you could square that away before you head out today.'

'Head out? We'll be staying in.' She cups his face and wiggles her nose against his.

And that's enough of that for one day. Well, until our family of six from Germany come down for breakfast. I only hope these two are gone by then.

42

20 DECEMBER

Margaret has her feet up on the chaise in Library Anaïs. From her red-rimmed eyes, it's obvious she had no sleep after reading Chloe's manuscript. When she goes to smoke her vape, I yell, '*Non, non!* One of our guests already set off the smoke alarm, in the early hours.'

'It's not smoke, it's a vape.'

'*Please.*'

She heaves an impatient grunt. 'Fine. Firstly, this manuscript is dynamite. It's going to be huge. Chloe's made careful notes about publishing it according to her wishes and, because you own the hotel and its chattels, that makes you in an enviable position, Anais. What will you do with the proceeds? Because this' – she waves the precious notebook – 'is going to be huge. A hundred-year-old literary mystery solved, and the real author of those literary classics that are still studied to this day will get the attribution they deserve.'

'I'm going to give all the proceeds away.'

Margaret sits up straighter on the chaise. '*What?*'

I take a seat in the bergère chair beside her. How to explain just how moved I was by Chloe's memoir? Because that's what her last novel is: a story of heartbreak and loss, hurt and pain, until Lily-Louise made a last-minute decision one fateful day to stop at the Chateau Beauchêne when her driver had automobile trouble, because they knew the author Benjamin Marceaux lived there. She'd vaguely known him from various cultural soirees in Paris.

Lily-Louise didn't factor in meeting his wife, Chloe, and sensing the woman was in trouble. And so began their clandestine communication by letters, which Chloe hid from her abusive husband. And those letters blossomed into love. Where good triumphs over evil and love wins. 'Why would you give the proceeds away?'

'It's not my story, it's Chloe's. So what right do I have to profit off her words? I'd be no better than her husband, would I? Noah and I had a long discussion about what to do with it and came up with a plan. We're in the process of setting up the Chloe Boucher Literary Foundation. A fund that will help and support women and girls with education, books, literary studies.'

'That's lovely, Anais.' Margaret swipes away a tear. 'This memoir will go to auction, and it'll generate many offers. Are you sure you'd be happy to give it all away? You could pay off the hotel with what this will earn.'

'*Oui*, I know, but I don't want that. I have a feeling the hotel is going to earn enough money to pay its own way when the memoir is published. Chloe has left her touch here by keeping suite nineteen, the secret library, a time capsule. I *will* capitalise on that, not only for financial reasons, but because it's what Chloe deserves. Awed visitors pulling back a curtain on a hundred years ago and peeking into the place she wrote her memoir. The secret library where she wrote on her MAP typewriter that still sits there today. Visitors will be able to gaze in from the doorway, like they do with Gustave Eiffel's secret apartment at the top of the Eiffel Tower.'

Margaret raises her hand for a high five.

'You're very demonstrative today,' I say with a laugh.

'Don't tell anyone or my reputation will be in tatters. And suite twenty, what will you do with that?'

I flash her a smile. 'I'm going to make suite twenty available as a guest suite just as it's been left but with a very hefty price tag for the privilege, and that will help fund another idea...'

'More brillance from Anais De la Croix?'

'Well, Noah came up with this one all by himself, so credit should go to—'

Margaret waves me away. 'Let's not be too hasty giving a man too much credit. You've seen what it did to your ex-husband. The man, the myth, the legend, all in his dreams.'

I laugh, which soon turns slightly hysterical because, unbeknownst to Margaret or Manon, Francois-Xavier is inside these hotel walls as we speak... And I'm not quite sure how to evict the guy without causing a further scene.

'Well, we thought we'd name a suite on the second floor the Lily-Louise suite. Her literary patronage provided financial aid to struggling writers from all walks of life, so I'd like to follow in her footsteps and help aspiring writers too. We'll offer the suite as a Writer in Residence Programme for successful applicants, and we'll fund this from renting suite twenty as is, for a premium. Writers who stay can help keep the library organised as part of the conditions, and can help with the tours of suite nineteen. We also hope they'll return one day when their work is published and allow us to host their book launch. All this is dependent on the success of suite nineteen and how many people come to visit the secret library, of course. It might take us a year to formalise, but it's the long-term goal.'

'This is far too wholesome for me, Anais. But, wow, it sounds bloody brilliant.' A small sob escapes, which she tries to disguise with a cough, but I let it go. If Margaret is moved, then the sky is the limit.

'So, I guess what I'm saying is, I'm keeping the hotel. And I'm going to make Manon's dreams of becoming a hotelier come true.'

43

21 DECEMBER

Manon gives the reception desk a wipe down while I arrange a bouquet of colourful Christmas blooms Margaret picked up at the market this morning.

'What is he doing here?' Manon hisses as Francois-Xavier saunters past, lifting his head in hello as if we're all on good terms.

I pull a face. 'He's staying with Renee. She's updated her booking to include him and I didn't quite know how to handle that because Renee is a guest and I'm terrified if I say no to her she'll leave an awful review or make a scene for our other guests, and that would not bode well.'

Manon's shoulders slump. '*C'est terrible.*'

I nod. 'It is. Unless you have any ideas on how we can boot him out and keep her happy?'

'I should have held the choke. A jury of my peers would surely have forgiven me.'

'Violence—'

'*Is never the answer,*' she groans. 'I know, I know. But it would be *so* satisfying. What's he doing? Trying to make you jealous? Snooping? What?'

'I presume he wants to see if the hotel is a money maker? Money that he would gladly offer to take off my hands.'

Manon squints at him. There's a touch of danger about the look, as if she is truly plotting an evil deed. 'Hmmm. I have a plan.'

'Does it include ending his life?' I whisper. 'Because, if so, I'd prefer you didn't, even if you're *certain* you can hide the body and it will never be found.'

'OK, I have a *new* idea.'

I roll my eyes. 'It's probably best if we let this play out. I don't want to risk a scene in the hotel, especially with the German family also staying here.'

'I'm glad they're on the third floor, well away from him. And Renee – why is she so demanding? This morning she told me she expected fresh sheets on her bed every day. *Every day*. That's a lot of washing, when she's booked to stay for three weeks.'

'*Oui*. Time consuming, washing and ironing too. Did we do those notecards about our green initiative?' Manon and I have brainstormed so many plans for the hotel that our spreadsheets now have spreadsheets and I struggle to remember if we actually printed the notecards and placed them on the desks in the remodelled suites.

'I'm sure we did, but I doubt she cares. Do you think the incentive is enough?' Our green initiative offers guests a daily hotel credit to opt out of housekeeping services, in an effort to reduce water use, conserve resources and save staff time. It might not matter so much now, but it will when we're at capacity.

'It's enough. The incentive can be used for a *fromage* platter, like who wouldn't want that? Her sheets would be changed every fifth day, with or without the incentive. Anyway, there's not much we can do except bear it.'

'With a bright, welcoming smile.'

Margaret joins us, her vanilla perfume wafting over. 'Who do we hate?' She leans her elbows on the reception desk.

I laugh. 'Renee has moved Francois-Xavier in, if you can believe that. But he's expecting theatrics, so I don't want to rise to the bait.'

'His tan is even more orange, how is that possible? When he was lying in a heap after Manon strangled him, I swear I was looking at a twice-baked Christmas ham.'

We fall about laughing, which is very unprofessional of us, as our other guests, the family of six, wander over.

'*Bonjour*, how are you enjoying your stay at L'Hôtel Bibliothèque Secrèt?'

The father speaks up. 'Very good so far. We loved our special Parisian memoir, *Paris Letters*, by Janice MacLeod, and the children are enjoying the games and the books in the kids' section.'

'*Merci*.'

'There's one small problem – the lights don't work in the bathroom.'

'Ah – sorry, I'll get that fixed right away.'

'Thank you. It's only that the kids will need to bathe later and there's no chance they'll do that in the dark or by torchlight.'

'Not a problem, we'll do it right away,' I say as my stomach twists in knots. How hard can it be to fix? It's probably just a blown fuse or something.

'Great. We'll be back later.'

'Enjoy your day.'

Once they leave, I face Manon. 'Can you call JP and ask if he can send his electrician to see what the issue is?'

'On it.' Manon moves to the side of the desk to make the phone call.

Margaret touches the delicate leaf of the red poinsettia. 'When that's sorted, can we have a little chat? How about lunch? My treat.'

A little chat. When Margaret uses that phrase, it's always something big. 'You hate the chapters I sent you? They pale in comparison after reading Chloe's, don't they? Put me out of my misery and tell me now.'

She lets out a guffaw. 'It's nothing to do with your chapters. I haven't had a chance to read them yet, but it is to do with biz.' Margaret raises a brow to imply it's important but she obviously doesn't want to discuss it here.

Just as I go to ask more, Manon hangs up the phone and says. 'No can do. His electrician is away on holidays. And the one who subs for him is in hospital. Must have cut the red wire; everyone knows not to touch the red wire.'

I swing from Margaret back to Manon. 'So did he have any other ideas?'

'I have to find a local electrician and he will square away the invoice as it's a fault in their work.'

'OK, well that's easy. Find a local electrician and mention that time is of the essence, *non?*'

'Sure.'

'Margaret wanted a chat. Will you be OK here while we go out for lunch? Then we'll make up the rooms when I get back and you can have a break after that?'

'I get breaks now? Is that only because Margaret is listening?'

'Very funny.'

'I'll be fine. Go have fun!'

44

21 DECEMBER

Margaret and I arrive at Le Vieux Bistrot in the Latin quarter. It's a small family run cosy restaurant that serves raclette and fondue and, while these dishes are slightly old fashioned, visitors to Paris usually delight in the theatrical nature of the experience.

'I hope you like *fromage*.'

'I could live on it.'

We're seated at a table for two and order wine, French onion soup for entrée and raclette for main.

'This place is divine,' Margaret says, taking in the cave-like aesthetic of the small space. 'I sometimes wish I lived anywhere other than London.'

Things have been so hectic; I haven't noticed the change in my agent's demeanour until right this second. She's usually swearing and blustering in her high energy way. I'd figured she was here solely to get her hands on Chloe's manuscript, but now I take a moment to study her, I sense it's more than that. Her shoulders are high, and there is a certain stiffness about her that's out of character.

Our wine arrives. I take a sip, enjoying the swirl of the robust red while I wait her out. Soon, two steaming bowls of French soup are deposited on our table, and a sweet fragrant smell permeates the space between us. If there's one thing Margaret is, it's forthright, so it won't take long for her confession, now that we're alone.

Margaret swizzles her wine and then blurts, 'I've left the agency.'

Shock knocks me sideways. 'What!' Margaret has been at Thames Literary her entire career of forty-odd years. Is there even a Thames Literary without her? While she's not the owner, she's the face and has the biggest stable of well-known authors who have been loyal to her.

'But... why?'

'That celebrity "author" was the nail in the coffin. I couldn't stand it another minute. Why do we have to bend and scrape on one knee like a sycophant to the likes of him? Sure, his cosy mystery has sold well, but so what? We're allowing a guy to swan in, behave horribly, and we can't say a word, because the rules don't apply to him.'

My mouth falls open. 'Did he do something when you met him that was a catalyst for this?'

She takes a sip of wine. 'He told my new assistant she'd be gorgeous if she had her teeth fixed. And it devolved from there. He went into detail about a sex act she could perform... Actually, I'll leave it there. It was *heinous*. She was in tears and quit that afternoon. I talked to the powers that be and can you guess what they said?'

I sigh. 'Something like "She's too sensitive. She'll never make it in the biz if she can't take a joke. He's known for his 'humour'. He doesn't mean anything by it." Shall I continue?'

'No, you've summed it up. And so I lost a fantastic staff

member due to him and there was no point even telling her to go down the legal route, because I understand he's got a prestigious law firm on his side, and she won't be able to fund the fight against that behemoth.'

I know that feeling of powerlessness. 'It's awful. And so... you also quit?'

'Not before I threatened them with going to the press with details about what they let slide, because they figure he might be their new cash cow and I'm supposed to turn a blind eye to his behaviour. It's not just him. It's all the reality stars, the two-bit celebs, or big-name male authors and the deals they get and how I'm to allow them to treat our staff badly because they bring in the most money.'

'You went to the press?'

'I bloody well did.'

'But I haven't heard anything about this news breaking? I've been distracted with the hotel and my deadline, but I would have thought my industry friends would have told—'

'I got legal advice first, found out where I stand. What I'm risking and how to best survive the onslaught when it does go to the press.'

'Smart. So when will that be?'

'An hour ago.'

'What!'

'Yeah. I did an in-depth interview with *The Times*. And spoke on the record to several tabloids too. He and the agency will be feeling the pinch right about now, I would guess.'

If I raise my eyebrows any higher, I'll fall over backwards. 'So you're hiding out here while the dust settles?'

'God, no! Do I look like the hide-out sort?'

I laugh. 'No, you don't.'

'I'm ready to fight with everything I've got. Who wants to

risk their own neck in situations like this? But, if not me, then who will? The same rules should apply to all in publishing and I for one am over it.'

'I'm dead proud of you.'

'Good, because that's my other reason for coming here. I've started my own literary agency and I'd love to take you with me.'

It's a no brainer. 'You're my agent and always will be.'

'Thank you, darling. But that doesn't mean you can expect deadline extensions in the future. I'm not going soft or anything.'

I let out a bark of laughter. 'I wouldn't expect anything less. And your old assistant, the one who quit?'

Margaret gives me a dazzling smile. 'She has a sparkly new title of Executive Assistant.'

'Nice. I've got to check this interview out.'

'It's online already.'

I take my phone and swipe it to life. The article is titled *Juggernaut Agent Quits!* It goes into depth about publishing scandals over the years and how certain celebrity or big-name male authors have behaved disgracefully with no comeuppance. I go to Twitter and have a look at what my publishing pals are saying about Margaret's exposé about the industry as a whole. Which is *a lot*. My feed is full of retweets and a running commentary about people who have had interactions with the debut author and none of them are positive.

The hashtag #CelebsAren'tRealAuthors is trending, with authors from the same publishing house demanding the debut cosy crime writer be cancelled.

I open the latest message from an author friend, Tully Davies:

Your literary agent has finally silenced that sleaze! I hear she's on the hunt for new authors. Put in a good word for me, would you? I'd happily switch agencies for one with a woman like that at the helm.

45

21 DECEMBER

Back at the hotel, Manon is clutching her hair while she speaks fast on the phone. She hangs up with a loud sigh. 'I can't find an electrician in all of Paris who can come today!'

'Oh no!'

'We better go make up the rooms, including Renee's, before they come back. Leave the calls for a moment.'

'I'll watch the front desk,' Margaret says. 'I can catch up on my socials.' She throws me a devilish grin.

I fill Manon in on Margaret's exposé and what that means for me. 'She is an icon!'

'She is.'

'What about the electrician, what will we do?'

We open the family suite on the third floor and go to the bathroom. I flick the switch and the light comes on. 'It works!'

'How can that be?' Manon frowns. 'I tried it a number of times and it didn't switch on at all?'

'It might be a fuse on its way out, so it's going off inter-mittently.'

'OK, one problem solved for the moment.' Manon exhales.

'We need to hire a local handyman for things like this that crop up. Guests will expect things to be fixed instantly.'

'*Oui*, that's a great idea. And let's still get the electrics checked in here to make sure there isn't a fault. Maybe JP might know a local handyman?'

'I'll ask.' We spend the next hour making beds and tidying up the family suite.

'Renee's suite next.'

'Urgh. Cleaning up after that man is the worst.'

We unlock the door and find the room in disarray. The bedding is pooled on the floor in a messy heap. 'Our white linen, left disrespectfully like that,' Manon says.

I pick it up and put it in a washbag. The quicker we do this the quicker we can leave. I go to the bathroom and wipe down the surfaces and replace the towels, as requested. When I come back, Manon is rifling through Francois-Xavier's bag.

'What are you doing!'

'Looking for evidence. Watch the door, will you?'

'Manon, that's not—'

'Aha!' She brandishes a folder full of paperwork. 'It's documents relating to the purchase of the hotel.' She thumbs through them, speed-reading while I stand just outside the door, heart racing at the thought of being caught out but also curious about his motivations.

'And?'

'There's a letter from his family firm, instructing him on how to get this place back.'

I gasp. 'But how? The divorce is finalised. He can't do that, surely? And why?'

Manon's face pales. 'He knows about suite nineteen. They mention it here.'

'Oh no. They're going to win the hotel back, aren't they?

They're going to bury me so deep in litigation I'll go bankrupt. Worse, I'll lose Chloe's manuscript and he'll make a mockery of the whole thing. He won't preserve their story. He'll sell it to the highest bidder with no care or concern for...'

Manon takes her phone from her pocket and snaps pictures of the paperwork.

Once that's done, we make up the suite with shaking hands. Now what? Will I lose to him again?

* * *

That afternoon, I sink into despair, pasting on a smile when the family of six arrive back, cheeks pink from the cold and the excitement of the Christmas fete. 'The light is working but please let us know if you have any more trouble.' We found an electrician, but he can't get here until tomorrow, so I hope the light works in the meantime.

They go on upstairs when Manon appears behind me, making me jump in fright.

'I've got an idea and I'm sure it'll work. So be ready.'

'OK,' I say glumly. I wanted to surprise Manon on Christmas Eve with my decision to keep the hotel and make her manager. If everything went as planned with Chloe's story, then I figured it would be a safe bet and Manon would be able to keep her dream alive in the place she finally feels like she fits. I'd get to stay too and, at night, I planned to write in suite nineteen and hope some of Chloe's literary genius rubbed off on me.

Now that's all been threatened with Francois-Xavier's scheming.

'Manon, I want to keep the hotel. And now...'

Her face dissolves into a grin and she claps a hand to her

mouth. 'Say no more. Keep it, we will. We owe it to Chloe and Lily-Louise, and I will not let that king of idiots steal it from us.'

'But how?' I've been down this road before. 'The legal fees alone...'

'Leave it to me. First, I need to set up a hidden camera.'

'A hidden camera? Is that legal?'

'Sure, for security in the hotel. Perfectly legal.' I swear I wouldn't be surprised if Manon did some kind of spy-like commando roll across the floor.

* * *

That evening, Francois-Xavier and Renee return, kissing and canoodling as they go, which I'm sure is for my benefit because it looks rather awkward to kiss like that in motion.

Manon stands in front of them as they are about to go upstairs. She gives me a surreptitious nod, which is my signal, but to do what I'm still not sure.

'Francois-Xavier,' she says in a saccharine voice that is very unlike Manon. 'Can I have a private word with you?'

'What about?'

'The hotel.'

Renee goes to protest but he reassures her with a kiss and sends her on her way. 'I won't be long, *ma cherie*.'

He follows Manon to a table in the dining room and sits. She motions for me to join them. 'It's come to our attention that you've made enquiries about the hotel and are subsequently trying to win it back, even though you were the one who agreed you should get the apartment.'

'I was railroaded, so we're going to appeal; but how do you even know this?'

'Lawyers talk.'

It's all I can do to keep from screaming at him. But I trust Manon. She must have an ace up her sleeve. 'And one other thing I found interesting is that you knew your family would bury Anais in paperwork that her lawyer would have to respond to, costing her a fortune in legal fees.'

He grins. 'So—?'

'Well, I find your family's support rather surprising after all the things you've said about them over the years.'

'Like what?' he asks.

Ah, now I see where she's going with this. I say, 'You said to me many times that "for well-educated prominent lawyers they are dim-witted and dull". That they'll always bail you out because they're "easy to manipulate" and they can't tell when you were lying right to their faces. Who *says* that about their own family?' And why did I not run when I heard him speak in such a way? I'd put it down to him feeling spiteful about their success and his lack of it but now I see it for what it is. Calculating and cunning behaviour.

'So? They are all of those things and more. Successful, *oui*, but boring and brainless. All I have to do is run home with a pained expression on my face and yet another dilemma is fixed by Père, who has no idea it's his money I'm after.'

'So you admit it?'

'*Oui*. But who cares?'

'We care,' I say. 'We care about this hotel and everything inside of it. You're not getting it back.'

'Wait and see,' he smirks.

'I don't think so.' Manon sends him a cold smile. 'Just so you know' – she points to a camera above – 'we have cameras situated in here for the safety of our guests and I'm sure we've got what you said on record and I think it's best if we share it with your family, so they know exactly what they're dealing with.'

'You wouldn't!' He finally loses his composure, his face turns puce with worry.

'We will if you try to take the hotel back. It'll be the very first thing we do. We'll send the video to every single person at your parents' firm, so they *all* know what they've been dealing with over the years.'

'Fine, fine! I'll stop. You can have the hotel. But promise me they'll never see that video? They will disown me and then where will I be?'

'Where you deserve,' Manon says. 'On your own.'

He deflates. 'I'll go. But not before I tell Anais how much I love—'

'Save it,' I say.

After he's gone, I ask Manon, 'How did you come up with that idea?'

'True crime podcasts. They catch them all the time like that. Wasn't that fun?'

'I'm not sure if I'd call it fun but I must admit it was a little thrilling to see him cave so fast. He'll be terrified of his family finding out all those things he's said about them over the years. We might have seen the last of him!'

'And now I get to run the hotel! We're keeping it?'

I grin. 'We're keeping it!'

46

CHRISTMAS EVE

'Shoes for Santa?' Noah asks.

'*Oui*, it's tradition in France. We leave our shoes in front of the fire, with a carrot for Gui. And, if we're lucky, we'll wake up in the morning and find the carrot has been replaced with a gift.'

'Ah,' Noah says. 'I see.'

Manon and JP join us in the library wearing matching Christmas jumpers. 'Yes, we're already at the matching clothes stage. I've heard it enough already,' she says.

'Shall we open presents now?' I ask, standing in front of the crackling fire. Soon our guests will join us for Christmas Eve drinks and nibbles.

'*Oui*,' Manon says, and she takes a present from her pocket for JP. He opens it to find a key. 'The key to my heart.' I'm stunned silent, wondering what the punchline is, because this is *Manon*, but instead, she steps towards him and gives him a kiss on the cheek. 'Look after it.'

'Aww.' I'm genuinely choked up by her gift to him, but try not to show it or she'll harp on about me and my feelings again.

I go to the tree and find a small box with a gift card bearing Manon's name.

She tears off the wrapping with no concern for preserving the paper. She squeals. '"Manon De la Croix – Manager",' she reads from the small A-frame desk nameplate.

'I thought I'd make it official.'

'I love it,' she says, giving me a hug.

'And for you,' Noah says, handing me a gift.

I open it to reveal a stamp. It reads: *A gift from L'Hôtel Bibliothèque Secrèt.*

'It's a book stamp for the books you gift your guests, so they remember their stay here.'

It's the perfect bookworm gift. '*Merci*, Noah. It's sweet. And for you...'

I find a large gift-wrapped box and pass it to him. Unlike Manon, he takes his time unwrapping the gift. 'A bucket?' he queries.

'There's more!'

He falls back laughing when he figures it out. 'A new squeegee?'

'Not just any squeegee – it's a brand new and improved one that will leave you with a streak-free shine, even in winter.'

'I do like a clean window.'

Juliette and Kiki join us, bringing a bottle of wine. 'Merry Christmas! Timothee and Zac will be here soon. They're just finishing their very last shift at the market.'

'Great. Let me get the Christmas charcuterie. We can eat in here.'

'I'll help you,' Juliette says.

We return with platters full of cheese, cured meats, olives, terrine and fresh baguettes, and our family of six joins in the fun. The children are busy leaving their shoes by the fire and demanding more carrots for Gui. Even Renee joins us, giving me a tentative smile when I offer her a glass of wine.

Margaret arrives, smiling. 'Anais! Your manuscript! Messy, yes, but what a feat! It's going to be your biggest yet!'

I have Noah to thank for that. It turns out my neighbour makes a very dashing hero when I don't kill him off in the second sentence.

We spend the evening playing Christmas games with the children before they go up to bed. We continue the festivities, including partaking in the thirteen desserts, a French Christmas tradition.

47

CHLOE'S LAST LETTER

I write this last letter and enclose it in my manuscript. This manuscript is my most important work to date. It is more than a memoir; it is a love story that I hope will last through the ages.

It is the story of my life, my marriage and subsequent disappearance. It's about a man who terrorised me and took my voice away. And then my beloved found me. Lily-Louise appeared when I had given up all hope. I escaped to her family hotel and assumed another name so he could not find me. I left a note for him, alluding to the fact I was taking my own life and hoped he would believe it.

I was always happy to hide in suite nineteen if it guaranteed my safety and allowed me to stay by Lily-Louise's side. Our love was all that mattered. It is all that matters now, although I lost Lily-Louise some time ago.

The heartbreak after her death was almost too much to bear, but bear it I did. What else could I do? Her family grieved like I did, and we supported each other as best we could. I spent hours in suite nineteen, honouring her by telling our story, the one in the enclosed pages. At first, I only wanted to write about Lily-Louise; however, that would not be the full picture and, as a writer, I owed the reader the truth. I suppose I did not want to give my husband any further thought, any more of my time. He had tried his best to break me and almost succeeded. And, yet, I persisted writing novels for him to claim as his own. Anything to survive. Anything to keep him at bay.

Once I'd made my escape, I could not write fiction again. I felt as though, even if I published under a nom de plume, he would find me. He would read a novel by a debut author and sense my voice, my style and know I was alive and come looking for me.

I have done my best to stay after losing Lily-Louise so many years ago, but now I am much aged and my time here is finished. I have a concoction to drink and soon I will meet her again, wherever souls go after here. Her dearest brother Jean has assured me that, if anything were to happen to me, he will keep our memories safe. I trust him; he's a good man.

And so I bid my adieus with one final request. Please keep my soul in peace and my manuscript safe. Please tell our story so Lily-Louise may live forever in print.

EPILOGUE

'Noah! Have you seen my pink heels?'

He gives me a sly smile. 'Last I saw them...' He winks.

I smother a smile. 'Right. It's all coming back to me. Why you insist on serving those petrol-flavoured drinks is beyond me.'

He nuzzles my neck, which doesn't help matters. We're already late and now I'm feeling weak at the knees, like my legs might give way under me.

'Why you kept drinking those supposedly petrol-flavoured drinks is the real question.'

'Peer pressure.'

He bends and finds my heels kicked under the bed. 'Hurrah! The princess shall go to the ball.'

'*Merci*.'

I swipe on lip gloss and check my reflection in the mirror.

'You are beautiful, Anais. Stunningly beautiful.' It's been a full calendar year with Noah by my side and still these compliments have the ability to make me melt.

'*Merci*. You're pretty damn hot yourself.' He's dressed in a black suit and is every inch the hero I dreamed he would be. He kisses me and I fall against him, losing track of time again.

'Oops, lipstick.'

I fix my makeup before dragging him out of the suite.

It's an important evening for us. The book launch of Chloe's memoir hosted by Margaret at Shakespeare and Co. A fitting tribute for our author.

In the lobby, Manon is dressed in her hotel uniform, smiling as she serves a guest. 'Ooh, have fun, won't you! I can't wait to officially open suite nineteen for tours tomorrow!'

Manon has made the hotel a success, even without the world knowing suites nineteen and twenty exist. But, as soon as Chloe's memoir hits the shelves tomorrow, I have a feeling we're going to be run off our feet and our boutique literary hotel will be filled with bookworms wanting to see where Chloe Boucher and Lily-Louise Toussaint lived and loved.

And where another writer, Anais De la Croix, now lives and loves.

Outside, we wait for our taxi. Noah takes his jacket off like the perfect gentleman and wraps it around me. '*Je t'aime*,' he says.

Stars sparkle in the inky night as Noah hugs me close. I breathe him in and wonder, not for the first time, if the magic of suite nineteen is responsible for bringing us together.

'*Je t'aime*, Noah.'

ACKNOWLEDGEMENTS

Thank you to my editor, Isobel Akenhead. You've made this story so much bigger and bolder. Your advice for the L. L. and C. thread made it so very special. I still tear up at that ending. To team Boldwood, my sincerest thanks. And to my copyeditor Jennifer Davies and proofreader Paul Martin, thanks for your amazing efforts. Shout out to Niamh Wallace, the cleverest marketing wizard I ever did see. Nia Beynon and Amanda Ridout, you are superstars.

As always, huge thanks to my readers. I appreciate every single one of you. I love our chats online and I feel very lucky that together we've created a supportive environment to chat about books and life and everything in between.

And to my family. You are the best of the best. Without you, I wouldn't have been able to keep up the pace. Thanks, legends.

ABOUT THE AUTHOR

Rebecca Raisin writes heartwarming romance from her home in sunny Perth, Australia. Her heroines tend to be on the quirky side and her books are usually set in exotic locations so her readers can armchair travel any day of the week. The only downfall about writing about gorgeous heroes who have brains as well as brawn, is falling in love with them—just as well they're fictional. Rebecca aims to write characters you can see yourself being friends with, people with big hearts who care about relationships and believe in true, once-in-a-life time love.

Sign up to Rebecca Raisin's mailing list for news, competitions and updates on future books.

Follow Rebecca on social media here:

 facebook.com/RebeccaRaisinAuthor

x.com/jaxandwillsmum

instagram.com/rebeccaraisinwrites2

bookbub.com/authors/rebecca-raisin

tiktok.com/@rebeccaraisinwrites

ALSO BY REBECCA RAISIN

A Love Letter to Paris

Christmas at the Little Paris Hotel

LOVE NOTES

LOVE IN EVERY CHAPTER

WHERE ALL YOUR ROMANCE
DREAMS COME TRUE!

THE HOME OF BESTSELLING
ROMANCE AND WOMEN'S
FICTION

 WARNING:
MAY CONTAIN SPICE

SIGN UP TO OUR
NEWSLETTER

https://bit.ly/Lovenotesnews

Boldwood

Boldwood Books is an award-winning fiction publishing company seeking out the best stories from around the world.

Find out more at www.boldwoodbooks.com

Join our reader community for brilliant books, competitions and offers!

Follow us
@BoldwoodBooks
@TheBoldBookClub

Sign up to our weekly deals newsletter

https://bit.ly/BoldwoodBNewsletter